A FLAME OF STARS & MIDNIGHT

USA TODAY Bestselling Author

EVE L. MITCHELL

A FLAME OF STARS & MIDNIGHT

This one's for my friend, Renée.
She tells me that she's proud of me almost every day, she writes
ridiculously long emails when she knows I need reminding that I'm good
enough and she sends random gifts "just because."
She also demands all the words that I write, because she's greedy like
that, but she also listens to my harebrained ideas, and when I say, "I'm
thinking of writing this..." She says "Do it!" Because she has complete
faith in my ability to write.
These words are for you; thank you for being my friend.
Love ya, Nee x

Note from the Author

There are terms and words within this book that are not contained with the dictionary. This is a paranormal romance book—I reserve the right to make up names and words at my leisure (as my editor will attest to).

Please note that I am a British author, and although I have tried to make this as universal as I could, there will be some British spelling, phraseology, and terminology that I can't (and won't) eradicate from my writing, and I'm okay with that.

If swearing offends you, I recommend you stop reading now.

A Flame of Stars & Midnight

I will make them pay.
The demons who sealed my fate and betrayed me.
I may be just a witch, but I will revel in their ashes.

Waking up in the underworld left me reeling, tricked, enraged…
I confronted a prince of hell and believed I had won.
It was all a lie—all because I refused to lift a blood curse.
The demons who betrayed me will *bleed* for their treachery.

Forming an uneasy truce and unlikely alliance with a teacher
who is willing to help, I will do whatever I need to get out of this
infernal pit. To seek revenge on those who ruined me.
For hell hath no fury like a witch scorned…

*A Flame of Stars & Midnight is book 2 in the Watcher Series and ends
on a cliffhanger.
If you enjoy reading paranormal romance packed full of action, adventure, and heat, with a funny, sarcastic heroine and a deeply dark anti-
hero, then this series is for you.
This book is recommended for audiences of 18+ due to the terminology,
language, and sexual content.*

CHAPTER 1

There was only pain.

The pain of betrayal.

Betrayal.

They killed me. No, *he* killed me. That demon bastard killed me, while the others stood and watched. They *watched.*

They watched me die, and Hound took my soul to hell.

I felt the flutter of my eyelashes as the tears slipped out from under my closed eyes and silently slid down the sides of my cheeks.

I'm crying?

Of course I'm crying. I got stabbed in the heart, it fucking hurts.

It hurts? Yes! A big pointy, stabby thing knifed me in my heart.

Pay attention, it shouldn't hurt. I'm dead.

Then why am I crying? Why am I aware that I am crying? How do I feel this pain?

"Your thoughts are really very entertaining."

My eyes flew open as I sat bolt upright in the bed, my hand instantly shielding my eyes from the room, which was beyond clinical white and was painfully bright.

"Who are you?" My voice sounded croaky, and I realised that I needed a drink. "Am I in hell?"

"Who I am is not important right now; yes, you're in hell; no, you're not dead, well, not much."

Not much? "What? I'm only a little bit dead?" I snarked as I opened my fingers to peek through.

"They said you were funny."

Dropping my hand to the sheet, I braved the neon white light to glare at my companion. "They?"

He was beautiful. Thick brown hair the colour of chestnut

brushed back from his too handsome face. A clear smooth forehead, warm chestnut brown eyes, with thick dark lashes, a perfectly straight nose, full lips that split into a smile as I admired him, showing perfectly white, straight teeth.

"Why can you lot never be ugly?" I grouched as I swung my legs off the bed. My screech was ear-splitting as I dived back under the white silk sheet. "Why in the name of God am I naked?"

"You're dead."

"You said I was only dead a little bit," I reminded him with a glare, pulling the sheet to my chin. "Even a little bit dead, I should have clothes on."

Chestnut tilted his head to the side as he studied me. "Why?"

"Why should I have clothes on?" I asked him in bewilderment. "Manners? Decorum? Courtesy? Because I don't want to be naked?"

"Odd."

I watched him as he watched me. He was gorgeous and massive, like Hercules massive, and now that my eyes were adjusting to the brightness, I could feel the slow throb of power that surrounded him.

Looking around the room, I took in the bed, the dressing table with chair, and the seat he was in. That was it, but the room was huge. He sat in one corner as he waited for my slow perusal to be over.

"Why am I here?"

"Where would you like to be?" he asked me as he crossed his legs. Propping his elbow on his raised leg, he dropped his head into his hand as he watched me with a casual, almost *playful* curiosity.

"I would like to be *alive* in my cottage."

"Not possible."

Taking a deep breath, I considered my next words. "I thought I would be in the Land of the Souls."

"Why?"

"Why not?" I countered as I narrowed my eyes at him.

"It's currently…indisposed."

Noticing his hesitation, I leaned forward. "Why?"

"Watcher business."

Watcher… My rage was returning. "The Watchers are in the Land of the Souls?" I demanded as I stood, pulling the sheet with me and wrapping it around my body like a shield.

Chestnut ran his eyes over me in amusement as he leaned back in his seat. "What are you doing, Star?"

"I'm going to the Land of the Souls to cut a certain demon's heart out."

His finger twitched, and I was back in bed under the sheet. Incredulous, I met his amused stare. Stubbornly, I got up, wrapping the sheet around me again.

"I want to leave."

Throwing his head back, he let out an almighty laugh. "Don't we all, Star, don't we all." Lazily he stood, and I had to force myself not to let my weak knees collapse under me. A white button-down shirt was half tucked into fitted black trousers, and the silver buckle of his belt shone brightly. His shirt had two, maybe three, buttons undone at the neck, and I could see the smooth skin underneath.

"You need more sleep," he told me.

"I'm dead, do the dead sleep?" I asked him with an arched brow.

"Star, why are you being so difficult?" he asked me with a lazy smile as he crossed the space to stand in front of me. A single finger lifted my chin, tilting my head back so I could meet his gaze as he stared down at me.

"A bunch of Watchers betrayed my trust, then he…*one* of the bastards stabbed me in the heart, a hellhound took my soul to hell, and now I'm naked with a silk sheet around me in a room of astonishing brightness with *another* demon, who is telling me nothing."

He grinned. The perfect white teeth matched the brightness of the room.

"You need to dial that shit down," I muttered as I tried to step back.

"Go to bed, sleep. Heal. I'll be here when you wake up."

A shiver ran down my spine as he spoke. "That's what worries me."

Another laugh as he stood back and turned to return to his seat.

"You're just going to sit and watch me sleep?" I demanded as I watched him take his position.

"You're chaotic. It's peaceful."

What? I shook my head to clear any lingering cobwebs as I sank back down onto the bed. "I'm a paradox?"

"Yes."

"Who are you?"

"I can be anyone you want me to be, Star." His smile was cocky as his eyes danced with humour.

"I'd rather you just be yourself," I answered as I thought about the last demon who tried pretending with me. "Can I leave?"

"No."

"Because I'm dead?"

"No."

"I'm alive?"

"No." He grinned again.

"But I'm not dead?"

"No."

"So can I leave?"

"No."

"Because I'm alive?"

"No."

He reminded me so much of *him* that I knew I was going to punch him soon. "You're one of them, aren't you? A Watcher?"

"No."

"Oh for the love of all that's holy, is *no* the only word you know?"

"No." His eyes were brimming with laughter as he settled himself into his chair and observed me.

"Did he send you?" I asked quietly.

His laughter died and he sobered as he watched me for a long moment. "No."

Screaming in frustration, I flung myself backwards on the bed. "I already hate you, well done."

Laughter echoed through the room as I felt a tingle on my cheek. "Sleep."

The laughing Hercules put a sleep spell on me.

Wanker.

THE NEXT TIME I woke up, I was on my side, facing the wall. I was aware of his presence before my eyes were fully open, and as I turned to look over my shoulder, he met my stare with that grin.

"You were restless," he observed.

"Imagine that," I muttered as I rolled onto my back and stared at the white ceiling. "Some creepy fucker watches me sleep, and you criticise I'm restless."

"Your disposition is sour," he commented.

"No shit, Sherlock," I said to him as I sat up. "Why am I still naked?"

"Because you have no clothes on?"

I was going to take great delight in smashing his head off

something hard if he didn't stop grinning at me. "You have clothes on."

"Would you like me to take them off?" His hand reached for his shirt buttons.

"No!" Dropping back onto my pillows, I felt like crying with frustration. "Can you stop it?"

"What do I need to stop?" he asked me gently.

"This." My hand wavered as I moved it up and down in his general direction. "Just be straight with me or leave me alone."

When the room was unbearably silent, I sat up and looked around. He was gone? Leaping out of the bed, I wrapped the sheet around me like a toga, and I was racing to the wall. When all I was faced with was white wall, I searched the other one, then the next, and on the final wall, I reluctantly accepted that I was in a doorless room.

"How did he get out?" I wondered as I looked up at the ceiling. "Winked?" I wondered as I thought about the ability to *travel* by winking in and out of places. Reaching for my powers, I wasn't really surprised to find my powers gone.

I kicked at the wall and then had the fun time of hopping on one foot as I tried to soothe the pain and hold my toga up at the same time.

"Death sucks," I grumbled.

"What are you doing?"

Spinning on my one leg, I met his curious look. "How did you get in?"

"Magic." He winked at me. "You should sit. The sheet's see-through."

Clamping my lips tightly together, I marched to the bed and sat on the edge of it. "I want clothes."

"You said."

"I want out of here."

"You said."

"I want *answers*."

That slow sexy smile crossed his face as he leaned forward with a gleam in his eye. "And what about what *I* want?"

My gulp was loud in the silent room, and I shifted uncomfortably on the bed. "Unless it's my new toga dress, I have nothing to give you."

His head cocked to the side, and he took a long slow look up my body. "I prefer pants."

"Me too, but someone is being reluctant with sharing the clothes."

Standing abruptly, he looked over at one of the walls. "I have someone here to see you."

My mouth was open to protest, worried it may be *him*, but my jaw dropped further when a large, black, scary as fuck hellhound appeared in the room. My back hit the wall at the top of the bed as I scrambled up it, away from the four-legged demon that brought me here.

"You remember my assistant, don't you?" he asked me with a small smile.

Hound stared at me with faintly glowing red eyes, and I couldn't push down the fear as he took a step towards me.

"No." My protest was a whisper as Hound dipped his head at my word. Slowly he turned and walked through the wall. Panic clawed at my throat as I fought to remain calm, and closing my eyes, I willed myself to breathe.

"You are scared?"

A small snort escaped as I pressed my hands into my eyes. I could still feel Hound's teeth as they sank into my neck. My hands felt and checked the skin as I worried over the events that brought me here.

"You will not be harmed."

Opening one eye, I fixed him with a glare. "Yeah, that's what the last lot of demons said, right before they stabbed me in the heart."

"Samyaza had his reasons."

I was on my feet, my rage infinite as I crossed the room to confront the demon in front of me. "You do not say his name! Ever," I seethed as I glared up at him.

"Your aura is fascinating."

"You said the hellhound is yours?" I changed the subject. Pretty men with pretty observations could go suck a rock.

"Well, of course."

"Dude, seriously, if you don't start speaking in sentences that *say* something, I will not be responsible for my actions."

"Start asking me things I can answer."

"You irritate me more than Zel; I didn't think that would be possible."

"An insult?" he queried.

"An observation."

"You are amusing." Swiftly he stood. "I must go, my servant will remain."

He was gone and Hound was back.

Wordlessly I stared at him, and the hellhound stared back. "You freaking killed me." I felt a tear slip over. The hellhound shook his head as he sat on his back legs and watched me. "You're arguing?" I asked incredulously. "Are you saying you didn't kill me?" Hound nodded. The hellhound *nodded,* and I wondered which part of my brain was accepting this. "You took me here?"

Hound nodded.

Rolling my eyes, I turned away from him. "I don't need you here, please go away." I lay back down on the bed. "You've done enough."

I heard Hound settle on the floor, and closing my eyes in despair, I did my best to ignore him.

How the hell was I going to get out of here?

CHAPTER 2

WHEN I WOKE FOR THE THIRD TIME, THE ROOM WAS STILL AS painfully bright and also as unwelcoming. Its guests hadn't improved either, I noticed, as I glanced around the room. Hound still sat on the floor, watching me, which was creepy.

Turning on my side, I stared at Hound, and he stared right back. "I can't get out of the room," I told him. "I don't know why you need to be here. I cannot get *out*." I narrowed my eyes as he watched me. "Did you just raise your eyebrow at me? Seriously? You're giving me attitude?"

Hound snorted. The hellhound legit *snorted* at me. I stared at him in disbelief. Sitting up swiftly, I swung my legs over the side of the bed, the sheet wrapped around me, and got to my feet.

Leisurely, almost coolly, the hellhound rose too. I was too pissed off to be intimidated by his size or his past actions. I may be dead, or not dead, or whatever, but there was no way in hell I was taking attitude from a fluffless giant-jawed dog.

"You killed me. You wrapped those gigantic jaws around my throat, and you took me here; you do not get to give me attitude!" I yelled at him. "You stupid mutt, I trusted *you*, and you killed me."

"Actually, it was the dagger to the heart that did it; the hellhound merely carried you to safety."

Whirling around, I saw Chestnut with his back to the wall, his shoulders against it, as his legs stretched casually out in front of him. He was eating an apple and wearing a white suit with a white shirt. He looked like a really bad eighties album cover in his white room, white clothes and dark hair. Glancing down, I noticed his bare feet. It was a stark contrast to the suit and the perfectly styled hair.

"Safety?" I looked around my cell. "You call this safe?"

Chestnut looked at me and the bed. "Even you can't hurt yourself in this room."

"You make me sound like a hazard. I'm perfectly capable of being in a room with more furniture and not hurting myself," I said to him with an angry glare.

"You make bad choices."

"In furniture?" I asked as he pushed himself off the wall and walked towards me.

"No." His look was mocking. "In your choice of whose company you keep."

"Says the Wham reject in front of me."

His head tilted slightly as he looked at me, and then he looked past me to Hound. "You may go," he told him.

I hated that I held my breath in anticipation as I waited for Hound to leave. As I waited, I watched Chestnut and saw his eyes narrow so slightly I was sure I had imagined it, but then I remembered I didn't have that active an imagination.

"You can talk to Hound?"

"You knew this," Chestnut replied as he walked past me to stand beside the bed.

"Does he talk back?"

His huff was derisive. "Back chat is his favourite thing," he muttered.

I looked at the wall Hound had walked through. "Can he shapeshift?"

Chestnut laughed out loud. "Are you worried he's one of your demons?"

No, because I hadn't thought of that, but now the idea was in my head, I was scared of the answer. "It would just be my luck the hellhound was a Watcher in disguise."

Chestnut was chuckling at my expense as he sat on a chair

that hadn't been there before. "The Watchers do not have the ability to change form to that extent."

Remembering well the ability some had to change parts of their appearance, I felt my anger rise. "Yeah, well, they think they can take whatever they want."

"Still so angry." Chestnut watched me curiously.

"What are you then? Another Watcher?"

"What I am and who I am is of no importance, just know that I am protecting you."

"Demons have protected me before," I snapped angrily. Holding out part of the sheet, I showed it to him. "Look how that worked out."

"You are so young," he mused as he watched me. "Angry, full of passion, and if you must call me something, Star, call me by my name. *Chestnut* makes me sound like a snack."

The fact I immediately thought about snacking on him made my cheeks burn when his eyes sparkled with humour. "Shut up," I muttered as I sat back on the bed and waited. And waited some more. "Do I need to beg? What's your name?"

"You may call me Cross."

"Cross?" I squinted at him. It didn't suit him. "As in 'you're angry' cross or as in the old wooden cross that they…" My eyes widened and then squeezed shut as his bellow of laughter echoed in the sterile room.

"I'm not the son you fear," he told me as he crossed his leg over his knee and watched me like I was his favourite show.

"Are you a Watcher?"

"No."

"Are you an angel?"

"I'm in hell the same as you, Star."

"Are you a demon?"

"Are you?"

"What?" I knew my mouth was opening and closing like a goldfish. "You know I'm human."

"You *were* human. Now…" He hesitated.

"Now? Now what?" I was on my feet again. "Are you saying I'm not human?"

"You're so…flighty."

"What?" What the fuck did flighty mean? "When do you start answering questions?" I demanded angrily.

"When you start asking questions I can answer."

A wave of fatigue washed over me, and I sat back on the bed, my head dropping into my hands. "You tell me nothing, you speak in riddles, you may as well tell Sa—*him*—and his cronies I'm done."

"Samyaza is not here."

Lying back on the bed, I stared at the ceiling. "Whatever."

"What do you want, Star?" Cross asked me quietly.

My sigh was louder than I intended as I closed my eyes and fought the tears. "I want to go home. I want to have never met them that night at the cemetery, I want to forget it all and go back to my psychic readings on a Friday night and a Saturday afternoon. I want a cup of tea. With some shortbread. And I want to hug my mum and dad and tell Mum I did not get struck in the heart by a deceitful demon. I want to go to work on Monday and never ever complain about the printer jamming again. I want to forget them, him, and I really, *really* want to not be dead. Or a bit dead. Or whatever the fuck I am. I want out of this room, and I want away from all hellhounds. I want my life back." The tears crept out from under my lashes and slid down into my hair as I lay there wishing everything was different.

The room was silent, so silent I thought Cross had left, so I turned my head to look and met his deep chocolate brown eyes. "Is that all?"

His tone was gentle. His eyes…kind? Turning away from him,

I looked back to the ceiling. I had been fooled by kind eyes before. "I want to be free."

"I cannot give you freedom."

"Shock." Moving on the bed, ensuring the sheet covered my modesty, I gave him my back.

"You need to rest more. Your strength will return."

I didn't hear him leave, but I knew that he did. I felt more tears spill, and I angrily wiped them away. "Why are you crying?" I asked myself. "You let them in, you wanted to work with the demons, you helped them. It's your own fault they betrayed you."

With an angry sniff, I pulled the sheet higher. My rationality tried to tell me that my choice in the beginning was limited. That they made me work with them, but even in my anger, I knew I would not be able to blame them solely for all of my actions. No one made me sleep with Sam. No one made me think they were protecting me because they *cared*.

Screwing my eyes shut as if to block out the memories, it was no use. It was all very much alive and wishing to be heard, dissected, and analysed in my brain. They protected me not because they cared, but because they needed to use me for their own gain.

Bastards.

They *didn't* care. *He* didn't care. He used me. They *all* used me.

The Watchers' betrayal hurt, it did. I had been fooled into thinking I was important to them, and I had been, but not because of some spell. Because they needed a sacrifice. Sam's betrayal cut deep because, well, that was obvious. What had I been thinking, falling into his trap? Sleeping with him, caring for him, loving him. *Dick*.

But it was more than just Sam's betrayal that hurt, I realised as I lay there. *Chaz*...swallowing hard, I opened my eyes. Even I couldn't shut that pain out. I had trusted Chaz the most. But his hard voice the night they killed me; I could hear it now. I could taste the fear they caused me as if they were in front of me.

But they weren't.

Sitting up, I looked at the wall that Hound disappeared through so easily.

Why weren't they here? Why was not one of those dickhead demons here right now? They used me. I knew those demons, okay, maybe not as much as I thought, but I knew them. They did nothing without an agenda. The end game for them…what was it? To stab me in the heart under a blood moon? Was that *it*?

Nah. That wasn't the pricks' style.

Hound walked through the wall towards me, his low burning red eyes as always fixed on me.

"Why would they kill me?"

He sat on his haunches as he waited.

"It makes no sense." I chewed the end of my hair as I thought about it. "They would have a bigger agenda." I chewed my lip as I thought about it. "Wouldn't they?"

Hound lay on the floor, his head resting on his mammoth paws as he watched.

"Or maybe I'm still a stupid little nobody that thinks the best of dirtbags," I said with a groan as I flopped back onto the bed. "I want to go home." My heels kicked the bed in frustration. "I'm so sick of being someone's pawn, I want to go *home!*" I screamed the last bit in frustration as I searched for my powers.

Had Cross cut me off from them? Were they gone when I almost-kind-of-not-quite died? What did almost-kind-of-not-quite dead mean?

"Am I dead?" I asked Hound as I turned to him. He shook his head as he sat up. "Am I alive?" He shook his head again. This time with a snuff, like I was wasting his time. "So you didn't kill me, but I'm not living?"

Silence. Obviously. I couldn't communicate with him the way that Cross could.

"If I go home, will I die?"

Hound lay back down and closed his eyes. Huh. So that was his reaction to what? A question he can't answer or a question so stupid it didn't warrant an answer?

There were too many questions!

"You're a really irritating dog," I muttered into the silence. "And if I'm not dead and I'm supposed to be dead, then well, you're a shit hellhound too."

I ignored the snort from the floor.

Dipping into that place inside me again, I searched for my pool of tranquillity. The pool of my powers. Zel had cut me off before; had he cut me off again? I reached and felt nothing but emptiness. Did I lose my powers when they killed me? It would be so completely like them to cut me off from that as well as everything else. They knew anger fuelled my ability to do anything, and that rat bastard knew I was planning on coming for him. I recalled my last words to him.

"I will see you burn in hell," I seethed at Sam as he pulled me closer.
"I'll be waiting."

I remembered the feel of the blade as it pierced my skin, sliding through tissue and flesh as it found my heart. The agony as pain flooded my body, but it was his betrayal that broke my heart.

"Where the fuck are you, Watcher?" I asked the quiet of the room. "You said you'd be waiting. Were you lying to me? Again. I bet I'm just one big, giant joke to you, you arrogant dick." Swearing at Sam even when he wasn't here was satisfying, but it was a short-lived satisfaction. As I thought about that night, I remembered what Gran had told me before she'd left me in the lounge.

Asmodeous was burning souls, in rage, *at me.* How did you

even burn a soul? A cold shiver ran over me as I thought about it. I needed out of this room. I had so much to fix and, feeling the void inside me, I needed my powers back. I recalled the other thing Gran had told me.

"The tree is all that can save you from him now."

Who was *him*? Sam? Or Asmodeous? Where in hell, pun intended, did you put the tree of life? Was it even in hell? Why would the tree be in hell? That made no sense. Had she told me this, or had I just leapt to that?

Gran couldn't have known what Sam planned. Could she? But the tree of…life? I was dead but not dead. Was the tree for me?

"Oh my God, Gran, did you know what they planned and never warned me?" I whispered in the quiet of the room. "Why would you let this happen?"

There was too much that I didn't know, and so much I needed to ask, but all I could think of right now was, how do I get out of here? Which was the original question.

"Okay, Star, new plan. Stop moping. Get out of here, find the tree, and then stab that bastard in his black heart." I frowned at myself as I lay there. What a list of impossible things. Where did I even start? With Cross?

Tiredness pulled at my eyelids, and I fell asleep, feeling pissed off and alone. Again.

CHAPTER 3

WHEN I WOKE LATER, IT WOULD HAVE BEEN STUPID TO GUESS THE time, never mind the day. This room was so depressing. I was surprised that Hound wasn't with me. Had I been alone at all since I woke up here? Why was I alone now?

As I got out of bed, it took a moment before I realised that I now had a dressing table. No mirror, but there was a dresser. As I crossed the floor to it, I noticed for the first time that the marble white floor was warm.

They had underfloor heating in hell? What the fuck?

As I laughed at my preposterousness, I actually completely lost it. Tears were streaming down my face as I ended up bent over the dresser, holding myself up, one arm wrapped around me, clutching at my sides.

"What amuses you?" Cross asked as he came into my room, wearing a half smile as he watched me.

"Underfloor heating," I gasped as I tried to calm down, wiping my eyes as bursts of irrational laughter burst free.

His quizzical look was enough to set me off again. "I feel you need to share," Cross told me as he casually sat on the edge of my bed.

"Underfloor heating?" Shaking my head as if I were clearing it of my hysteria, I pulled my hair away from my face. "Underfloor heating in *hell*? Seriously? Nothing?" His expression told me he genuinely wished he got my joke. "Dude, I'm in hell. Of course it's warm…fiery pits of hell? No? Nothing? Seriously?"

"Are you envisioning wild flames, burning lava and red-skinned males running around with pitchforks?"

"And goats."

Cross blinked. "What?"

"What?"

"Why goats?"

"Demon goat gods."

"I ask this with complete respect, but what are you talking about? Are you okay?" Cross asked me seriously.

"Um…yeah? I guess so." I checked my sheet-covered body. "You know, for being naked, in hell, and kinda dead. Honestly, it wasn't in my five-year plan, but shit happens, demons stab you in the heart, and your life is over at twenty-four."

Cross looked perplexed as he considered my words. Why did they all need to look like *GQ* magazine models? Where were the ugly buttfaced *minions* of hell? Or the skin-peeled demons that horror movies had been promising me for my entire teenage years?

"I understand all of that," Cross spoke suddenly. "But demon goat gods?"

"No gods for goats?" I asked as I opened one of the drawers on the dresser and almost wept when I saw the hairbrush. When he pinched the bridge of his nose and closed his eyes, I fought my smile. "I'm disappointed."

"Of course you are," he groaned as he stood. "Well, I do have news."

My humour vanished as he addressed me. "If *he's* here, he can go fuck himself."

Cross was once again looking at me with that mixed look of his, the one where he was both amused and appalled at anything I said. "You have no visitors," he confirmed. "But I thought you may want to come out of your room?"

I took a step eagerly forward and then hesitated. "Why?" I asked cautiously. "What's out there?"

"Molten pits of lava, volcanic fire, buttfaced minions of hell," he deadpanned.

"And you want me to go out into that?" I asked him incredulously. *Buttfaced?* "Hey! Stop listening to me!"

"You want me to ignore you?"

"No, I want you to stop listening to my brain."

"But it's so enlightening." Cross looked entirely too smug, and I realised he would have "heard" me when I was referencing him as a model.

"Well, it's rude," I mumbled as I looked towards the white wall he usually walked through to get here. "What's out there?"

Cross looked at the wall with reservation and then back to me. "Well…"

"It's really bad, isn't it?" I asked fearfully.

"Yes." His nod was sombre. "Are you ready?"

Was I? No. Never. Suddenly the white room with the bed I'd slept in for who knows how long, was comforting. "Okay."

Cross extended his hand, and I was proud of the fact that my hand gave only the slightest tremble. His grip was firm and strong. Wildly, I thought my dad would approve. Cross led me to the wall, and stupidly, I braced myself for impact.

Opening my eyes, I looked around. White marble floor, soft white walls, two large sofas, a white throw rug between them with an intricately carved coffee table with a glass top. A huge white fireplace was the feature, with the most beautiful stonework I had ever seen. The far wall had two huge floor-to-ceiling windows that let in—"Daylight!" With a cry, I ran to the windows and looked out and immediately jumped back. "Holy fuck!"

I heard his chuckle behind me as I inched back to the window and looked out.

"Where are we? Is this hell?" I asked in wonder as I looked down. The room seemed to be poised right on the edge of a cliff. There was nothing but air outside, and far below, like a *long* way down, was an ocean. "I don't understand."

"Disappointed that there is no fiery pit of hell?"

"No. Yes?" I turned to face him and saw him sitting comfortably on his sofa, with a cup and saucer in his hands. "Coffee?"

"It is, would you like some?"

Nodding eagerly, I crossed to the sofa and sat down across from him. "I haven't peed."

Cross, who had been in the process of lifting the cup to his lips, paused briefly at my overshare and then continued to take a drink. "Thank you for the update," he murmured as he placed the saucer back on the coffee table.

I could feel my cheeks burning as I stared at the intricate carvings on the coffee table, eager to avoid his gaze. "I mean, I haven't felt hunger or thirst, and therefore I haven't had any, you know...bodily function requirements." My eyes narrowed on the design as I leaned forward. "Oh my God!" I suddenly realised what I was looking at. It was one mass orgy of...things. Sexually active things, and holy crab cakes, were they moving?

Cross boomed with laughter. His head was thrown back, and he was outright laughing at me. "You are so refreshing." Shaking his head as he looked at me, he gestured to the tray with the cafetière and cups. "Please, help yourself."

Yes, I'm in hell. Maybe. Yes, I'm dead. Possibly. Yes, I'm scared. Who wouldn't be? Coffee? Come to mama.

Once my cup was fixed, I took a tentative drink. Holy caffeine. I think I actually moaned.

"Oh," I said as I licked my lips. "Now I know I'm dead. That's...heavenly."

"Wrong dimension, but I'll accept the compliment."

Cross didn't miss my flinch at the reminder of where I was. "Are we on earth?"

"No."

"What ocean is that?" Looking to the windows, I stared out at the sky and realised it wasn't exactly blue. Curious, I walked back over towards the wall and paid more attention to the details. The sky was more green than blue, and the sun, I couldn't see. There were no clouds. Looking down, I noticed the water was closer than before, and it was dark, almost black. "This isn't real?"

"I like it," Cross answered calmly. "It's soothing."

"It's an illusion? Hiding…what?" I asked him as I turned back to hear his answer. Cross appeared to be a male in his late twenties, perfectly groomed, stunningly attractive, but as I paid attention and waited for his answer, I saw the deep ancient wisdom in his gaze. It was unnerving. What was he?

"Look again," he instructed softly.

I suddenly didn't want to, but I knew that I needed to turn back. My mouth dropped open as I tried to take in what I saw. Walls that ran with—no, they didn't run, they *oozed*—fire. Red fiery walls, black clouds of smoke everywhere and…what in the name of all that was holy was that? "People?" I gasped as I pressed to the window and looked out. "Oh shit, is that people?"

"Souls."

"No." Shaking my head, I didn't realise I was crying until a white handkerchief was handed to me. "Why aren't they in the Land of the Souls?"

"Maintenance issue."

"I swear, if you say the elevator repairman is out of commission, I will shove this handkerchief so far down your throat you'll be able to wipe your arse with it."

Cross's laughter at my anger only made me angrier as I returned to look at the misery outside the window.

"How can you let this happen?" I demanded as I felt him leave my side. I took a step backwards as I suddenly saw them. The dark cloaked wraiths moving amongst the souls. "Cross? What are they?"

"Reapers. Soul takers. Messengers of death," he answered casually. "They have so many names."

"Are they one of your illusions?" I whispered as I stared at the very lifelike dementor wannabes moving slowly through the lines and lines of souls, all who were trudging downwards. Down to what? That I couldn't see.

"No, my reapers are very much real."

Whether it was his mention of them or my open horror at witnessing them, they all seemed to stop moving, and even though they were more shadow and mist than corporeal, I realised that they were all staring at me.

"Come away from the window, Star. You'll only excite them."

"They're staring at me." I could hear the tremor in my voice as I watched the wraiths move forward.

"Star, please." Cross's voice was firmer, and suddenly the wraiths and fiery scene were gone, replaced with sky and sea. "Your coffee is cooling."

I had no doubt that they could still see me, and I felt incredibly uncomfortable that I couldn't see them as I returned to the sofa. "What do you want from me?"

"Nothing."

"I don't believe you." Today, he was wearing his white trousers, but instead of his white shirt, it was a pale blue. He looked as if he should be walking across a beach in the Caribbean, not lounging on a sofa, drinking coffee with me while hell literally happened outside his window. His feet were still bare, I noticed.

"You don't need to believe me," Cross answered, easily interrupting my inspection of his feet. "Nor do I ask that you trust me."

"Then why am I here, Cross? What do you want from me?"

The man—no, he wasn't a man—the male in front of me sat back and looked me over head to foot. I was still in the stupid bedsheet, but his look was clinical; there was nothing "off" about it. "My desire is to keep you safe."

"Where were you when I got a dagger in the heart?" I muttered as I adjusted uncomfortably on the sofa.

"I was here."

"Well, that sucked for me," I snapped.

"My servant was with you."

When had Hound come into the room? Sitting in the corner, watching us both. "I know he was *with* me—I can still feel his teeth on my neck." My anger was surfacing, and I struggled to fight it down. "I want to go home."

"No."

Inhaling deeply while fighting for calm, I stretched my neck as I rolled my head on my shoulders. "Then let me go to the Land of the Souls."

"No."

"I can't stay here."

"Actually, you can." His smile was benevolent and showed his perfect white teeth. "This is exactly what you will do."

"So, I am a prisoner."

"You may label it however you see fit."

"It's not a label, it's a fact. You won't let me leave. I'm here against my will. Therefore, prisoner."

"Fair enough." Cross stood as he walked over to the bookcase that wasn't there earlier.

"Nothing about this is fair," I mumbled as I watched him.

"Very true," he said as he glanced at me over his shoulder. "But then, life rarely is."

"So, I can't leave and I'm not dead." I waited for him to nod. "So, what's your plan?"

"I thought you may wish to be taught."

Of all the things I was waiting for him to say, that wasn't it. "Huh?"

"You can continue to be an ignorant, bumbling mess," he

began, "no offence intended, and please note, whilst it *is* incredibly endearing, it's also frustrating."

"Well, excuse me for not being fucking incredible."

Cross was suddenly in front of me, and I shrank back at the wildness in his rich brown eyes as he leaned down, his eyes level with mine. "But, Star, you *are* incredible, and I want nothing more than for you to realise it."

"How?" What had been in his coffee?

"I'm going to teach you."

"Teach me what?"

"How to kill a prince of hell." His wide smile scared me. "Or two."

Cross was insane. Of course he was. Fan-fucking-tastic.

CHAPTER 4

"You want me to kill a prince of hell? Maybe two?" I asked him as he straightened and went back to his bookcase.

"Yes."

"And how do you propose I do that?" What harm was there in entertaining his madness when I was already dead anyway?

"Well, we need to fix your powers for one," Cross told me as he searched his bookcase.

Honestly, it was about eight shelves and perhaps a meter, maybe a meter and a half, wide. It wasn't the British freaking Library he had in front of him. It had to hold about three hundred books, maybe more, maybe less. My nosiness was getting the better of me. "Okay, one, how? And two, what the hell are you looking for?"

"One, with a spell. Two, a book."

"Isn't it fun that you're some kind of insane comedy genius?" My voice dripped with sarcasm as he reached out to a book.

"You're delightful," he said with a wide smile before he turned back to the book. "Yes, this one."

"Have you any clothes for me?"

Cross looked up and looked me over as if he had forgotten I was still rocking bedsheet fashion. "Of course."

Looking down, I saw that I was wearing white jeans and a simple white button-down shirt. Lifting the shirt away from me, I stared down at my chest, which was supported with a plain white bra, and I was aware that I had underwear on. "I know you don't know me well, but me and white…that's a recipe for disaster." My clothes were black. "Well, that just blew my mind."

"Happier?" Cross asked as he sat down.

"You could dress me the whole time?" I asked suspiciously as I retook my seat.

"Yes."

"Then why was I wearing a sheet for so long?"

"I thought you may have grown attached to it."

I gaped at him. "Like a blankie?" He looked slightly confused, and I fought the eye roll. "Like a comfort blanket," I explained.

"Ah, yes."

I'd lost him again to the book. He just dressed me with magic...or something. Was it also an illusion? "If I were to walk down the street, would people see these clothes?"

I heard him fight his sigh of irritation, and I was perversely glad that I was annoying him. "They wouldn't see you, Star. So, no."

"Okay, grumpy grumpison, but if I was able to be *seen*, would they see these clothes, or am I a delusional emperor?"

Cross closed the book. His hands rested on it, one over the other, and I swear, if he wore glasses, he would be peering over the rim. He was projecting very strong headmaster vibes.

"I knew you would be a challenge," he told me. "You are not the emperor, you have not been duped by crafty tailors, you are not walking around naked. The clothes are real. The fact that I can manifest them is because I am capable of doing so. Can you please stop focusing on small inconsequential things; your method of coping is...distracting. If you need to, just let it all out."

I felt both scolded and infuriated. It was a weird feeling. My emotions were high, my temper was bordering on rage, and my inner wellness was a thriving pit of uncertainty. He wanted it all out?

Fine.

The scream made him jump. A small petty part of me felt immense smugness at the unflappable demon reacting to my pitiful hurt. I screamed until I lost my voice, and then I screamed some more.

When I opened my eyes, I was on the floor, my knees drawn up to my chest. Hound was in front of me, his eyes a dull red, and carefully, he placed his head on my knees. Without thought, I reached out and scratched his ear. Hound moved forward, and my head dropped to rest atop his.

We sat like that for a long time. A former clairvoyant, an almost witch, a broken soul, and the hellhound who took me to hell. The tears slipped free, and when Hound raised his head, we sat forehead pressed to forehead and just…were.

I knew Cross was gone, and I was glad. I had no doubt that he was still watching me, just as I knew the horror that lay beyond the glass was not a green-tinged sky and deep ocean, but a nightmare that would make every person topside rethink their actions if they knew what was waiting for them below their feet.

Nothing was real, but everything was real. Nothing was the same, but everything felt familiar. Hound was not my friend, but right now, he felt like my only ally.

Sensing I was over my meltdown, the hellhound sat back and regarded me with an almost nervousness?

"Hey," I said to him as I wiped my eyes. "Guess I needed that, huh?"

Hound nodded.

"You know I'm still pissed at you," I told him. "And it just shows you how fucked up my life is that I'm still talking to you."

Hound's nose nudged my leg, and I huffed out a laugh. "I am. You don't get to go all cute on me; you're still a scary ass hellhound, not some cute golden retriever."

Hound rolled his eyes.

"A scary ass hellhound with attitude," I mocked him as I stood. "How come I can't talk to you?"

"Because the hellhounds are mine to command," Cross said

conversationally from behind me. He was back on his sofa, this time with a glass of wine.

"That *is* red wine and not blood or some other bodily fluid that's going to make me barf?"

"It's the flesh and blood of…Napa Valley grapes."

"You're a dick." Flopping down on the couch, I looked over at him and then pointedly at his glass. "Share."

The second glass appeared on the table, and still avoiding the antics of the carved figures on the table, I reached over, picked up the glass and took a long drink. "So, where were we?"

"You were screaming, and my soldier asked me to leave so he could give you comfort."

My surprised stare caught Hound's. "You asked?" I was grateful to the hound that killed me. Yup. That was pretty much my fucked up life. "Thank you."

"He didn't kill you. The dagger allowed you to come here," Cross explained.

"Did *he* mean to kill me?" I asked quietly as I sipped my wine.

"It was Samyaza's intent for you to cross over."

"Cross over…" I suddenly understood his name. "This is where you tell me your name isn't Cross?"

"I have many names. I like Cross. It has many implications. Both spiritual and penalising."

"And I'm going to avoid that conversation," I told him truthfully. "My brain is close to breaking as it is."

"Wise choice." His smirk was playful.

"Did your book answer your question?" I changed the subject.

"Hmm, perhaps."

"Don't tell me: I'm on a need-to-know basis, and I currently do not need to know?"

Cross surprised me when he said, "No. You need to know everything."

"Well, that's new."

His low chuckle made me relax more. "You need to know it all, but not all at once."

"And there it is," I said with scorn as I took a drink of my wine. "Keep me dangling, a game I no longer want to play."

"Did you ever *want* to play?"

With a snort, I half lay on the couch, clutching my glass. "No, but I wasn't in charge of the rules."

"You had more control than you think you did. You just hadn't been taught to know it."

"And you can teach me?" I asked the enigmatic male curiously.

"I can and I will." Cross emptied his glass and set it on the table. "Have you tried reaching for your powers?"

"Yes, they're gone."

"They're not gone, they're just out of reach," Cross told me as he crossed his legs and looked towards the windows, where the illusion was now showing a darkening sky.

"Is that the illusion, or were the fiery depths of hell the illusion?" I asked him curiously. A small smile played around his lips, but he didn't answer me, and I think I already knew he wouldn't. "So…my power is…where?"

"When Samyaza stabbed you, you entered a state of…limbo, shall we say? You are not dead, but to be here, you are not fully alive either. As you have not died, you cannot go to the Land of the Souls. As you are not alive, your powers think you are, in fact, dead."

"My powers *think*?"

He grimaced as he thought about his word choice. "Obviously, it is not separate, but you are aware of it being *aware* of you, are you not?"

I almost snapped at him to say no, but then I remembered that time when they told me to *take them*, they were *mine*. "I think I know what you mean."

"At present, they are absent, for want of a better word, and we need them to come back. Yes?"

"Yes."

"There is a catch," Cross said, and I knew it was coming.

"There always is."

"If we are successful and they return, he *will* be able to find you."

"Sam?"

Cross nodded. "He will be able to track you the moment you hold your powers again."

Asshole.

But then I thought about it. "Wait," I said as I sat up and looked at Cross with wide eyes. "They don't know where I am?"

Cross grinned at me as his glass seemingly refilled itself. "You thought they knew where you were?"

"I thought they would know," I admitted. This was great, he wasn't coming for me. Wait. This meant no one knew where I was, and I had no power. Cross was far too amused to not have been listening to me again. My eyes flicked to Hound, who was lounging in front of the fire. "Hound hasn't told them?"

"The hellhounds are mine to command; no one else has the ability to do so at present."

"So, when Hound and the other two were with the Watchers, they were there because you sent them?"

"Hellhounds carry souls. It is not usual for them to be requested when death isn't the end game."

"What are you saying? The Watchers *did* mean to kill me?"

"No, that was not their intent."

"Are you saying that me being here is a fluke?"

"Happy coincidence."

"Happy for who?" I asked in bewilderment. "To see a hellhound means death," I reiterated the old adage as I stared at him. "Has that changed?"

"No." Cross looked past me as he considered his words. "A hellhound is many things, but the main purpose really, is that of a soul carrier. A psychopomp, are you familiar with the word?" When I shook my head, he nodded thoughtfully. "It's derived from Greek, basically meaning a guide to souls or of souls. Many animals and deities are guiders of souls. Angels, obviously; spirits of loved ones already passed; for some it is a raven, a crow, a vulture; animals or creatures with wings seem to be common." Cross smiled briefly. "But in some cultures, it's a horse, a deer, perhaps even a dog."

"A hellhound?"

"Yes, in ancient Egypt, the god Anubis was considered the deity that took your soul to the underworld, a man with a canine head. Or perhaps you prefer the fabled ferryman to whom you pay your pennies to cross the waters, or the messenger of the ancient gods. The Norse had their Valkyries; every culture has their own belief. All can be true or none at all, but whatever their appearance, a soul needs to be carried to cross the veil."

"Why did I get a hellhound and not an angel?"

"You are a witch. I believe your Watchers already explained your destination was downward."

"Hound was always my end?"

Cross shook his head slightly. "You were struck by a Watcher; Samyaza is more than capable of carrying your soul. You forget what he once was."

"An angel," I whispered as I looked away from Cross's knowing stare. "He's no angel now."

Cross laughed at my comment as he leaned back in his seat. "Your Hound stepped in and took your soul instead, and here we are."

"Here we are," I repeated as I watched Hound yawn widely. "He intervened?"

"He did."

"On whose command? Yours?" I asked suspiciously.

"No, he made the choice."

"So…" I didn't understand any of this. "You weren't expecting me?"

"I was not." Cross looked far too pleased with this.

"Then let me go."

He was wearing a huge grin now and looked delighted with my suggestion. "I cannot. You need your powers."

"When I get them back, can I go?"

"No."

I felt my frustration rising, and I wanted to scream again.

"But, when you get them back *and* you can use them, *then* I will let you go."

Staring at him, I felt hope rising within me. Was he serious? Actually honest to goodness serious? "Promise me?"

"You have my word."

"And your word is…?"

"My honour."

Well, when he put it like that, how could I get this wrong?

CHAPTER 5

SOMETHING CROSS SAID TO ME WAS NIGGLING, AND AS I DRANK MY wine, my eyes kept returning to Hound. "I can command the hellhounds."

Cross looked up from his book that he was once again skimming through and gave me a nod in confirmation. "You've called them before."

"I called Hound. I thought…" Wetting my lips, I considered my words. "I thought it was my anger."

"You are a necromancer. A very strong one. You command the dead, the souls, and the ones who carry them."

"All of them?" I asked eagerly.

His slight smile made me smile bashfully in return. "The angels, even the fallen ones, answer a different command."

Rubbing my hand over my knee, I gave a rueful shrug. "A girl can hope," I murmured as I took a sip of my wine. "Why can't you take me to the Land of the Souls?"

"It is not safe for you there," Cross answered easily.

"I need to see Gran." I shifted uncomfortably. "I need to speak to my mum. Like seriously need to talk to my mum." Mum would be freaking out. "I need to tell her I'm not dead. Completely."

"I can send the hound."

Was he crazy? "Are you insane?" I asked him incredulously. "To see a hellhound *means* death; are you trying to kill my mum?"

"You're being very"—his head tilted as he considered me— "dramatic."

"You just offered to send a being that *carries souls over the veil* to my mum!"

"Your mother wouldn't see him," Cross explained patiently.

"Your mother holds power, albeit slight, but it's there. She would understand the message."

"Well, next time, lead with the non-death bit." I looked over at Hound who was, as always, watching me. "Can he shift into something else?"

"The form he is in now is his preferred state."

"Were you an angel too?" I asked Hound softly. Red eyes stared back at me. "When I can command them again, will..." I hesitated. "Will I also be able to talk to him?"

"You can talk to him now," Cross stated simply.

My eye roll was legendary. "Will he be able to communicate with me? And don't say he communicates with me now, I mean like he can communicate with you."

"No."

"Oh." Should I have felt so disappointed? Probably not. *Did* I feel disappointed? Yes. "When can you teach me how to shield my thoughts from others?"

"When your powers are back."

"Okay, so to get them back, I need to do what?" I asked him. I was eager to start. "Also, how do we fix my non-alive state?"

"We start with meditation."

I'd had a very bad feeling he was going to suggest something like that. Me achieving inner peace with the way I was currently feeling? Not likely. "And plan B?"

"There is no plan B."

"And this is where you will fail, my young padawan."

"What?"

"No sci-fi down here, I'm guessing?" I joked as I involuntarily looked towards the windows, which were now showing a midnight dark sky. "I guess when you're living in the fantasy, it's hard to differentiate."

"I try to keep abreast of many things that the human world fixates on, but I fear you have lost me."

"Nope, not lost you, you're still right here." Cross looked… cross. I bit back my grin. "*Star Wars*, I don't think it's your thing," I said easily as I finished my wine.

"Your brain is never at rest."

"Is anyone's?" I asked in surprise.

"Meditation will be good for you." Cross stood and looked to the wall we had "walked" through earlier. "You need more sleep."

"All I've done is sleep," I grumbled as I stood.

"Your energy needs to recharge. Before I can teach you to run, Star, I must teach you how to walk."

I'd been staring at the "sky" outside, still unsure what was real and what was not, before I turned to Cross. "Did you just *baby step* me?"

"Do you mean encourage you to take it slow?" At my nod, he smiled. "Yes, I did."

"How long does meditation take?"

His look was enough to suggest that, for me, the answer may be too long.

I HAD BEEN in the room for an unknown number of days before Cross had let me out for a visit to the living room, I guess it was called. In the times I had woken up in the stark white-walled room, not much had changed. White marble floor, white walls, one bed with white bedding, and then on his previous visit, I had a dressing table with no mirror, and my other décor consisted of one moving-through-walls hellhound.

When I opened my eyes this time, blue-green sky greeted me as I peered up at a skylight.

I had a skylight.

With a weird sky.

In hell.

"I wonder, if I ask, if he'll get me a pool," I said to the empty room as I sat up and got out of bed. Last night, well, I don't know if it was actually night, but last time I saw him, he gave me the softest, most comfiest jammies I had ever worn. Also white. The man had a thing for a colour-free zone. "His shirt was blue," I reminded myself as I padded across the floor. "And I got black clothes."

Staring at the wall, I closed my eyes and walked towards it, promptly banging my nose off it and bouncing back a step.

"Platform nine and three-quarters you are not," I said bitterly. "Cross!" I yelled. "I need coffee, I'm awake. Let me out!" Cocking my head, I waited as I listened. "And toast! I want toast and marmalade."

"I'm not a drive-thru at a fast-food chain." I didn't hide my jump as he spoke from behind me, and he didn't bother to hide his smile at my reaction. "Star," he greeted.

"Cross," I mimicked. "I'm hungry."

"Interesting."

"Because dead people can't be hungry?"

"You're not dead," he reminded me as he took a hold of my arm and walked me through walls again.

"How come you know fast food, but you didn't know *Star Wars*?"

"Is this how we're starting this session?" he asked me as he walked over to his sofa and picked up his already steaming coffee cup.

Today, he was actually distracting me with his clothing choices. Worn faded jeans, a simple white tee and those damn bare feet. He was pulling off sexy incredibly well, and I hated that I noticed. Demons had done enough to ruin my life.

"What kind of marmalade?"

"Seville orange," I answered automatically as I walked over

and saw toast and condiments appear on the table. "Is this you, magic or invisible minions of hell?"

"Invisible minions." He held my stare.

He's bluffing.

What if he's not?

Don't you dare ask him!

"You serious?" I blurted out. My inner voice was disgusted with myself.

"Deadly."

It was the tone. The unblinking stare. My eyes narrowed. "Are you serious about *this*?"

"Invisible minions of hell?" He grinned widely. "No."

"You're a dick."

"You're a gullible idiot."

I paused as I reached for the golden toasted deliciousness and then shrugged. "Been called worse."

"Your marmalade is apricot."

"I asked for orange."

"You prefer apricot."

"That's creepy." It was creepy, but it didn't stop me from reaching eagerly for the crystal jar of thick juicy yumminess and eagerly spreading it on my toast.

"Once you have eaten, we will commence."

"You speak weird." My voice was full of toast and marmalade, and I knew that bothered him, but I also didn't care.

"Says the guttersnipe on my sofa."

"Oooh, what's a guttersnipe?" I asked before I took another huge bite.

"Star."

"Mm-hmm?"

"Let's stop the bullshit."

My mouth fell open, and I looked at him as he blanched and

averted his gaze. Hastily, I swallowed my mouthful of toast and tried to clear my throat so I could speak, only I choked instead.

"You truly are a walking disaster."

Cross handed me a glass of water, which I took and gulped down the contents greedily. "You swore at me!"

"You swear from the moment you open your eyes to the moment you close them, and even then, there are several swear words just floating in your subconscious."

"You watch me *sleep*?"

"I *hear* you sleep. There's a difference."

"I think you may be creepier than the other lot," I tell him as I finish my toast. "When do I start to need the bathroom?"

Cross shook his head slightly in mortification. "Where do you think your waste is going to go?"

For a moment, I was stumped. I genuinely had no words. "Hell has no indoor plumbing?"

"I am not about to start talking to you about waste processing plants and sewerage, but just accept, as long as you're here, you won't need any…relief."

"Sexual too?"

"I'm ignoring you."

"Most people do."

"When you've finished thinking you are hungry, we can begin training."

"I'm finished." Eagerly standing up, I looked around. "Any chance you have a pool?"

Cross had risen to his feet slower than I had, and I heard his heavy sigh. "Yes, I have three, water's so easy to come by down here."

"Hmm, swearing and sarcasm." I gave a light laugh. "I think I'm rubbing off on you."

"You have no idea how terrifying that thought is." Cross

pointed to the far corner of the room where I saw mats had been placed.

"You serious with the meditating?" I asked him as I walked over there.

"Yes."

"Is my mum okay?" I asked him, trying to be casual and failing badly.

"Yes."

"You sent Hound?"

"He is familiar with Jean."

My head snapped up to meet his gaze. "Don't do that." I fought my temper down. "Don't be *familiar* with my mum."

"Even for you, that sounded…sordid." Cross gracefully sat down and assumed a position I was sure would break my knees.

"Shut up." I grunted as I landed heavily on my ass, and looking at his legs again, I decided to pull mine up to my chest instead.

"What do you want, Star?"

"To go back to the way that it was before and be no part of any of it," I answered with no hesitation. "Of *them*."

"That ship sailed. You are where you are. The choices made are in the past. What do you want *now*?"

My head was lowered as I stared at my knees, but I felt it, coursing through me, rising, raging, eager to be free. "Revenge."

"Against?"

"Them. *Him*. Asmodeous. All of them. Yeqon." My frown deepened as I thought about his awful trickery. "*Especially* Yeqon."

"He's in the pit."

"What's that?" Dimly I remembered a night not that long ago when some of the demons ran to get Sam, worried he would be *thrown in the pit*.

"There are seven circles of hell, each more depraved, dangerous and deadly than the last, do you know this?"

Nodding, I sat up straighter. "Yes, Gran told me."

"And with each level, there is a prince."

"Yes, Asmodeous, his level is lust." It still annoyed me that the Watchers worked for him. Of course, now it made more sense. It was definitely *lust* that got me into this mess.

"The Watchers are not tied to any level," Cross reminded me as if he read my thoughts, and because it was him, he probably had. "They watch. They step in when order needs to be restored. Soldiers."

I snorted. "Of course they are. Zel's the bossiest bastard I've ever met; makes sense he's on a power trip." Cross said nothing as I thought about the demons I had so willingly interacted with and trusted. Bastards. "Why would they be allowed to order princes around?"

"They fell first. They led the rebellion against heaven, but they did not want to rule. They wanted only to live with those whom they watched."

"Coveted." I glared at the wall. "They *coveted* humans. They basically said fuck you to the Ten Commandments and are all dicks."

This time, Cross laughed at my outburst. "You are so delightful. Your anger burns so brightly it's mesmerising."

"I'm not a log fire, and quit laughing at me." I concentrated on trying to make my legs do what Cross's were, but my calves weren't meant to sit on my thighs like that. "So...do I need to know all the princes?"

"No," Cross said as he shook his head.

Oh shit, he was going to make me ask him. "Are *you* a prince?"

"You know I'm not."

"I don't know a lot, remember?" I muttered as we watched each other. "So, you're not a prince, and I won't meet any more? Why?"

"Some have moved on and some are no longer seen."

"Moved on? Where else can they go?"

Cross ignored me; he was good at that. "There are seven levels of hell, and then there is the pit."

Uneasiness uncurled in my stomach. "At the bottom of it all?" I asked, knowing it was true.

Cross ran his eyes over me: my blonde hair tangled and uncombed, lying over my shoulders; wearing my comfy white pj's that he gave me; my feet bare like his. His expression gave nothing away. I had no idea what he thought when he looked at me, but I knew I would never play poker with this man. He made Sam look soft. "It's called the pit for a reason," he said as his dark eyes watched me.

Wetting my lips, I couldn't stop the look over my shoulder to the wall showing a clear greenish sky. "What level are we on?"

His smile was deadly, his eyes dancing with cold amusement. "*We* aren't on any level."

Fear clutched at my throat. "I'm in the pit?"

"Welcome to hell."

CHAPTER 6

"I've been in hell for days—how many days? Actually, tell me that later." Pulling my hair over my shoulder, I tried not to freak out. "I knew I was in hell, so it's quite anticlimactic to say *welcome to hell* when I'm already in hell and have been in hell for *x* number of days"—I held my hand up to stop him interrupting me —"no, I'll cope with all your weirdness after I'm done with my rant." I noticed his look. "Shut up, this is *my* rant. This is my breakdown, you don't get a say." *Breathe, Star,* I told myself. "Welcome to hell…was that your mic drop moment?" Cross said nothing, and I knew I was going to commit bodily harm to him soon. "How long have I been here?"

"In human terms?"

"Yes!" Wait. "There's other terms? What are the other terms?"

He leaned forward, his elbow on his folded leg and his hand resting on his chin. It was impossible for that position to be comfortable, yet he looked as relaxed as if he were lying stretched out on a couch. "Time moves differently here."

"Oh my God, I've fallen through the back of the wardrobe."

"Hmm, possibly more akin to falling down the rabbit hole more than a winter wonderland." His smirk was hovering, and I knew he was trying to be playful. "Bit hot here for winter."

"Cross…I'm going to throttle you soon."

"I know, it's endearing that you think you could." He turned to look out the window. The sky was bright and welcoming. I no longer knew what was real and what was illusion, how could I? Everything was an illusion. He looked to be watching something intently in the sky, and I wondered what it was that Cross was seeing through the window.

"You okay?" I asked as I looked between him and the window. "What can you see?"

"Trouble."

"Who?"

"You." His smile was blinding. "Can we meditate now?"

"No," I stammered incredulously. "Explain terms, time, stuff!!"

"In human terms, you have been here for two weeks."

"Two *weeks*?"

"Do not screech, Star. I am not deaf, and I would prefer to keep it that way." Cross picked imaginary lint off his jeans.

Closing my eyes, I tried to push the panic down. "I'll have lost my job. My mum's going to have been going insane with worry. Oh God, Dad will have a search party out. I bet he's already had them out. Ruairidh, oh my gosh, Ruairidh will be distraught—"

"Please, can you stop? Your Watchers have taken care of it all: your work gave you leave, your dad has been exchanging text messages with you daily, and your mum has been informed you are fine. Your friend…I believe he thinks you are on vacation."

"I'm on holiday? With who?" His suppressed smile caused my jaw to drop. Again. "He thinks I'm with *Sam*?"

"Your love is very convincing." Cross sniffed dismissively. "Star, focus. You are here, they are there, they believe you have come to no harm. We need to work together to get your powers back."

Squeezing my eyes shut, I fought my scream back. I needed to focus; Cross was right. I needed to get my powers and then get out of here. "How long have I been here in demon terms?"

"Slightly longer."

"Cross," I warned him.

"Four weeks, give or take. Time moves differently here."

"I've been with you for a month, and they haven't come for me?"

"They do not know you are here, and hell is a vast place." Cross looked as if he was ready to call it a day, and I reached out and grabbed his arm.

"No. I'm sorry, I'm ready. It's a lot, but I need to be able to adapt." Nodding to myself, I rolled my head from side to side, loosening up my neck. "I'm ready."

"Very well." He settled himself back into his leg pretzel pose. "I asked you what you wanted, you said revenge." Cross closed his eyes and took a deep breath and held it. As I watched him, I felt pressure in my own lungs build. Realising I had inhaled with him, I let out my breath in a rush as I fought not to choke. Cross carried on as if I weren't a three-year-old toddler being disruptive. "You seek to harm a prince of hell. You seek to harm some Watchers. I can help with that. You seek to return home. I can help with that, although you may not want to return when all is said and done."

"What do you mean? Why wouldn't I want to go home?"

He slowly opened his eyes, and I was captivated by his deep chocolate gaze. "When you have more understanding of who you are, what you are capable of, then you may find the world you know is too mundane for your tastes when you are in full control of your powers."

"What kind of magic are you going to teach me?" I asked softly. I knew a blood spell was cast on Asmodeous, and I knew I couldn't read it, but I somehow knew I could cast it.

"The best kind."

"You mean dark, don't you?"

"Black magic is more fun." Cross closed his eyes again. "Let's begin."

"I don't want to know dark magic. I want to know what's right."

"There is no right and wrong when you command the dead,

Star. Stop being a naïve child. Do you think Asmodeous, if he finds you, is going to treat you kindly? Fairly? Justly? You destroyed the spell that can set him free. He will have you burning in oil as he peels the skin from your body before he flays the very flesh from your bones. Every day. He will share your body around his soldiers who will feast on your flesh while you scream in pain and pray for an end. You'll wish for death, and death will not come. No Watcher will save you, child, when he claims his right to you."

I was going to be sick. "That's quite the picture you paint." My voice was hoarse, and I felt a shiver of fear run over me as I saw no sympathy in Cross's eyes.

"It is your reality. Unless you shut up, stop being a child, and learn. I can teach you all you need to know, but you need to learn. You need to *want* to learn."

"Of course I want to learn!" I snapped angrily as I struggled to my feet. "You think I want to be here, with you? With Hound? I want out of here as much as you want me to leave. I just don't want to have to spill blood to do a spell or sell my soul to a devil in the hopes of revenge."

"The devil is not interested in you; you have nothing to give him. Plus, Samyaza already marked you as his."

"He did *what*?"

"They know you're somewhere in hell, but they don't know where."

"And that makes it okay to *brand* me? Hasn't his *seed* withered and died like he should?"

"Your voice becomes unnaturally high when you talk of him. Do you want him to find you? I can let them know where you are."

"Don't you dare."

"Very well. Can we commence?"

"I don't think I can meditate," I huffed at him as my anger continued to soar. "They make me angry."

"Sharks or rabbits?"

"What?"

"If you don't stop acting so petulantly, I will put you either in a pool of sharks or a pen of rabbits." Cross's smile had no humour and lots of teeth. "Pick. Your ridiculous fear or your irrational hatred?"

"I pick meditation." I hastily sat down.

"Wonderful choice." He waited until I was back with my legs crossed simply in front of me and watching him for further instruction. "Now, you need to close your eyes, clear your mind, and just attain clarity."

I lasted perhaps a second before my question tumbled out. "What the fuck does that even mean?"

"You achieved this with Azazel."

"I was reaching for my powers."

"And what, pray tell me, are you trying to achieve here?" Cross asked me with amusement.

Oh.

"Oh. Why couldn't you say that?"

"I thought I was." His sigh was heavy, and I closed my eyes. "Well, it's a start."

"How do I clear my mind? Silence makes me edgy."

"I'm shocked," he deadpanned. "Instead of thinking on every whimsy or flight of fancy you get distracted with, instead of chasing down errant thoughts, think of nothing at all."

"Is nothing black?"

"What?"

"Do I just think of blackness, like a giant hole?"

"No, why are you trying to visualise nothing?"

"Well, it can't be nothing, it has to be *something*. Nothing has to look like something, else how would we know it was *nothing*?"

"That's ridiculous. You are absurd. I may just feed you to the sharks myself."

"Should I lie down? I may be better at this lying down." Without waiting for a reply, I lay down on the cosy shaggy fur rug. Stretching out, I relaxed. "Okay. Hit me with your magic."

"Achieve a sense of calm."

This was stupid. The man, male, demon-like person, had been with me for what did he say, a month? He'd already told me I was chaotic. However, it was either try or die. Wow, that was sobering. Pity I wasn't drunk. Maybe I needed alcohol?

"No." Cross's tone was dry and brooked no argument.

"I didn't *say* anything," I protested.

"I'm leaving. Stay there. Concentrate. Relax."

"Paradoxical."

"Shut up." He sounded grouchy, and I wondered if he actually left.

When I peeked through half closed eyes, I saw he was gone. Instantly I was on my feet and lying down on the sofa. Closing my eyes, I yawned widely. A nap was the best way to clear my mind.

Trees loomed over me, a low mist covered the ground, and looking down, I saw I was in another white billowy dress. Great, I was re-enacting music videos again. My hair was loose, and as I turned slowly to take in my surroundings, I sensed no breeze. Which was odd as the leaves on the tree branches swayed to a silent beat.

"Please, God, let me be dreaming." I took a step forward, and then from my peripheral vision, I saw it. The small cyclone heading my way. "Wind!" I greeted it enthusiastically as I looked around again. This wasn't the Land of the Souls, was it? I hadn't seen a forest before. Wind scooped me up and took me where it wanted to. I was under no illusion I was controlling it.

When I was where it wanted me to be, I was set on the

ground, and I faced the Waterfall of Solitude. Only it wasn't the waterfall I knew. The world was grey. When I had been here before, it was always white, which Sa—*dickhead*, I corrected myself—had said was unusual. He saw colour when he was here. Why would I now see white to grey? Was I soon to see it in colour, or had the land been affected as I had been?

Was this Asmodeous? Stepping forward, I realised it was. The land wasn't grey, it was covered in ash. He had burned it. Or someone had. Where were the souls?

"Wind? I need to go to the Plains of the Dead."

Wind picked me up and carried me to the cliffs, giving me a view of the plains. They were empty. "No." I spun on my heel and jumped back in fright when I came face-to-face with the demon I wasn't ready to see.

"Witch."

"Demon." I was surprised and gratified my voice was steady.

"You're hiding from me."

"And yet here you are." My heart was racing. He looked as he always did. Cold. Hard. Impossibly handsome.

"Where are you, witch?"

"Where are you?" He didn't know where I was? Could he not see me? Stepping forward, I realised he was not looking at me but through me. Sam may be in front of me, but I was not in front of him *that he could see.* I had the advantage?

Well, that was new.

His longish black hair sat curled on the collar of his black tunic. His leather trousers hugged his thighs as always, and his shitkicker boots had two handles protruding from them, not the only weapons he wore. My eyes caught and held on the dagger at his side. The one that stabbed me. His fingers ran over the hilt as he looked at me. Deep green eyes glowed faintly with power, and I realised suddenly how *normal* it felt to be within his reach.

Taking a step back, I cautiously took my eyes off him as I

looked to see what he was looking at. There was nothing there. Turning back, I almost swallowed my tongue when I realised I was almost pressed against him. His breath caressed mine, and I was scared to move.

"Where are you, little witch?" he whispered to himself.

As I stood still in front of him, I held my breath. There was a tightness around his eyes, I noted. He looked…*tired*? Was he exhausted looking for me? Good. I hope he never slept again. His conscience should weigh him down. The guilt should choke him.

"I'm right here," I taunted him as he looked around, and I feared I made a mistake when his fingers stilled their movement on his dagger and his other hand was raised to his lips. A soft caress of his thumb over his lower lip had me wetting my own, much to my disgust.

"I can taste you," Sam said into the quiet. "I know I am close, but I don't know where. Help me, witch."

"Never," I swore as he took a step back.

"I will find you, Star."

My heart leaped. Sam had never called me by my name to my face. He had said my name to my parents, but never addressed *me* as Star. I was always witch. Although I knew he wasn't talking to me right now, it was the closest I had ever gotten to hearing my name on his lips when he was talking to me, even if I was a hidden figure.

Emboldened by his inability to see me, I stepped closer. "You will never be this close to me again," I whispered in his ear, and I heard him inhale sharply, somehow sensing me even though he couldn't see me.

"Tricks, little witch?" Sam rumbled, and I felt his chest shake with amusement as I realised I had reached out to touch him. My hand lay against his chest as I had reached up to talk to him. "What cleverness have you learned, my little witch?"

"I've learned you're a dick and a prick, and I wonder if this hurts, demon?" Taking the dagger from its holster, I looked at it as I ran my thumb over the blade. "Let's see how you like it," I hissed as I plunged the dagger into his chest.

CHAPTER 7

UTTER INCOMPETENCE. THAT'S WHAT I FELT. THE DAGGER SLID through his clothing, into his flesh, sliding towards his dark blackened heart, and he didn't even blink. Sam looked down at the hilt protruding from his chest, and much to my chagrin, he threw his head back and laughed out loud.

"Witch, I *knew* I could taste you on the air." He looked around at the empty plains as we stood almost chest to chest, and I saw the shadows that had been under his eyes, as clear as if he were being freaking airbrushed in front of me. "I will find you, and when I do…" He plucked the dagger out of his chest like it was a wayward toothpick. "You will regret hiding from me."

Was he so completely delusional and arrogant that he thought I was playing a game with him? Did he think I wanted the back-stabbing—no, *front* stabbing—bastard to find me? Did he think I was flirting? Playing an elaborate game of hide and seek…in hell?

I may stab him again.

"Zel!" Sam called.

The dark demon was in front of him, and instantly his head lifted up as he inhaled. "You found her?"

"I think she found me," Sam answered him with amusement. "She stabbed me."

Zel grunted as he looked around. "Where is she?"

"I don't know," Sam mused as he studied the dagger. "But it was definitely her. I could almost taste her on my tongue," he said as he smiled knowingly at Zel. "And she does taste so sweet."

"I don't need to know the details of your perversions with the witch." Zel's eyes roved over the plains before he turned back to

Sam. "It makes sense she would come here. This is familiar to her."

"Dangerous. And stupid," Sam frowned as he criticised me.

"Exactly like her." Zel snorted as he crossed his arms across his chest. "He finds her, and you won't be smiling."

"He finds her and touches one hair on her head, and I will kill him and any who stand with him."

I took a step back as Sam's face changed, and I saw what I had witnessed only once before. *Samyaza the Watcher.* So fierce, so strong, his power… My mouth watered at the vastness of the raw power exuding from him. Had he always been like this? This…force?

"You cannot bring down hell for one silly witch," Zel scoffed.

"Be careful, Azazel." Sam's low warning tone to Zel had my eyes widening.

"She could be anywhere, someone will find her, and then we'll all have to listen to her screeches." Zel rubbed a hand over his jaw. "It's been peaceful without her yammering."

"She cannot fall into the wrong hands," Sam murmured as he looked at his tunic and the hole from where I'd stabbed him. "Did we not tell her that we were immortal?" he asked Zel conversationally. When Zel nodded, Sam chuckled. "Why does she never listen?"

"Because she's the most infuriating creature to have ever breathed?" Zel responded automatically.

Sam said nothing, but I saw his small smile. Like he was pleased that Zel said horrible things about me. *Zel*…another one that I would happily stab.

"I shall make Bara come here and patrol," Zel said as he looked to the sky. "If she came once, she may come again."

"We need to find her. When she realises why it's empty…"

As my eyes darted between the two of them and the

surrounding area, I waited for them to finish the sentence. *Why was it empty?*

"It will be hard for her," Zel agreed as he bent to pick up the ash, letting it trail through his fingers. "She's going to take the guilt as her own."

"It may break her."

"Probably. She's sensitive to this shit," Zel huffed in agreement. "I'll send Bara."

Sam nodded as Zel winked out of there, and Sam remained. "I know you're still here." His words were quiet. "You need to show yourself to me."

Not flipping likely. Was he insane? Had he forgotten he killed me?

Suddenly Sam spun on his heel, his attention on the water that lay beyond. "Interesting," he breathed just before he vanished completely.

"What? What's interesting?" Peering out over the water, I saw nothing.

"You play a dangerous game."

My scream frightened even me. Cross was beside me, his eyes hard as he too stared out over the water. "Jesus fuck, are you trying to just finish me off?" I demanded as I clutched at my chest, my heart racing.

"Showing yourself to Samyaza was foolish."

"He didn't see me," I corrected. "He only sensed me."

"Sensing you? You may as well have placed an arrow above your head and said, *I'm here.*" Cross looked pissed, and I studied him closely. He wasn't masking his frustration. Well, Mum always said I would test the patience of a saint.

"What is it that he sees?" I changed the subject as I looked back over the water.

"Trouble."

"Informative," I snarked as I twisted the end of my hair in my hands.

"Are you ready to return?" Cross asked me as he gave me his full attention.

"To earth? Absolutely," I replied even as I saw his frown. "To your doorless abode? Not so much."

"I keep you safe."

"From who?" I looked over my shoulder to the horizon. "They didn't seem to want to harm me." Which confused me; I had been thinking they were hell-bent on finding me to finish me off.

"And this is why you need me to keep you safe. You're a danger to yourself." Cross reached out and clasped my forearm. "Let us leave."

Pulling my arm from his hold, I looked down at the ash. "Why is it burnt? Was this because of me?"

Cross hesitated. "If you're asking if it's because of your choice to destroy the spell, then no."

"Asmodeous didn't do this?" Nothing made sense.

"He did not. The Land of the Souls is for the dead."

Sam had said I would take the guilt for it, and I knew I didn't want to ask but knew that I had to. "I did this?"

"You were not aware of it at the time." Cross sounded as if that made it alright.

"The souls who were waiting?"

"Were eradicated."

"I burned them." Horror dragged at my shoulders, and needles of terror raced over my skin, prickling it with the repulsion of my actions. "I don't know how." Stepping closer to Cross, I reached for him. "Cross, how? *How* did I do *this*?"

"Before Samyaza pressed the dagger into your heart, you told him that you would see him burn in hell," Cross said as his large hand patted my much smaller one.

"So…what?" I asked wildly. "I just *burnt* everything?"

"This is why I must teach you, Star. You cannot burn hell; it burns without aid and will burn for eternity. However, as a necromancer, you can command and destroy the dead. Your anger was very bright."

"My anger was at *them*, not the souls! My anger was at Sam, Zel, Pen and the others. Not the souls, *never* the souls."

Cross looked at me with sympathy. "You are untrained. You are powerful, but you cannot harm a Watcher. Yet. But you can cause harm to those at your command."

"I subconsciously burned them?" I felt the tears fall as I looked at the ash. "That doesn't make it better!"

"Your powers were unleashed and uncontrolled."

Sinking to my knees, I bowed my head. "This is not what I wanted."

"I know." His voice was gentle.

"How do I get them back?"

"They are gone, Star."

Shaking my head, I refused to believe it. "No, I can't…" I took a huge deep breath. "I won't accept that."

"Now do you see why you must train? And learn?"

After I nodded that I understood what he had said, he didn't say anything else. I felt them arrive, and I didn't care enough to look up.

"She was here," Pen said. "I can sense her."

"She knows," Chaz replied. On hearing his voice, I automatically looked up. His hair hung loose, his tunic was rumpled, and he looked weary. Like Sam had. The anger I felt for *Chaz* was frightening. "She won't understand," Chaz said as his fingers traced the air.

You're damn straight I don't understand, you spineless bastard.

"Her anguish was great," Pen spoke quietly. "We need to let him know."

"You go," Chaz said to Pen as he walked a few steps from me, which is when I realised he was searching for something.

"What is it? What are you looking for?" I asked as I turned to look at where Chaz was staring.

The spot where Cross had been.

"Something is not right," Chaz murmured as he reached out to let his hand hang in the air. "I don't know what it is, but there's…"

A firm hand closed around my upper arm, and looking up, I saw Cross looking down at me. He raised his finger to his lips, warning me to be quiet, and then we were back in his living room.

"What the hell is going on?" I asked as I took a seat on the couch.

"Chazaquel and Penemue are the more sensitive of their brethren. They note shifts in the atmosphere far more astutely than the others," Cross explained. "We cannot let them know where you are."

"Why?" I understood his confusion at my question as he looked at me. "I mean, yes, they killed me, but you're acting really dodgy. Why?"

"So, you're suspicious of me?" Cross looked amused. "*I'm* suddenly the danger?"

I thought about it for a nanosecond. "Suddenly? You've been the danger since I woke up. Them? Well, I learned the hard way not to trust them." As I rubbed my nose, I looked for Hound, spotting him in the corner. Silent. Watching. Waiting? "They're looking for me. Why?"

"I would be a far wiser man if I could understand the thought process of the Watchers," Cross told me drily. "How did you even get to the Land of the Souls?"

Settling back against the soft fabric cushions, I closed my eyes. How did I end up there? My powers were still out of reach, and I had gone to sleep. "Is my body still in bed?" I asked. The silence dragged on, and I opened my eyes to look for Cross, wondering if he had left me again.

He was still here, and he was looking at me with a conflicting expression. It was a mix of confusion, amusement and consternation. You know that look of I-can't-believe-she-hasn't-died-of-stupidity-yet look? That's the way he was looking at me.

"What?" I asked. "It's a reasonable question. You all wink me here, there and everywhere, so for all I know, I'm having an out-of-body experience."

"An out-of-body… Star." Cross took a deep inhale. "Where do you think your body is?"

Looking down at myself, I pinched my leg and flinched when it hurt. "Here isn't the answer that you're looking for, is it?"

"Your physical body is not here. Your *soul* gets carried over the veil; the husk is left behind."

"Husk? *Husk?*"

Cross and Hound exchanged a look, one that very much said, *told you she would overreact,* to which Cross was replying, *yes, I see what you mean.*

"Can you both quit it?" I snapped as I stood abruptly. "Where the fuck is my body?"

"It is safe."

"That *filthy* heart-stabbing demon has it, doesn't he?" My hands were on my hips. Or were they? If I wasn't here, then were my hands, my hips, my *anything,* here?

"I didn't think I needed to have this conversation. I forget how much you really do not know." Cross rubbed his forehead as he thought. "You have *so* much to learn. Can you *please* let me teach you?"

"Are you here?"

"Star."

"Just tell me, is that your body?"

"Yes."

"And it was *his* body."

"Yes. The Watchers and I are…different."

"Because you were all angels." I started to pace as I freaked out. I mean, it wasn't a big freak out—I had freaked out before—this was a mini freak out. Tiny. Hardly worth noticing. Yet Cross's eyes were wide. "Which angel are you?"

"This isn't important. And I am no angel." His look was amused, but his eyes danced with more than just amusement, and once again I was reminded that Cross was a very, very attractive man. Man? Demon. Male. Thing.

Ugh.

"I think *thing* is harsh," Cross murmured as he sat down. "You have the attention span of a goldfish."

"Stop reading my thoughts." I could feel my cheeks burning. Only they weren't, were they? I wasn't here. Just my soul. I jumped up and down and felt the very solid floor beneath my feet.

"Do I want to know what you're doing?"

"Why am I standing on the floor?"

"Because you stood up."

"You're a comedy genius." I snatched a cushion. "How am I picking this up?" I saw his mouth open to give me some smartass reply. "I will stab you, demon, if you say with my hands."

"You're making this more than it has to be." Cross sighed loudly. "Your soul is the essence of you. It makes you *who you are.* The body is just a suit."

"Essence…" Chewing my lip, I mulled it over. "That's why he doesn't know where I am. His *seed* did not contaminate my soul."

"Contaminate?" Cross was laughing at me again.

"Oh! You know what, fuck off." Storming over to the wall that we usually walked through, I was ready to go to my room. "I'm not talking to you anymore until you give me answers."

"I say stay," Cross taunted me as my body, or soul, was turned to look at him.

"I say fuck off." I wasn't real? This was *just* a soul, then walls shouldn't bother me. With a clenched jaw, I marched to the wall with purpose. *You're not real* was on repeat in my head. At the last moment before impact, I closed my eyes.

When I didn't land on my ass or break my nose, I opened my eyes warily. To look at my bed.

I'd done it. Holy crabsticks, I'd walked through the wall.

"Proud of yourself?" Cross asked as he perched against my dresser.

Scrunching my nose up as I thought about it, I gave him a shit-eating grin. "Yes!"

His rich laughter filled the room. "Go to sleep, stubborn girl. We start training tomorrow, *no* arguments."

"But…" He was gone. Could I follow? Maybe? Did I want to test my luck? No.

Take the wins where you could find them, however small.

This was my win.

CHAPTER 8

TIME HAD NO MEANING HERE. I SLEPT. I WOKE. I TRAINED. I SLEPT again. My sleep pattern was skewed. How long did I sleep? Who knew? Cross didn't exactly have a hotline to the world clock…or if he did, he didn't look at it.

Some days, we spent what seemed like hours sitting searching for the meaning of life. Okay, so I was being snarky. We searched for inner peace. When I told him that I had no outer peace, because you know, I was *bodiless*, he hadn't laughed. Hound had huffed, and I had taken it as a sign *he* at least found me amusing. How they thought I was going to achieve inner peace was beyond me; had they met *me*?

When I wasn't sitting across from Cross, with my hands upturned on my thighs and searching for the *calm* inside me, Cross actually taught me how to fight. He called it sparring, I called it getting a good ass kicking that happened on the street outside a pub after a bad night out.

I may not have a body here, but bloody hell, he didn't pull his punches. The upside was I didn't bruise. The downside was that we had no idea what would actually hurt me when I got put back in the *Star Husk*.

"Can you please stop calling your body the Star Husk?"

"It's like a good sci-fi name for a film." I raised my hands and moved them through the air like I was unveiling a banner. "Star Husk, coming to cinemas near you this summer," I quipped with a low voice in what I thought was the perfect imitation of a voiceover guy.

"I would very much like to gag you."

"I would very much like to see you try," I jibed back as I

bounced from foot to foot in front of the punching bag. "I'm pretty good at brawling now."

"You're akin to a Christian in the Colosseum, ringed by gladiators and about to be fed to the lions."

I stopped bouncing. "I'm Russell Crowe?"

His fingers pinched the bridge of his nose. "Star, can we just…not?"

"I've been training for how long?" I asked as I resumed bouncing from foot to foot.

"Two months. Maybe."

"Okay, and when am I done?"

"Never." Cross stretched his arm over his head before he bent it behind his neck, his other hand pulling it down. I was sure he was double-jointed.

"Uh-huh, and what do you think that means in reality? A week, two, maybe more?"

"Your craft will continually evolve."

"Fantastic," I said as I punched the bag of sand hanging from his roof. "And when do I leave?"

"We've spoken about this," Cross said as he set me with a hard stare.

"No, you see, *you* spoke and I listened, and then I ignored you. When do I leave?"

Cross ignored *me* as Hound came into the room.

"Are my mum and dad okay?" I asked the hellhound as he reported whatever back to Cross. However, I knew he had been to my mum, and when Hound studiously ignored me, I stepped closer. "Hound?"

"We may have an issue."

"Just one?" I bit out as I stopped hitting the punching bag. "What is it now?"

"Your mother is getting desperate," Cross said bitterly as he crossed the room to the window.

"Hmm, her daughter was killed by Watchers, and her body is fuck knows where because a demon dick hides it. Her daughter's body has been missing for *months*, and the whole time she's lying to her husband, her friends, her daughter's friends. I cannot *imagine* why she may be getting desperate."

"She reached out to the Watchers."

Oh. Oh well yeah, Mum was definitely desperate. "I can see why you would be pissed."

"Well, now I can sleep at night," he mocked with a wry smile.

"Shut up. We both know you don't sleep." I gave up the pretence of training as I joined him at the window.

Cross surprised me when he reached out and pulled me into him, his arm settling over my shoulders. "Are you okay?" he asked me gently.

Confused, I looked up at him. "What? You never care to ask me any other time. Why are you being weird?"

He booped my nose. Legit booped it. "You're so funny."

"You *just* wished to gag me." Turning in his loose hold, I looked up at him as I tested his forehead, pushing the thick hair back to place my hand on his forehead. I wasn't prepared for him to lean into my touch. "How do I know if you're hot?" I asked him, hating the way my voice went all throaty and stuff.

"You already think I'm hot." Cross gave me a cheeky wink as he spoke.

Despite myself, that made me laugh. "Dick. I mean a fever." I playfully pushed him away, but my smile faltered as I took him in.

Cross was looking at me. Not as in his attention was pointed my way, he was *looking* at me. A flutter low in my tummy happened, surprising me more than the way he was watching me.

"Cross?" I asked warily. Right before he kissed me.

I was being kissed by Cross.

And I was *not* objecting to the way he was kissing me.

The room was spinning, no, not spinning—*thumping*. In my confusion, I thought it was my heart, but I didn't have a heart, I only had my soul. The thumping was getting louder, and I finally found my common sense and stepped back from the hot demon who kissed me like I was a long drink of water on a hot day.

"Whoa," I began, just as the windows exploded.

Shards of coloured glass burst around me. Instinctively, I crouched, my hands covering my head as the room rained glass down on me. Deadly quiet spread out after the last tinkle of glass bounced off the marble floors.

"Shit," I whispered as I looked around at the debris before slowly rising to my feet, my back currently to where the windows were.

Cross was in front of me, his face blank as he faced outward with his expression completely closed off.

Turning to see what he was staring at, I saw *him*.

His Watchers were behind him with their hoods pulled low and their weapons ready, the red walls of hell behind them, framing them. They were in an arrow formation, *him* at the front with Zel and Ros on either side and then the others fanning out behind him. I saw them all, and I saw none of them.

My eyes were only interested in him.

Thick black hair hung too long, dense and heavy over his forehead. A long straight nose sat over full lips, which were currently pressed in a tight line of disapproval. Nice bone structure emphasised the fact no human man could achieve such perfection. Thick black lashes framed bright green eyes currently filled with…*fury*.

Was he kidding me? He was furious? What the hell was he angry for?

"Witch." Sam looked me over with scorching contempt.

"Demon." I returned his hostility with my own. I would not be intimidated by this dickhead.

"You invade my home, Samyaza?" Cross said quietly as he walked over to stand by me.

"You took what wasn't yours." Sam spoke to Cross, but his attention was on me.

"Did I?" Cross said casually as he stepped closer to me. "I would say Star is exactly where she needs to be."

"Witch, come," Sam directed.

"Fuck you."

"Witch—"

"You deaf, demon?" I asked him as I met his furious glare with my own. "You think you say come and I'll trip over my feet in my eagerness to stand by your side so you can kill me again?"

"Kill you?" Sam gave me a cruel smile. "You don't look dead."

"Do I look *alive*, you inconsiderate, heartless prick!"

"Star," Cross warned quietly. "Remember your training."

"You've been training her?" Pen asked in surprise. "Why?"

"Why I do anything is of no concern to you, Penemue."

"When it concerns the witch, it is," Zel grunted. He looked at me, ice blue eyes meeting mine. "Come."

"Suck a dick." I felt Cross stiffen slightly beside me. So, I may have bad terminology sometimes, whatever. "I am going nowhere with the scum who killed me."

"Your training methods are poor," Sam snarked to Cross. "I have no time for this, let her go."

Did Cross have to do what Sam told him? I didn't know. "You aren't going to let me go," I whispered to Cross anxiously as I watched the demons. There were seven of them, and I wondered why only Bara was with them and not Yeqon and the other one whose name I genuinely could not remember. Nevertheless, no matter who was there, the fact that there were seven of them was enough. They all looked formidable and slightly intimidating, and all that hostility was focused on me.

"No." Cross flicked his eyes to mine and smiled. "You remain here, where I can keep you safe."

"The witch is safe with me," Sam snapped.

"Are you out of your *mind?*" I demanded incredulously. *"You're the reason I'm dead!"*

"What?" Pen asked, amused. "You're not dead, Star."

"Do I look alive?" I snarled at them again. "Do you see my body? No. You only see my soul because you wankers killed me."

"What game are you playing?" Sam asked Cross coldly. "The witch belongs to *me.*"

Cross draped his arm over my shoulders, and I knew he was doing it to push Sam's buttons, and I was petty enough to let him, so I pressed into his side. Was I being childish? Yes. Was I poking the bear? Yes. Would this end badly for me? Most definitely. Did I care? Not one iota. After all, the fucker already killed me; what else could he do?

"Star," Cross began, and I loved that he called me by my name and not witch, "remains here, with me, where I can teach her all that she can be and allow her that empowerment of not having to rely on a demon."

Sam snorted his contempt and took a step forward, but I noticed that it was a step, not his usual stride. Was Cross holding them off? My respect for his badassery just increased. "Do not push me," Sam warned him as he glanced at me once, and the power of his rage made me gulp.

"You may go," Cross spoke, as if Sam hadn't just threatened him. "Next time, Watcher, wait until someone invites you before you barge into my domain."

The wall was suddenly back, the windows showing a rather stormy sky. There were no demons outside—that I could see—

and as I waited for the thumping to resume, I felt like I should hold my breath. Only I didn't need to breathe to be alive here.

"Did he go?"

Cross grinned at me as he moved away. "No. He will post a guard, I would think."

"He's such a dick," I muttered as I flopped onto the couch. "Can they see in?"

"No." Cross thought about it. "I don't think they all can... Samyaza might."

"Wonderful." I lay on his couch and closed my eyes. "Why did you kiss me?" I was only brave enough to ask the question when I wasn't looking at him.

"Curiosity."

My eyes flew open as I looked at him as he watched me with a small smile on his face.

"Excuse me?"

"I do try to, but you make it so very difficult."

Okay, that was funny. "Can you be your normal serious self, please?"

"You complain I'm too serious, now you complain I'm not serious enough." Cross relaxed in his seat, his long legs stretching out in front of him. "You're never satisfied."

"Funny, she's never complained to me about lack of satisfaction."

Cross was on his feet as I sat bolt upright on the couch. Sam was leaning against the wall, his arms folded as he watched us both.

"How?" Cross asked him as he looked around the room. "You shouldn't be able to—"

"Cross your wards? See through your illusions? Walk into your domain as if it were my own?" Sam sneered. "You cannot keep me out, and you have my witch."

"What more can you want from me?" I asked him in exasperation. "Haven't I given you enough?"

Forest green eyes met mine. "No."

"I have nothing left." It was supposed to sound firm, strong, matter-of-fact. Instead, my voice was soft, almost like a plea.

"You are mine."

"I'm *not* a possession."

"Yes, you are. You belong to me, witch, and you will realise that when you have stopped hiding from everything."

"I'm hiding from you!"

"Ridiculous." Sam turned to Cross. "Release her."

"No."

Sam grinned and it was frightening. "I was really hoping you would say that."

I didn't even see him move. All I saw was Cross flying across the room from the force of Sam's blow. Cross went crashing into the wall, and I was grateful he was supernatural, because the blow would have killed a mortal. Sam had his swords in his hands, the flames licking the length of steel, and I knew my mouth was hanging open when Cross reached over his back and a large dark scythe appeared, with a wicked curve.

"Holy fuck," I whispered as the two of them started to fight. Hound was suddenly in front of me. "Is he *death*?" I asked Hound as I watched the two males beat the shit out of each other.

Hound nudged my hand with his head, and I looked over at the other wall. He wanted me to run? A huge crack snapped my attention back to Sam and Cross, and I saw Cross slide down another wall as Sam smashed his fist into his face. Where did the swords go?

Hound nudged me again, and I placed my hand on his head. As much as I was fascinated with whatever the hell was happening between the two of them, I also knew I had no intention of leaving here with Sam.

Hound looked at me, and I nodded, and the room was gone.

I looked around at…nothing.

"Hound?"

Everything was dark, the ground was black, and the sky, if it was a sky, was grey. I suddenly felt very alone, even with Hound beside me. I knew that where we were was undeniably…empty.

With a snap, a crack and the sound of crunching bone, Hound straightened. He literally morphed into a two-legged…male.

"What in the name of hell…" I backed away as I watched his canine snout disappear into a nose and mouth, and I was reeling from the physical change.

"Star." His voice was gravelly, growly, and exactly what I imagined a hellhound would sound like…if they were a person.

"Are you shitting me?" I couldn't stop looking at him, and my mind was struggling to accept what my eyes were seeing.

"It has been too long to be like this." Hound looked down at himself with distaste. "I feel. Wrong."

"You're a man!"

"Demon," Hound corrected with his gravelly, gritty voice. "You are not safe."

I instantly stepped back, and now I knew where my four-legged friend got his attitude when his still-red eyes rolled at my reaction.

"I have never harmed you," Hound reprimanded me. "We have little time. It is no longer natural for me to be like this. I cannot shield us for long."

"Shield us from who?" I looked around wildly.

"Watchers will come." Hound rubbed his jaw like it hurt him. "You must train, you must learn your craft. You *are* a necromancer, and you are very powerful, but you cannot let them, *any* of them, manipulate you. Asmodeous is hunting for you, neither Cross nor Samyaza is your ally, but they will help keep you from *him*."

"That's a lot to take in," I mumbled as I stared at him. "How do I know I can trust you?"

"I choose you as my master, and I hope you choose me as your servant."

"You killed me."

"Samyaza struck you down. I merely carried you away from them all."

"Semantics." I knew I was perhaps having a mental break-down. After all…wasn't this a *dog*?

"Stop deflecting and avoiding," Hound chastised me. "You *must* learn."

"I'm doing my best!" I snapped. "It's a lot. You know. Like"—I waved my hand up and down in front of him—"a lot."

"What do you need?" Hound asked me.

There were so many things, how much time did he have? But instead, when I went to answer exactly that, my own words surprised me. "I need to find the tree."

"The tree?" Hound asked in confusion. "Of life?"

"Yes."

He was nodding as he thought it over. "He can take you there."

"Death?" I scoffed. "Can take me to the tree of *life?*"

Cue next eye roll from my so-called servant. "Samyaza. Only a Watcher knows the way."

"Fan-bloody-tastic."

Hound watched the sky. Was it sky? I was freaking out. My brain had separated from the obvious stroke I was having, and now my inner me was watching my outer me like I was uncon-nected, and my inner me was a bitch.

"They come."

"Sounds biblical."

"They were." Hound reached forward suddenly, and his long nails scratched my skin over the palm of my hand. Before I could even snatch my arm out of reach, he scratched his own hand and pressed our palms together. "Bound by blood we will be."

"Hang on a min—"

He was suddenly a hellhound again. "What is going on?" I screamed in frustration.

I am with you now.

Hound was talking to me. *In my head.*

"We are bound?" I whispered urgently as I felt the air shift.

Tell no one. I can protect you as long as you try to protect yourself.

"Why should I trust you?"

I am the only one who does not wish to use you for gain.

Well, when you put it like that, my life officially sucked, I thought just as a large hand clasped my arm.

"Are you death?" I asked Cross as he frowned down at me. "Because before they turned up, the kiss was quite nice, but now, if it's the kiss of death, literally…I don't think I'll cope. Plus, you know, I'm not all the way dead, so if you *are* the kiss of death, why are you trying to kill me all the way?"

"You are truly preposterous." Cross turned to look at the sky-like-thing-darkness. "We must hurry."

"Why is everyone chasing me?" I demanded as I turned to see nothing within nothing, and therefore, I would forever call this place the nothing…which reminded me of one of my favourite films of my childhood.

"We can talk more later." Cross nodded at Hound, who vanished, and then I was back in the living room. The walls were intact, the furniture rightened, and the windows restored. Storm clouds were gathering in the green sky outside, and I glanced at Cross.

"Feeling edgy?" Cross fixed me with a flat stare, and I fought the giggle. "Can we talk?"

"Can you be serious?"

I thought about it, I really did. "I want to say yes," I started. "But I think I'm having a psychotic break, so if I'm not in my right mind, then I don't think I can commit to giving you an answer."

"What?"

"You see, if I know I am not acting in my full mental health capacity, then if I say yes, am I saying yes based on who I was when I'm not, you know, undead, then is that right? And if not, if I'm actually flucked beyond all recognition, then saying yes will only be a lie, and why would you want me to lie to you? Or—"

"Stop."

"But—"

"No." He cut me off again. "You have answered the question, you cannot be serious."

"Oh." I looked at Hound, who was lying on the floor watching, and I realised I could feel him. I could *feel* the hellhound in my...soul? Holy shit. "Are you death? Like *the* death, the grim reaper, and why did you lie to me? You said you weren't an angel."

"I am Cross. You know me as such." Cross looked between me and Hound. "Why did you go to the Void?"

"Are you asking me?" I asked him, slightly surprised that he was looking at me and not the hellhound.

"I'm surprised, that's all."

"I thought you were used to me by now," I muttered as I crossed to the window. I looked out at the darkening sky and then down at the choppy waters below. What was that? I peered closer. I squinted and tried to focus. Was that...rabbits? The sea foam was white rabbits that were dancing over the dark depths. I almost laughed out loud, but I knew who was doing this, and I knew that they were watching.

He was watching.

"What amuses you?" Cross asked as he came to stand beside me, and I turned away before I got sent flying sharks. Because the demon was an asshole, and he would totally do that to me.

"Cross, can you answer my questions?" I asked as I walked back to the couch. "Just say it."

"I am Death," Cross said to me and smirked when my mouth dropped open.

"Like for real?" I hadn't actually expected him to say it.

"Like totally, dude."

My eyes narrowed on the smug dick's face. "You're not funny. Why are you hot?"

Cross laughed out loud as he took a seat and watched me in delight. "Would you prefer me to be a skeleton in a dark cloak?"

I gave it some consideration. "Yes, I think I would." Tucking my feet under me as I studied him, I kept looking him over. "You shouldn't be able to look like this; you should fit more into people's expectations."

"The people who expect skeletons and cloaks?" Cross asked with amusement.

"They don't expect a *GQ* magazine model with deep chocolate brown eyes that promise a good time. Not a deadly time! Not a you're-never-coming-back-from-this time."

"You don't seem to object to what I look like," Cross said confidently as he crossed his left leg over his right and slouched back on the couch. He looked so relaxed. Casual.

"Tell me how they found me. Tell me how he got in, and then tell me how I know they aren't getting in again. Then, when you're done, you can tell me about the Void and how the hell you are Death."

"We could do this another way," Cross told me as he leaned forward. "I am what I am because I have always been."

I waited. He wasn't saying anything else. "That's it? You are Death because you've always been Death?"

"You're screeching again, Star."

"Really? Colour me fucking surprised!"

"And here comes the swearing." He sighed in disappointment.

I can do this. I will not overreact. Calm down. I practiced my breathing to keep me calm. I am calm. I am calm.

You are not calm. You are freaking out.

Shut up, Hound. I am calm.

"Can we start this again?" I said with a cool even tone. *See? Totally calm.*

The corner of Cross's mouth turned up, and he nodded once.

"Can you explain to me how you are…Death? I thought the

angel of death was an, well, an angel. But you told me you aren't an angel."

"Where there is one, there is always the other. Where there is yin, there is yang. Where there is right, there is wrong. Where there is up, there is down. Where there is life, there is death."

What the hell was that supposed to mean? "So…you've always been?"

Cross considered the question. "Yes."

"So when God popped along and said, 'Let there be light,' you said, 'Screw you, let there be dark'?"

His laughter echoed off the walls as I shifted uncomfortably at his merriment. "Sure, let us say that was what happened."

"What else could it have been?" I waited and Cross didn't answer, much to my annoyance. "How are you not an angel?"

"Because I was not created by the maker."

"So who made you?" Again, I was met with silence. "Are you kidding me? It's a secret?"

"It is not necessary to know."

"What bullshit is that? Most things in life aren't necessary to know! I will never ever know why I had to know algebra. Not once in my adult life have I needed to know the value of *B* to get to the value of *C*. Ever."

"You use algebra in everyday life. Problem solving, logical thinking…" He paused. "You're right, you have never used algebra in your adult life."

Arsehole. "How do you know he won't come back?" I changed the subject before I hit him. "He's a general after all."

"Samyaza is a formidable warrior." Cross nodded in agreement. "It is what it is."

"I've been here for months, every day you jibber jabber at me, and today, when shit goes sideways and demons literally break your door down, you become Mr Less-Words-is-More."

"The Watchers are aware of where you are. They will keep

surveillance. I have ensured that none of them enter here again. You can return the favour by learning, training, and keeping inane questions, which we both know I will not answer, to yourself."

"I liked you better earlier when you were kissing me," I muttered and then realised how that sounded out loud. "You know I don't mean the actual kissing, I mean the earlier before now thing, like..." I stopped. There was nowhere to go. Cross was openly grinning at me, and as I heard myself, I realised I just needed to hand the shovel over before I dug a bigger hole. "Shut up, you know what I mean."

"I thought you were very pleasant to kiss also."

"Shut up." I threw my hands over my ears as he opened his mouth to speak again. "Seriously not listening!"

Cross stood and crossed the space between the couches. Gently he pulled my hands from my ears, and I looked up at him curiously. How could he be Death? He was not what I expected at all. "Stop thinking of me in a long black hooded cloak," Cross said playfully as he stepped back. "Go to bed. You've used a lot of energy today."

"Have I?"

"To get to the Void, it depleted your strength." Cross looked down at me. "They are out of sight, but they are there, and we need to show them that I am your best chance to survive what is coming for you."

"Why does anything need to be coming for me?" I complained as I stood.

"Because you infuriated a prince of hell, and the consequences for your action are high."

"If he cannot be killed, why am I training?" I asked softly. "I cannot be hidden forever. I cannot be not-quite-dead for the rest of my life."

"He can be defeated. Not every end is death."

I contemplated his words. "Does that piss you off?"

Cross groaned as he sat back down on his couch. "Star," he grumbled.

"I bet that drives your OCD nuts, doesn't it? Knowing there are unalive things out there that can't die."

"What drives me *nuts* is necromancers that can't be quiet."

I hesitated. The way he was looking at me, that headmaster look he wore so well, left me in no doubt that he meant me.

"Necromancer…freaks me out." I didn't look at him directly; instead, I focused on a spot just over his head. "I was just adapting to witch."

"Witch is incorrect."

Do not roll your eyes, Star, I warned myself. "It's an awful lot to deal with, very soon."

Cross was silent for a moment. For Cross, that wasn't unusual. "Very well. But the sooner you realise what you are and what you can do, then the sooner your training can match your needs."

I realised that he was away to start a lecture. Again. "I'll go lie down."

Without giving him a chance to reply, I went through the wall to the room beyond. Didn't matter how many times I did it now, I still turned to look at the solid wall every time, completely doubtful I had mastered the trick.

Sitting on the bed, I thought about today. It had started off the same as any other. I had gone through the wall and shared coffee with Cross. He had changed my clothing from a nightshirt to yoga pants and a T-shirt. I should probably ask him how he manifested clothing onto my body, but not only did I really not want to know, I was scared he would tell me. In detail.

Cross was a great teacher. He had patience, and most times, he was understanding. It made sense he was Death. He would wait you out to the very end. The literal end.

Lying on the bed, I stared out of my skylight. Darkness lay beyond, and I knew not to look for the stars or the moon. It was an illusion. Nothing was real.

Everything was real.

Was there a Watcher watching me as I lay here? Would they know that I had a skylight? Was there an actual skylight? Or was that also an illusion?

Tiredly I closed my eyes, and I felt when Hound joined me. I also felt my clothing change, and with surprise, I looked at the black silk pyjamas. Usually I got a sleep short set or a long night-shirt, but tonight I had black silk pj's on. They were nice, with a lace trim on the camisole top and matching lace trim on the bottom of the legs.

"Nice," I said as I showed my leg to Hound, who nestled his head on his paws and closed his eyes. "Be like that," I snipped as I settled on my duvet.

"Is Nessie real?" I asked out loud.

No.

I'd actually forgotten that Hound could communicate with me. How do you forget you can talk to hellhounds? My life was obviously so insane that talking, shapeshifting hellhounds were now mundane.

Okay, even for me, that was an exaggeration.

As my mind mulled over the actions of the day, I drifted off to sleep.

I should have known I would find wherever Sam was. He was sitting on a chair. It was more like a throne if I were honest, but Sam on a throne was one thing my brain instantly rejected. The large black *chair*, with intricate carving and a long back piece, actually towered over Sam as he sat in it, with his head resting against the wood. His eyes narrowed in concentration. Turning, I looked over my shoulder. Who was he looking at?

When I saw the woman, I was sure my eyes just bugged right

out of my head. Who the fuck was she? Long red hair, flawless skin, a dress that left nothing to the imagination, with two deep slits to the skirt, and a deep drop that exposed a fair chunk of her ample chest and navel. Her *navel*. Why the hell bother wearing anything if you were putting it all out there anyway?

"He has fortified his wards."

She even sounded like sex. Bitch.

"It was to be expected." Sam rubbed his finger over his top lip as he stared at her. "Can you get through them?"

"You know he shunned my kind a long time ago," she answered him with a throaty voice that on earth would have made her a fortune as a phone sex worker.

"Which is why it is your kind that will get through his wards," Sam grunted.

"She is just a witch." The woman actually pouted.

"She's mine."

Fuck you, arsehole.

Sam's head snapped in my direction, his eyes searching behind me. "Go."

Did he mean me? Vaguely I was aware that slinky call girl had left.

"Witch?" His lips twitched slightly as he looked everywhere around me. As if he could see me. "You hide from me."

Who'd have thought it? I mean, he wasn't an imbecile; he had to know why I wanted to have nothing to do with him.

"You are vexed with me," he spoke softly as he leaned on the arm of the throne, *not* throne, big chair.

Well, obviously, you complete ass, you stabbed me.

"Little witch, what did Asmodeous say to you?" Sam's elbow was on the armrest now, his hand cupping his strong jaw. He was also staring right at me.

Like he could see me. He couldn't see me, could he?

"He said, and I quote, *there is nowhere on this earth that you can hide from me,* so why would you think I would leave you on earth?"

"What?" I snapped, forgetting he couldn't hear me.

He did this to me to *protect* me? He unalived me so I would not be on earth?

"I don't believe you," I whispered as I stood there in the shadows. Looking down, I saw Hound appear. His look spoke volumes, and I didn't need his voice in my head to tell me he did not approve of me being here.

Turning, I went to walk away, confident Hound would know how to get me out of this…wherever this was.

Sam's next words made me stumble. "Nice pyjamas."

I was still reeling when I was back in the room, away from him. He could see me? That changed everything.

CHAPTER 10

WHEN I WOKE THE NEXT MORNING, AFTER A VERY FITFUL NIGHT OF sleep, of dark demons hunting me through the woods in the rain, I felt like I hadn't slept at all. As soon as I walked through to meet Cross, I knew I was in trouble. Wearing jeans and a loose black button-down shirt with the sleeves rolled up, his feet bare, he looked good. Well, he would look good, but Cross looked pissed. Tilting my head slightly, I considered him. Nope, not pissed, apoplectic. Ah shit, he knows.

"Yes, I know."

"Morning?" I tried for casual, confident, completely at ease. Unfortunately, I heard the squeak in my voice and knew I hadn't fooled the male in front of me at all.

"Why would you go to the very demon you are trying so hard to convince me that you want to stay away from?"

"In my defence, I don't know how I ended up there either. It's not like I jumped up and decided to go visit the demon that killed me. I go to sleep, I wake up near him."

"Hmm, I didn't fully consider the hold he has over you. He is pulling you to him, and that we cannot allow."

"How do we stop it?" I asked as I sat on the couch. Cross wasn't unreasonable. I knew he was trying to help me, mostly. I was sure there was a reason that I would hate or a favour I would need to return at a later date, but he had some conviction that I was worth teaching, and although I knew that I was completely hopeless, he was trying.

Some days, he was more trying than others, but the guy was Death. I was sure he could handle an awkward, untaught witch from the Highlands of Scotland. Couldn't he?

"Yes, I can teach you, and yes, I can handle you, and yes, I can stop Samyaza pulling you to him. What I can't seem to teach you, it seems, is the ability to shield your thoughts."

"I thought they were," I muttered as I reached for a croissant and a cup of coffee. Cross had given up trying to explain to me that I didn't need food. I'd accepted I didn't cough, splutter, or need to go to the bathroom, but my body expected to be fed and watered in the morning, so he fed and caffeinated my soul to keep me quiet. The whole fact that Sam had my body, I was now ignoring. "Oh." Had I just had a revelation? "It's because he has my body, isn't it?"

"No."

Oh. "Wow. Just shoot me down with no explanations."

Cross sighed. He did that a lot with me. "It's because you are bonded to him. You have shared…experiences."

"I'm stuffed because we had sex." Perhaps I could have worded that better.

Cross was trying to keep a straight face. "Basically."

"Can I just have sex with someone else?" I asked as I took a large bite of croissant. "You know, would that get rid of him?"

"No."

"Why?"

"Because he holds your heart."

"Eeew." I dropped my croissant. "That's so gross, and I was going to put jam on my other croissant!"

"You foolish child, I mean he holds your affection." Cross shook his head in despair before he took a sip of his own coffee.

"Ohhh." I giggled at the mental image I had immediately conjured. Picking up my dropped croissant, I took another bite. "I was completely visualising him walking about with my almost dead heart beating in his hand."

"For someone with such an active and vivid imagination, it's frustrating that you never channel that energy into your learning."

I stuck my tongue out at Cross and grinned when he chuckled. "He told me that he had to kill me because Asmodeous said there was nowhere on earth I could hide."

"I know."

"You know what he said, or you know that's why I got stabbed?"

"Both."

"Why would you keep that from me?" I demanded. Cross said nothing as he drank his coffee. "I mean, that's vital information for me to have! I have been freaking out for months, thinking I'm a hostage and all the things, and now I know it's because I was being kept safe!"

"I have told you from the beginning that I was keeping you safe," Cross countered.

"Did you tell my mum this was why I was here?"

"I believe one of your Watchers did."

"Pen," I grunted. "They have a weird…understanding."

"Yes, Penemue enjoyed Jean when she was younger."

Choking on my coffee, I gasped for air as Cross's loud laughter echoed around the room. As I fought to get my breath back and wiped the tears streaming down my face, I glared at him. "What the hell?"

"He enjoyed *teaching* her, Star." Cross winked at me and laughed again when I threw the remainder of my croissant at him.

"That is so not what you implied, and you know it."

"I said what I said. What you *heard* is entirely out of my control."

"You're so bad," I chastised him as I reached for another croissant and more coffee. "Okay, I'm fed up with the eavesdropping on my mind. Once you yell at me for Sam last night, then we can do more on my mind blocks later. Yes?"

Cross stood fluidly, and I gave a little yelp as he did so. It was so easy to forget he was "other" when I spent time with him. We had formed an easy relationship as we cohabited in his domain, and the pleasant decor, soft furnishings and weird but now familiar sky outside made me sometimes forget that I was in the pit of hell and I was spending my time with Death.

"You're overthinking," his soft voice warned me.

"I know. When you move with such speed, it reminds me who you are and where I am."

"You should never forget," was his expected retort.

"What can I say, I like to block out bad times and concentrate on the positive."

He'd been bending down, giving me a nice view of his fine ass, but he straightened as he turned to look at me. "You think of me as a positive?"

"Well, apart from the job description, you're not bad," I teased him as I got up and walked over to the corner of the room we usually meditated at. "Can you swap my clothes out?"

"You surprise me so often, Star," Cross said as he turned back to his task. "And more often than not, it isn't in a good way. I expected this to be difficult, but I did not expect to enjoy it."

"Well...that's kind of sweet." When I saw him go to speak again, I cut him off. "Please don't ruin it!"

Laughing, he ran his eyes over me, and I felt the change in my clothing. "What I was going to say was that I didn't expect to be your fashion designer."

"Clothes by Death." I thought about it. "To-Die-For Clothing. No...Drop Dead Designs."

"What are you doing?"

"Thinking of your fashion label."

"For what reason?"

"None at all." I grinned at him as I straightened my pink workout top. "I feel excited about training today."

"Then you've been possessed by a soul I do not know."

"Ha. Har de har. Side splitting."

As I settled on the floor and assumed the position, I waited for him to join me. When he did, he looked once over my shoulder and then focused on me again. "The dream visitations need to stop, you going to him. I can control the repercussions, but when he gets enough control over you, the Watcher will be able to enter your thoughts with no invitation from you."

"I don't like what's behind door number two."

Cross frowned at my comment but carried on. "Shielding your thoughts also allows you to shield your mind from all attacks."

"Sam would attack me?"

"He has a poor track record, no?"

I dropped my eyes from Cross's knowing gaze. He saw too much, this male in front of me. "He hasn't been the best boyfriend," I joked awkwardly. "Since he isn't a boy. Or a friend, really." I rubbed my hands over my thighs. "And is really possessive. And bossy. Actually, he's a complete dick."

"Shielding is easy. As you would raise your arms to protect yourself from a blow, you do the same to your mind." Cross reached over and took my hands. "Now, it's a fact that you cannot actually deflect a blow. We all know what happened to you last time," Cross teased.

Snatching my hands out of his, I hit his shoulder. "That is totally a low blow." I felt the punch in my gut. "Ow!"

"*That* was a low blow, and again, you did not protect yourself."

"Why are you hitting me?" I protested as I rubbed my tummy.

"Your days of being handled with kid gloves are over."

I knew he could see my disbelief. "You think you've been soft on me until now?" I asked him incredulously.

"Star, I am Death. You are in the very pit of hell. You're surrounded by those that would hunt you and use you for their own gain and not care if you were wearing silk pyjamas whilst doing so." His look was challenging. "Honeymoon's over, time to face reality."

"This has not been a honeymoon. And if it has, I want a divorce."

"Not happening." Cross smiled as he closed his eyes. "You're a necromancer, therefore you're mine. Now concentrate."

I couldn't. All I could do was stare at the male in front of me. He had protected me, had sheltered me, but my eyes flicked to Hound, who sat close by. His head dipped in acknowledgement. Wetting my lips, I looked back at Cross, who was now watching me.

"I keep getting claimed. Only yesterday someone else was telling you I was theirs. Why must I be anyone's? Why am I not my own?"

"Valid points."

Valid points, but he wasn't disputing it. "I may be a witch with powers that lean more to the dead, but I am still my own person."

"Okay."

"And I am naïve, and I am untaught."

"Agree."

"But I am not entirely stupid." I paused while Cross's lips twitched. "And I know, since the time I had six demons show up at my door, looking for a descendant of the witch who cast a blood spell on a prince of hell, that no one, not one supernatural creature, has done something for nothing."

"And what do I want, Star?"

"I don't know." I searched his face, but he was as expression-less as a statue. "But if you're Death, like *the* Death, without the cloak, then I have no idea why you would want to help me. A prince of hell…is nothing to you? The Watchers, I think it must be them, but I don't know why."

"It must be them what?"

"I don't know. But to thwart their plans is the only thing I can think of why you would help me."

"What if I'm just bored and like to have a pretty blonde female in my bed at night and on my couch during the day?"

"That's your bed?" I asked him in surprise. "You don't sleep." He waited.

"Oh fuck me, you put me in your bed to fuck with *him*?"

Cross's smile was wicked.

"That's such petty *human* bullshit."

Cross cackled. Actually cackled. He was delighted with himself. Men. I didn't care what form of male it was; they were all pricks. "I can't believe you did this to make him jealous!"

Cross stopped laughing and leaned over to place a soft kiss on my lips. "It wasn't just for *his* benefit."

The walls shook and the floor vibrated. "I think you need to stop doing that," I whispered as I stared into Cross's gaze.

"For his sake or your own?"

I wasn't sure. "I don't know," I told him truthfully. Cross nodded and leaned back once more.

"Close your eyes, clear your mind, and imagine nothing."

I'd been to *nothing* yesterday. Now that I knew what to imagine, I slipped into the meditative state quite easily.

In the Void was Hound. As I looked around, I sensed nothing else, only the hellhound. "Hey," I greeted him softly. "Is it safe?"

It is.

"My morning's taken a turn," I told him as I crossed to him and sat beside him.

You play a dangerous game.

"You're not the first to tell me that." I thought back to the time at my cottage after Yeqon, *arsehole*, and Der told me the same thing. "I'm not playing, it isn't a game. To me at least."

You feel stronger today.

"Am I shielding?" I asked with delight.

Yes.

"From everyone?"

Neither of your consorts can hear. You have completely shielded them. But you have completely left your awareness behind.

"I'm split in three?" I asked in horror. "There won't be much of me left at this rate."

The Watcher keeps your body, your awareness is with Cross, but your soul is still very much your own.

"For how long?" I asked quietly as I rested my head against the hellhound's flank.

The prince will shred it.

"Charming," I quipped as fear slithered over me.

It will not be charming, it is excruciating pain.

I flinched as Hound spoke. "Firsthand knowledge?" I guessed softly.

Yes.

"I would like to avoid that."

Hound huffed his response, and I smiled in the Void, surrounded by nothing. I was completely at peace.

"Is it wrong that I like it here?" I looked around. "I mean, a splash of colour wouldn't go amiss, but I feel myself here." Hound had stiffened when I spoke, and when I finished, his huge head had turned to look at me. "What did I say wrong?"

That you feel at peace here, tells me that you are right.

"Right? For what? I'm never usually right—have you seen my love life? I make bad choices."

You will do well, Star Elizabeth Archer.

My doubt was shown when my nose scrunched as I thought about it. "Do I need to envisage here when I want to shield? And how does that work if my soul comes here but my awareness is left behind?"

The feeling you have now, that is what you need to channel.

"That makes sense."

Hound turned to face forward again.

"Did you know that's why they sacrificed me?" I asked hesitantly.

They would never have struck you, Star, had it been in malice. I would have killed them all.

Wow. "Um, thanks."

It is my honour.

I sat a little while longer. "Hound, you do know it's me. I mean, I'm *just* me. I'm not really all that."

All what?

Shrugging, I sat up, hugging my knees to my chest. "Whatever it is you think I am worth protecting." My chin dropped onto my knees. "I'm just a clairvoyant with an old crush on her best friend, who fell for a demon who killed her."

You are exactly who you are supposed to be. You just need taught.

"I think you need to prepare yourself for disappointment."

Hound looked upwards, his muscles tightening.

Be prepared.

Standing, I braced myself for Sam. Or Cross.

The demon in front of me was not who I was expecting. Twin scars ran over steely blue eyes.

"Whore."

"Arsehole."

"It's time to talk."

CHAPTER 11

"And if I have nothing to say to you, what then?" I snapped as I stared at Zel. "And why am I whore again?"

"You were always whore."

"Fuck you, Zel."

"No, you've fucked enough."

The Void gave me peace because there were no dead here. If there were, I would have given this demon two more scars after I cut his balls off. Hound sat patiently at my side, and I saw Zel's eyes flick to the hellhound. "I haven't missed you."

"Likewise."

"Then what do you want?" I demanded as I stood with hands on my hips.

"I have been sent to reason with you."

The Void had fantastic acoustics, and my laughter sounded eery as it echoed all around us. "*Reason?* You? Have they all lost their minds?"

"I am the best soldier for the job."

"No, you're really not. Go away."

"I am adept at entering hostile territory," Zel spoke as if I hadn't.

"I'm definitely feeling hostile."

"Are you done?"

"With you? Absolutely." I turned my back, and I heard Zel's snort of contempt.

"Your face or your back, it makes no difference to me." I heard his mockery, and I refused to rise to his taunts. "You heard the prince as much as the rest of us. After all, he said it to you. If you remained on earth, he would find you. So we took the only action that we could."

As I whirled on him, my fury was uncontrolled. "You performed some weird sacrifice, and I was stabbed in the *heart*! And as I lay bleeding on the ground, you fucking wankers stood over me and watched me *die*."

"The blood moon demands a sacrifice. It was not supposed to be you, but when you destroyed the spell and the prince threatened you, you left us no choice."

"There is always a choice."

"Not this time."

"I don't believe you."

"I don't give a fuck." Zel watched me impassively. "You done?"

"I already told you that I was."

"You think I like being here? With you? You think I enjoy the fact my brothers are either miserable, furious or pissed off with you."

"Furious? Pissed off? None of them should be that way with me, the hypocritical bastards." Was he kidding me? "And they *should* be miserable!"

"You forgave the hellhound," Zel pointed out in a reasonable voice.

"Hound is actually sorry for his part in that night."

"So we'll say sorry." Zel's mocking tone pissed me off. "You need to leave Cross."

"Fuck off."

"So you're in love with *him* now?" Zel sneered. "It's kind of your usual practice."

I pressed my hands to my cheeks as I looked at him with open loathing. "Oh, my God. I forgot how much you drive me crazy. No, I'm not in love with Cross, you imbecile. But he has protected me, he has kept me from Asmodeous and you!"

Zel's snort was uncomplimentary. "You're even more foolish than you were before."

"Ugh, you know what? You won't leave, I will."

"Have I ever lied to you, witch?"

His words stilled me. *No.* He was horrifically, callously honest. "No." I forced the reply through my clenched teeth.

"Then why would I lie to you now?"

Hound?

He has no ill intent.

I hate my life. "What is it, be quick."

"We need to free our brother from Asmodeous. You were the key. If we got you to lift the spell, in return, the prince would release Araqiel. You didn't perform the spell, you destroyed the spell." A look of contempt flashed my way. "We had no choice but to protect you, and of course, Samyaza is all…out of sorts over you." A disdainful sniff.

"What was actually cast on him, and what does he need it lifted for?"

"He is tied to hell."

"I assumed."

"No, he is *tied* to hell, he cannot leave other than for a short period of time. He was only at Dunnottar as we called him for your spell. He yearns for freedom."

Nodding, I flexed my fingers as I bowed my head. "And if I had cast his spell, what then?"

"We would have kept you safe."

"Because you knew he would kill me," I stated flatly. They thought I was naïve, and that may be, but I wasn't stupid. Obviously, Asmodeous would have killed me as soon as I set him free. "You get me to perform the spell, I do, then the prince of hell, *of hell*, is free, and in return you get another bloody Watcher to waltz through life causing havoc. And me, in the meantime, I still die!"

"You are not dead."

"Where's my body?" I demanded as I looked around. "Have you seen it? Is it here? Is my soul resting in it?"

Zel avoided looking at me.

"Exactly, you bastard. You're all bastards. The end game for me where you were concerned was always death. Are you freaking serious? You come here, '*We* need to free Araqiel,' and the whole time, you had an agenda to kill me. Go fuck yourself."

"Cross is using you."

"Everyone else has, why shouldn't he?"

"Why are you crying?" Zel asked me in confusion.

"Because you all ripped my heart out!" I wiped my eyes hurriedly, not realising that my anger had spilled over. "I *trusted* you. All of you, even you, though fuck knows why."

"Well, that was foolish," Zel said quietly.

"Ya think?"

"Chaz is very distraught, he will do something stupid."

"Good," I snapped.

"You are more than this, witch," Zel reprimanded me.

"You see, that's where you're wrong, I'm really not."

"You are the witch who took *herself* to the Land of the Souls. You are the witch who struck a general and lived. You are a witch who looked a prince of hell in the eye and took away his only chance of being free from hell. You are a witch who resides with Death and eats and drinks beside him as if he is a trusted friend." Zel stepped closer. "I *do* see, and I see a witch. *So* much more than a *witch*."

I narrowed my eyes as I considered him. There was no pretence with Zel, what you saw was what you got: a demon with striking blue eyes, a physique to envy, and a no-fucks-to-give attitude. It only highlighted to me Sam's complete ability to manipulate, that he knew to send this demon to me.

"I hate you all."

"How you feel about me is irrelevant to the conversation."

Tilting my head back, I looked at the Void. "I am still inclined to tell you to shove it, but before I can do it, what do you actually want?"

"Free Araqiel."

"How?" I turned my head as I looked at him. "Hand me to Asmodeous on a platter?"

"You're so dramatic," Zel scoffed. "We need another prince's aid."

"More aid since plan A failed," I griped.

"You think you were plan A?" Zel chuckled. "Witch, you weren't even plan Z."

Oh. Jesus. "Which prince?"

"For that, you need to speak to Sam."

"Which means I'm going to lose my shit, doesn't it?" Shaking my head, I reached out for Hound. "I'm done. It wasn't nice seeing you. But"—I hated him even more for this—"thank you for your honesty."

Hound.

We were back in Cross's living room. The male in question reclined on his sofa, dark eyes watching me as my soul and awareness merged.

"Should I be concerned you can split yourself even further?" Cross asked me casually.

"Probably," I muttered as I flopped onto my couch. "I've been speaking to demons."

"Which Watcher did they send?" Cross asked with barely concealed amusement.

"Azazel."

"Bold choice." Cross nodded. "And are you going to assist them?"

"No." I grimaced. "Maybe." I peeked at him from under my lashes. "They killed me."

"They did."

"They said they did it for my safety."

"They did."

"Was it?"

"Probably."

My eyes were wide as I stared at him, and he returned my look with a warm one of his own. "You aren't helping," I admitted quietly.

"You never asked me to lie to you," Cross told me just as quietly.

"Wouldn't it be terrible if Death was a liar?" I mused. "I always thought Death was no nonsense and maybe, not always, brutal… but definitely honest. Truthful."

"Thank you."

Smiling at his attempt to lighten the mood, I stared at the ceiling. "I said always, as in previously. Now that I know you, I know I was an idiot."

Cross chuckled across the room, and we both lay on our respective couches as we considered the wonders of life. Okay, that was bullshit. I was considering if I should help the ones who struck me down.

"You need to be careful. They are powerful, but they are not infallible," Cross warned me.

"I know." Turning my head, I looked at him. "Will you be with me?"

"No." Cross's smile was gentle unlike the sharp stab of panic I felt when he spoke.

"Why?"

"Do you want me to be?" He pushed himself up into a half-sitting position. He looked far too interested in my response.

"Yes."

"Why?"

"Because you need to keep my soul safe." *Liar.*

He watched me, and I knew I needed to look away. Only I

would be attracted to the entity that was Death. There really was something wrong with me. I was wired wrong.

"You did well today." Cross changed the subject as the awkwardness hung between us.

"I did?" I asked in surprise.

"You will master the Void, and when you do, you will have the capability to shield fully."

"I like it there," I admitted as I rolled onto my side to look at him.

Cross nodded as he mimicked my movement. "You should feel at peace there."

"Because it's empty?" I said with a sad smile.

"No, you'll see with time and *practice*."

We lay like that for a long moment. Me on my couch, him on his, our eyes holding each other's across the space. Even the carvings on his coffee table were still. What was happening?

A warning rumble shook the room, and I turned onto my back, breaking eye contact.

"I can ignore him if you can," Cross joked lightly as he sat.

"I can." No, I couldn't. Cross knew it and so did Sam. Fucker.

"You should rest."

"Okay." Standing, I headed to my room. "We'll try for inner peace tomorrow?"

"I'll be here."

With my back to him, I turned my head as if to look at him over my shoulder, but I stopped myself from turning back to him completely. "Thank you." My whisper was almost inaudible, but I knew he heard me.

With a heaviness I hadn't felt in some time, I went to the bedroom.

When I finally entered sleep, he was waiting for me.

"Witch, are you trying to make me jealous?" His black tunic was free of weapons. His leather trousers were snug, and I may have lingered too long on his thighs before I met his stormy gaze.

"You look…different." I glanced down at myself, surprised I was still in yoga pants and a T-shirt.

"Do I?" Sam had been leaning against a wall as if he were waiting for me. Now he pushed himself off it and walked towards me. I didn't step back, tired of this demon thinking he intimidated me. "How do I look different?"

In hindsight, I should have stepped back, because where I hadn't given an inch, this demon had taken a mile. He stopped right in front of me, causing me to look up to meet his eyes. "You're crowding me," I protested.

"You're flirting with death."

It wasn't even hypothetical. I really had been, and as I giggled, Sam's eyes narrowed. "You lost any claim to me the day your dagger pierced my heart," I snapped at him as I looked away from him.

"And what about when *you* pierced my heart?" Sam asked as his finger caressed my jaw before tilting my head back to look up at him. "Hmm, little witch, what about then?"

"Sam—"

His kiss was featherlight and so soft and gentle. I froze. It was everything Sam had never been. He was hard, demanding, possessive. Gentle? No. Soft? Never. His mouth moved over mine tenderly, and it was so light, so sweet, I swayed forward. Sam took my lack of protest as encouragement and deepened the kiss. An arm slipped around my waist, pulling me into him, as his other hand slipped through my hair, cupping my neck as he pulled my head closer.

The low growl behind me brought me to my senses. Pushing away from the Watcher, I stepped back, wiping my mouth with the back of my hand. "No. No! What are you doing?" I demanded as I reached out to Hound.

"Reminding you that you are mine."

"Do you stab all your girls?" I bit out angrily.

"Only the ones I want to save."

Speechless. I was speechless. "What?" I struggled to find my voice as my eyes widened. He grinned and I vowed to make him suffer for eternity. "You're a dick."

"I know, you've told me." Sam stepped back and looked to Hound. "Morax, you can stand down."

I looked between Hound and Sam. "Morax? Is that your name?"

"He no longer answers to it," Sam said with a sneer.

"Then why would you call him it?" I asked in confusion. Sam's cold stare made me shake my head. "So I would know? Know what? That Hound was an angel, like you?"

Sam looked away, and I imagined several long swords being thrust into his body simultaneously as he screamed in pain. "Violent, even for you," Sam spoke casually, and I flushed at being caught.

"Any more tricks?" I asked him with barely concealed contempt.

"I never tricked you, I didn't need to." Sam smiled smugly.

"And you have nothing further to say that I need to hear." I placed my hand on Hound's shoulder. "Stay out of my dreams."

A large hand grabbed my arm, and Sam roughly pulled me into him. "Listen to me, you obstinate little girl, I am trying to save you from the wrath of a prince of hell. While you eat pastries and play with Death and his minions, *hell* is hunting for you. Not to join you for yoga and fucking cookies. Asmodeous will find you, and while you continue to exist in denial, I and my brothers are doing everything to save you and your family and even that limp-dicked prick you claim is a friend." If he noticed my wide eyes or the whitening of my face, he didn't care. "You think we're playing a game? You think that Cross cares about you? Wake the fuck up."

Wrenching myself free of his hold, I took several steps back as I rubbed my arm and glared at him. "Wake the fuck up? *Wake the fuck up?*" I screeched. "*You* wake up, you complete dick. You stabbed me. With no warning. A prince of hell is hunting *me*? You brought him to my door! I was fine, I was living my life before you shattered it. I'm in trouble because *you* threw me into the pot."

"And I am trying to get you out of the *pit* before you kill yourself."

Ha, I saw what he did there. "I don't *want* or *need* your help."

Sam laughed. "Fuck, witch, you're even more delusional than before." His humour left him as he looked me over. "This is serious. I will lose no more brothers for you."

I had been about to snap at him when his words penetrated. "Who?" I asked, all anger leaving me.

Hard eyes glittered with anger. "Chazaquel."

He was the one I was mad at. Even more than Sam. "Where is he?"

Sam's look was scathing. "Asmodeous."

"No."

"Yes," Sam bit out. "Now are you ready to stop pretending?"

"I wasn't pretending," I snapped.

"I don't give a fuck about your denial! I need my witch." Furious shards of emerald glared at me.

They put me here. They involved me in this shit show. They only had themselves to blame. I felt like screaming. "I am not *your* witch."

"You're no one else's either."

"At last, we agree."

Warm fingers tangled in my long blonde hair. "Help me help

him." Sam dipped his head, his mouth a hairbreadth away from mine.

"Sam…"

His lips brushed mine. "She's busy, Cross."

Sneaky bastard.

CHAPTER 12

PUSHING AWAY FROM SAM, I WINCED AS MY HAIR GOT TANGLED around his fingers, but it didn't stop me from moving away from him.

"Everything is a game to you," I said as I pulled my hair over my shoulder.

"Not everything." His eyes were dark and full of promise, and I hastily looked away. Sam messed with my head, thank Christ my heart was somewhere else.

"Are you well?" Cross asked me as he walked over to me, his hand lightly running down my arm.

"Yes." I reached up to touch his hand, and somehow that made our fingers intertwine.

"You keep your hands to yourself, Cross," Sam warned.

"His hands can go wherever they want." *Whoa, Star, let's calm down.*

Sam's head cocked to the side, and I met his appraising look with a challenging look of my own. "Is that right?"

I knew I was in trouble. I knew it, and I knew not to push it, but he had no right over me. He killed that the night he killed me. "That's right."

"The whispers tell me Asmodeous gained another Watcher," Cross spoke as if I wasn't having a pissing contest with Sam.

"He has." Sam frowned. "Chaz is rarely impulsive"—his eyes flicked to mine again—"but certain things push us further than any can predict."

"You're blaming me?" I asked him incredulously.

"If you feel guilt, then you should ask yourself why."

Cross squeezed my hand, which I realised he was still holding.

"Star is not to blame. Chazaquel has been rash, and Asmodeous capitalised on that, as he would."

Sam grunted but his attention kept drifting to Cross's and my hands. "Zel said you need another prince to help you."

"Did he?" Sam shrugged. "It is nothing."

"You cannot take her to him," Cross said, suddenly in shock. "Samyaza, he will demand too high a price."

Sam looked away, but I saw his shoulders tense, like the weight he was carrying was too heavy for him.

"I thought you weren't answerable to any of the levels?" I asked quietly. "That you were Watchers, and the levels and the princes who ruled them had no sway over you."

"They don't," Sam answered. "The princes are bratty little shits that Father was glad to be rid of."

"So no love lost then," I snarked. "It seems to be your common theme."

"The princes are powerful." Cross squeezed my hand as he spoke.

"But they were all angels, no?" I asked as I turned to look up at Cross.

"They were. I know why you avoid the obvious choice, but you cannot take her to *him*."

"Then you come," Sam said, and I shook my head as I saw how he had once again manipulated the events to his desire.

"Cross is not getting involved." I took a deep breath, why I didn't know, but I did it anyway. "I'll go. It's me you need. Right?"

Sam smiled in satisfaction, and I realised that I had done exactly what he wanted. "Right."

"I'll go with Zel."

Sam's smile grew wider. "As you wish, though I should tell you, Satan and Zel have a violent history."

"Zel has a violent history with…" I stalled. Did he say Satan? "*Satan?*"

"Yes."

"The devil?"

"Prince of hell," Sam corrected casually.

I blinked. "I can't go to Satan!"

"Why?" Sam was enjoying this too much. "He's just another demon."

"Sam! He's *Satan!*"

"He really is just another prince," Cross said in a low soothing voice.

"And his level of hell is?"

Sam's grin was lethal. "Wrath."

Of course it was. "You want to send me to the Prince of Wrath with *Azazel*, the angriest fucker to have ever breathed?"

"I did mention there was some past conflict, but I'm confident they moved past it." Sam was far too relaxed for my liking, and amusement danced in his eyes as he watched me reach the inevitable conclusion.

"Fine." I shrugged, trying to be casual, but even I couldn't stop my head from shaking in disgust at his manipulations. Even I knew I would never survive a meeting with Zel and…yeah. "You win, I'll go with you."

"It sounds like the best plan." Sam nodded solemnly, but his eyes still sparkled with laughter.

"Do we go now?" I looked to Cross, who was watching Sam with narrowed eyes.

"No, you need to train," Sam said abruptly. "A few more days, I expect improvement."

The audacity. "Well, I'll do my best, Mr Motivator," I snarled at him.

"Of course you will, I'll be there."

Both Cross and I gaped. "You can't come into his home."

"His home? What lies you feed her." Sam turned from us as he held his hand up for silence. I felt Cross stiffen, and I strained my ears to listen. I heard nothing.

"What is it?" I whispered to Cross.

"We dally." Cross snatched my hand. "Come."

I'd never met anyone who said "dally" before. Sam looked at me quickly before Cross whisked me back to the bedroom. Waking up, I looked up at him.

"I split again?" I said as I sat up.

"The hold that he has on your soul is stronger than I thought."

"Is that how he pulls me to him?" I asked as I rubbed my eyes. "Also, I never get to sleep anymore."

"You can rest now," Cross said gently as he pushed my shoulder back onto the mattress.

"What if I can't?"

"I can lie beside you." Cross swung his legs onto the bed and settled beside me. "Relax." Because I could do that, with a hot guy beside me. I was not cool or collected enough to pull this off. "You're overthinking."

"It's a thing," I joked.

"I know."

"You don't sleep." I started to giggle as a song line popped into my head. "Sleep when I'm dead, but not you."

"I'm not going to ask," Cross told me as he got comfortable. "You used lots of energy today. I am glad that Hound is with you, but you still need to stop wearing yourself out."

"I'll do better," I promised the male beside me.

"Sleep."

For the second time that night, I did, and my soul recharged. In the morning, when I went stumbling and yawning for coffee, Cross was already in the corner, training.

Bare-chested and wearing low-riding sweatpants. Why? Was I such a terrible person? Did I deserve this before coffee?

"You're drooling." I jumped at the voice behind me.

"Sam?" I glanced at Cross. "What are you doing here?"

"I told you that I would be here." Sam looked...poised.

"Um, right." I looked back at Cross. "Coffee?"

"On the table," Cross murmured.

"Okay." I waited for a second, and then I thought this would all make sense over coffee. Sam watched me closely as I lifted the cup on the table that was waiting for me. I zeroed in on the half-eaten pastry. "You ate my breakfast."

"Peckish for something tasty."

I needed to count to ten. "How did you get in?"

"How do you get out?"

Good question. "I don't know," I admitted as I debated about eating the rest of the pastry. Stuff it. I picked it up and polished it off in two bites.

He looked far too smug with himself. *Arsehole.*

"What are you planning to do here?" I asked him as I took a gulp of coffee.

"Help you focus."

Well, that wouldn't work. At all. "I think you may be a distraction that I don't need."

"Well, I disagree." Sam watched me as I shifted on the couch, my breakfast eaten and my coffee finished.

"Star," Cross called, and I was off the couch like a rocket, joining him at the punching bag.

"Hi," I greeted awkwardly.

"Morning." His smile made me smile in return. "Some light sparring to start us off and then meditation?"

"I'm ready."

Cross changed my clothing, and I pulled my hair up into a ponytail. "Okay, what ya got?"

We slipped into our normal routine, and I almost, almost, managed to forget the demon in the corner. Sam said nothing, but his eyes were on me the whole time, and the weight of his stare didn't unsettle me like I thought it would.

"You okay?" Cross asked me softly.

"Yes, I think I'm getting faster with my responses."

"Why does she still act as if she's in her body?" Sam asked from his spot.

"Star has not accepted certain aspects of her situation," Cross explained.

"Witch."

"Demon," I snapped back.

"You need to realise that you are not in your normal…form."

"I'm aware you're keeping my body," I barked.

"Then move faster." Sam lounged back in his chair. "You're being stubborn."

"Why are you even here?"

Sam pushed to his feet and crossed the room quickly. As he towered over me, I stared up at him in defiance. "Punch the bag." His voice was quiet. Gritting my teeth, I turned and punched the bag. Moments later, the bag swung insanely as Sam punched it.

"*Punch* the bag," Sam growled.

"Can I punch you?" I grumbled back as I took aim and hit the bag again.

"You've taught her nothing." Sam pulled his shirt off over his head, and I watched in rapt fascination as his muscles were revealed, his biceps bunching as he tossed the shirt to the couch. "Here." He didn't wait and pulled me into him as he ignored my squeak of protest. A large hand trailed down my arm, catching my hand as his other arm enclosed me, and his other hand formed my limp hand into a fist. His heat was immense, and being so close to him was causing me to lose focus, and for once, I was grateful I had no body as he would know exactly what he was doing to me. "Focus," Sam whispered in my ear, and body or not, I still got chills up and down my spine.

"Do you need to be touching me?" I asked him and was distressed by how throaty I sounded.

"If you want to be taught properly, then yes."

With my fingers formed in the fist that Sam wanted, he then drew my arm back and thrust it into the bag. The bag barely moved.

"This is how you punched just now," he said as he pressed closer to me. Drawing my arm back, he then shot both our arms out, and the bag moved significantly more. "This is with some of my strength behind you." His lips were still at my ear, and he was playing havoc with my senses. I needed him to step back before I made a fool of myself.

"Okay, so I can't hit as strong as you because I'm not a giant. Got it." I took a step forward, and the demon behind me pulled me back. As he did, he tugged my hair tie free.

"You are thinking about it as a human. You are not a human at this moment, you are a soul. Your body is not here, your body's limitations of height, weight, softness"—my breath hitched when his lips caressed my ear on *softness*—"all the human limitations are not applicable to you at this time." Sam moved slightly, and I naturally moved with him.

Was it hot in here?

"I don't understand," I admitted as I turned to look up at him, and I was trapped in his heated gaze.

"Samyaza means that you still think of yourself as human, but as you are separated, you are more. You are a necromancer, and your vessel is no longer holding you back."

"I will be able to return to my body?" I asked Sam, and his eyes softened as he smiled. "You will give it back?"

"I hold it only for you to return," he said gently. "You were not supposed to disappear on me, witch."

My brain knew all the bad things he was and what he did, but if my body had been here, it would have betrayed me. I couldn't let my soul fuck me over too. I stepped away from the demon who still held such sway over me. Shaking my arms loose, I looked at Cross.

"What am I doing wrong?"

"Punch, thinking not of how much you weigh, how fit you are, but punch with your intent to make the other hurt."

Frowning, I looked at the bag. "I'm not really good with violence."

"Your mum is being held by Asmodeous, and he has a knife to her throat," Sam said as he reached for his shirt. "The bag is Asmodeous."

I punched the bag. I hit it with a force much stronger than normal. "He doesn't, does he?" I asked afterwards, and Sam shook his head. "Okay, again."

"Zel wants to cremate you so you can never return," Sam said easily. The bag was hit with force that rivalled Sam's. He snorted.

"Again."

"Chaz went to Asmodeous to beg for him to let you live, knowing he would be captured and tortured." When I didn't hit the bag, Sam raised an eyebrow before he nodded thoughtfully. "It was Chaz who suggested that, to save you from the prince, we had to sacrifice you to the blood moon."

The bag broke off its holding and went flying through the air.

Panting, I glared at it before I turned my anger to Sam.

"Again."

"I struck you down to save you, knowing you would never forgive me or understand, and I would do it all again if it meant I was protecting you."

My fist connected with his jaw, and his head snapped to the side at the force of my blow as I bounced lightly on my feet.

"Again."

"You are truly the worst witch I've ever met but are an incredible fuck."

His head snapped to the side again when I hit him.

"Again," I growled.

"You're the reason my brothers are suffering, and you will help them, or I will destroy your world and everyone in it."

My fist swung and he caught it, pulling me close. I glared up at him as hard dark green eyes stared down at me. "I hate you."

"No, you don't, and that's what pisses you off the most," Sam said as he nipped my bottom lip. "And if your body was here, I would be inside you right now, and you would be begging me for more because, witch, I like this kind of foreplay, and I think you do too. Now stop playing games, learn your craft, and when I come back, you better be ready to get my brothers out of Asmodeous's clutches."

As he went to pull away, my hand reached out and grabbed a handful of his hair, keeping him close to me. "What if I don't care about your brothers?" I challenged him. "What if I hope they burn, that you *all* burn, for eternity?"

Sam moved so quickly I didn't even see it. I was against the wall, his arms pinning me in, his body pressed against mine.

"*If* they burn, you and all you love burn with them."

Our eyes locked on each other, and I could see nothing past the walls he had put up. I hoped I had the same skill, but I doubted it. Sam knew me too well, which really did piss me off. But I was supposed to be powerful. It was time to own it.

I reached up and whispered in his ear. "I think you forget what I can be."

Roughly I was pressed into the wall as he hooked my legs around his waist, his lower body pressing in just right. As his hands tangled in my hair, he bent his head to speak against my lips, "I know what you are, what you can be and what you will *never* be." His tongue traced my bottom lip, and I had no idea why this was making me so hot and horny.

I couldn't let him win. I couldn't let my attraction to him be my weakness. "What will I never be?" I asked scornfully. "Powerful? Capable?"

"Me." His look spoke volumes, and I froze. "You will never be *me*."

I hesitated as his eyes glowed slightly.

"You will never be me, witch, and you may thank my Father that I will never let that happen. So go ahead, play your games with Cross, try to make me jealous, but you will help me and my brothers because that is who you are. No matter what lies you tell yourself, and the lies to others, you know and I know that you will always, *always* be mine."

Sam was gone, and I stumbled as I caught myself from falling. My hands shook from adrenaline as I straightened myself, and I met Cross's look with a startled one of my own. I had completely forgotten he was here. "Oh."

"It's intense watching you both; that attraction is…interesting," he said, as if the insane almost-making-out session hadn't happened right in front of him. "How do you feel?"

Pushing my hair off my face, I twisted my hair into a messy bun. "Confused."

"Understandable."

"Angry."

"To be expected."

"Vengeful."

Cross stood a little straighter. "Tell me more."

"They will pay for what they've done to me. Once my body and my family are safe."

"Fighting talk," Cross murmured.

"I'm ready to fight." I looked at the punching bag lying broken against the wall. "My days of being weak are over."

CHAPTER 13

"What's bothering you?" Sam asked me a few days later. He had been showing up at the room sporadically, and he was annoying me more and more every time.

"I want to see my mum and my dad and Ruairidh."

"No."

I looked at Cross, who also shook his head. "It's a bad idea, Star," Cross told me.

"Why?"

"Is it your plan to gift wrap yourself for Asmodeous?" Sam asked as he lounged on Cross's sofa.

I was currently meditating, or I had been attempting to, but my thoughts continually drifted to my mum and dad. They would be missing me, and they were in danger, did they know? Did my mum know how messed up my current situation was?

"No," I sassed back at him. "I thought that was your plan."

Sam's grin made me want to commit violence on his person. Showing great restraint, in my opinion, I turned back to Cross. "Why can't I go? I'm better."

"You are," Cross conceded with a smile. "But not yet."

Sam snorted and I gave Cross a pleading look. He shook his head slightly. He seemed frustrated. Were his hands tied because dickhead was here? I turned my glare on the demon that pissed me off on a daily basis. "You could go."

"I could," he said casually as he stretched his long legs out over the couch and got comfortable, closing his eyes. He was in simple jeans and a shirt today. The tunic and leathers were gone for more casual attire. He looked normal. Well, as normal as someone like him could look. He would stand out anywhere; he was too attractive, too tall, and if you looked more closely, you would see he was too deadly.

"Why are you here?" I demanded as all sense of zen left me.

"To make sure your most recent admirer keeps his hands to himself."

"You're jealous?"

Sam snorted. "No. I know who owns you."

There was that word again, *own*. "When will you learn I am not a possession? I am a person. A being. Someone who deserves respect."

"I do respect you," Sam told me as he yawned.

"Ho—"

"Is this going to conclude soon?" Cross cut off the argument before it even began, as he maintained his cross-legged position. He'd closed his eyes again as he chased a sense of peace.

"Sorry," I mumbled as I tried to relax. I failed. "Why can't you just go see my mum for me?" I asked him.

"I've been."

My mouth hung open like a fish, and I stared at him as that slow smile spread across his face, his eyes still closed as he lay there with absolutely no cares.

"You've been? What do you mean, *you've been?*"

"What do you want me to say more than I already have?"

Is this what flabbergasted felt like? "You didn't think I would need to know, that I would *want* to know?"

"You're easily distracted, and you're going to focus on this instead of training."

"Sam!" I was on my feet and crossing the room to get to him. "Tell me how my mum is before I kill you."

"Or you could train, and as a reward, I can tell you later."

I leaned over to punch him when he grabbed my hand, and suddenly I was on my back on the couch, and the demon lay on top of me.

"You never learn, witch," he scolded as his thigh settled between mine. "You must be prepared at all times. Striking without being prepared ends badly for you and, well, *good* for me." His head dipped into the crook of my neck, and I felt his lips on my skin.

"Get off," I grumbled as I bucked my hips, trying to dislodge him.

"Mm-hmm, you keep that up, I just might." His teeth nibbled at the spot behind my ear.

I stilled as I heard his low rumble of laughter, and as Sam propped himself up on his elbows, he looked down on me. I realised he wasn't crushing me; being bodiless meant I didn't have the pesky rib cage crushing internal organs as he lay his body on top of mine.

"Could you stop it?" I asked as I tried one more time to move him. "And then tell me about my mum and dad?"

His look was one of fondness as he looked down at me, and I had to look away. "What do I get for telling you?" he teased me gently.

"To keep your balls?"

Sam moved off of me slightly to the side as he laughed. "You're funny." As I went to move, his arm caught me and pulled me back onto the couch. "Stay and I'll tell you."

"Bribery? We're going with bribery?"

"I like it." His smile was full of mischief, and as I stared back at him, it was easy to forget that this was the demon who took my life. I didn't care why he did it, he still did it. The fact he did it to save me was irrelevant.

"I don't like you."

"I know." Sam reached out and twirled a lock of my hair as he watched me. "Ask me, and I will answer if I can."

"Are they okay?"

"Yes."

"Does Mum know you were there?" I wouldn't put it past him to ghost her.

"She does, she summoned me."

I felt like my eyes popped out of my head as I stared at him. "She did what?"

"Well…" Sam seemed to be distracted by my hair. "She summoned Pen, but I went too." Sam sighed as he dropped my hair and picked up another piece. "You have so many tones of honey in your hair," he mused.

He wanted to talk about the colour tones of my hair? I jabbed him with my elbow, and his green eyes snapped to mine in irritation. "Focus," I hissed.

"Your mother summoned Penemue. You know Penemue, he's more chivalrous than the rest of us, so he went." Sam picked up my hair again. "I miss the smell." He sounded surprised, and I was scared to move as he twirled my hair in his fingers. "You smell good. I don't like your current fragrance."

I heard Cross snort, and I felt Sam stiffen. What the hell was going on now? I had no idea, and I decided it was for them to be weird over. All I needed to know about was my mum. "Can you please, for the love of God, finish this story, and I'll let you sniff me later."

He gave me that sly smile, and I just *knew* he had made it dirty. "Promise?"

"You're a dick." Wiggling free, I yelped when he caught me to him again and pulled me down onto his chest. "Sam…"

The heat in his stare stopped me, and I looked down at him as my hair slowly fell around us, veiling us from everything else. From Cross.

"Your mum called for Pen. I am protective of my brothers at present, so I went with him to ensure there was no trap being laid." He hurried on when he saw me about to protest that my mum would never do that. "Jean was really fucking pissed." He grinned in remembrance. "I now know where that temper comes from." His cheerful smile was playing havoc with my insides. "I told her what had happened, and well, let's say that I thought *you* could swear."

"And when she calmed down?"

"We explained you were safe, and she demanded your body, of course."

"I'm with Mum?" I asked in excitement.

"No." He actually rolled his eyes at me. "As if I would let you be with anyone other than me."

"That's stalker talk," I snipped at him and gasped as he tugged me further down to him, our lips barely inches apart. "Don't you dare." I was not kissing him. It was bad enough that I was straddling him on Cross's couch.

"Pen has been in regular communication with her. She isn't happy, but at least your mother understands that what we are doing is to protect you."

"Because she doesn't know everything," I snapped at him. "She won't know you sacrificed me on a blood moon."

"She does know."

Well...I wasn't expecting that. "You told her you stabbed me?"

"I did."

"And you aren't dead?" Fear clutched at my throat. "Did you kill my mum?"

Hands too large to be so gentle slipped into my hair as he pulled me closer, and his lips caught mine. "No, she's fine," he said as he pulled away.

"Stop kissing me," I whispered. "You're trying to distract me."

"Is it working?" Sam asked as he pressed a kiss to the corner of my mouth.

"No." *Liar.*

"Liar."

"Tell me about Mum," I pressed.

"She is keeping your father at bay with the aid of your friend. Although it is likely that your father may know more sooner rather than later."

"Why?"

"Your mother is a formidable woman, but your father knows her well. I think he suspects, and I am sure it won't be long before she tells him everything."

"I need to go to them."

Sam's hands tightened in my hair as he held me still above him. He stared into my eyes, and I felt it deep in my soul. "No. It is not safe. You will stay here and learn what you need."

"I could be there and back again within minutes!"

"I said no." His voice was hard as he pushed me off him.

"I've said, many times, I don't care what you say," I countered as I stood and turned to challenge him.

"I will not tell you again," Sam warned.

"I think that's enough disruption for today," Cross cut in smoothly.

Sam's eyes flared with rage before he nodded curtly and then was gone.

"He vanished?" I turned to look at Cross. "Are you kidding me?"

"Samyaza knows when you won't be reasoned with," Cross said as he stood. "Unlike me, it seems."

"I can be reasonable."

"Of course you can," Cross said as he patted my shoulder while he walked past me.

"Where are you going?"

"I need to check something."

Before I could ask anything else, I was alone. "So everyone can pop in and out except me? This sucks."

Hound watched me from his usual post, and I looked around the room before I looked back at Hound. "Are we alone?"

Yes.

"You could take me?"

I could.

"But you won't?" I guessed.

It is not safe for you.

"Is here? Is anywhere?"

Possibly not. It changes nothing.

"I just want to let her see I'm okay." Sitting on the couch, I looked at Hound as he made his way over to me. "Can you not understand that?"

I can.

"But still you refuse?"

They will know if I take you.

I hadn't thought of that. "Of course," I mumbled as I stared at my knees. "I wish I knew how. I mean, I know how to get to the Land…" I stood. It made so much sense.

I winked. Travelled. Whatever. I did it. I was in the Land of the Souls. The world was ash, and it was an ash that I caused. But even through the ash, I could see the forms of the spirits. I may have burned this dimension, but souls were still taken here, and if souls were taken here to wait for—what had Gran called it, processing? If they were being processed, then I wasn't alone.

If they could still enter, I could *leave.*

I saw my wind tornado heading straight for me, and I eagerly awaited it to scoop me up. When it did, I let it take me where I wanted, and then I was in front of the Waterfall of Solitude. It felt surprisingly familiar.

"I didn't think I could do it," I said with a delighted laugh.

I felt the shift almost immediately. I wouldn't have before, my body too numb and untrained, but in my soul form, I was more attuned to this dimension and the souls within it. So when the world jarred as evil entered it, I panicked.

Asmodeous.

I needed to return to Cross, but I didn't know how. I had no idea how to get to the pit of hell. It was the *pit of hell*. I felt panic surge as I felt the prince get closer.

Squeezing my eyes closed, I willed myself to travel.

"*Star?*"

"Mum?" I looked at my mum in shock and then at her kitchen where the teapot shook in her hands. "Oh my God, Mum!" Racing forward, I flung myself at her and vanished.

"You've no body, girl, you aren't corporeal."

"But they touch me all the time!" I protested as I reached in vain for her one more time.

"And they are demons, and you are on a demon plane with them. Your soul will appear solid there, but here, on earth, you are merely a manifestation, my love." She looked at me with tenderness. "Lord, Star, what have you gone and got involved with? You have me worried sick."

"I know, I'm sorry." I kept reaching for her as I drank her in greedily. "Have they threatened you?"

"Threatened me? No." Mum looked confused. "Have they threatened you?"

"They're wankers," I answered and saw her understanding, but before she could speak, I felt it. Felt him. "Oh fuck, no. Mum, I'm sorry!"

I travelled. I could feel Asmodeous coming, and I could not lead him to my mum.

Opening my eyes, I looked at the familiar graveyard. Shit. I was in Slate.

"Well, look what I found."

Ah fuck.

THE PRINCE OF HELL LOOKED MORE FORMIDABLE THAN HE HAD that night at Dunnottar Castle. His suit was peacock blue, and it should look ridiculous, but he wore it so well I was surprised at myself as if I would doubt that he couldn't.

"Did I not tell you there was no place on this crust that I wouldn't find you?" His slow Southern drawl made his voice sound warm, inviting. A lie. It was all a lie, he was evil, and as he walked towards me, I knew what real fear felt like. Black eyes slithered over me, and I saw the smile form on lips that sneered at me. "Your soul? You think that you being in this form will deter me?"

No, I hadn't thought of anything except the need to see my mum and let her know I was alright. I simply hadn't thought, and Sam was going to skin my body when he got his hands on me.

"What do you want?" I demanded, proud of myself that my voice remained steady.

"You. Burning in the pit, along with every witch of your bloodline."

Gran. "What difference does it make if you have me? I never learned the spell."

"No one can read the spell," Asmodeous spat as he inched closer. "That's part of the original hex. The bitch who cast it cast another spell at the same time to erase the spell from memory as soon as it was cast."

"Wow, she must really hate you."

Asmodeous smiled as he looked me over. "She does." He shrugged. "And every day, I torture her."

"You seem to be rather dependent on her; do you think that's healthy?" I took a step back as he laughed. The tomb was still hallowed ground. I needed to put my feet on the concrete.

"I have been searching for you in hell, but none of my brothers have seen you. Who hides you, bitch?"

"Ever think I hide myself?" How I wished I could. How I wished even more that I didn't need to.

"Your Watchers are seeking you also, and Yeqon tells me you aren't with them. And I know Chazaquel knows not where you are, we chat daily."

"Because you captured him!"

"So someone told you, interesting." He looked thoughtful. "It may be that the Watchers are not as honest as they claim."

"The Watchers are bastards," I spat. Not a lie.

"They have their uses." Asmodeous looked me over again. "But you are stronger. I can feel it as you stand there, despite your pathetic attempts to get to the stone."

I wasn't being subtle in my intent? Fine. Turning, I sprinted for the tomb. My entire being jolted when I stepped on it, as if I was being electrocuted. Holy shit, was this what euphoria felt like?

"You think a weak benediction on a piece of stone will stop me?" Asmodeous asked in amusement.

"Weak is still *something*, and I think you cannot touch me if I am on it." I grinned. "And I'm a soul—I do not need food, water, sleep. I have all night, fuckface."

Asmodeous nodded as he shrugged off my insult. "You do." He threw a smile my way, and I felt my level of panic increase tenfold. "But do your villagers?"

"What?" I asked just as the first eruption happened. The ground opened, and as the nearest cottage fell down, the ground spewed *up*. "*No! Stop!*" I shouted as people came running and screaming.

"Stop what?" he asked me casually as the earth erupted again and the next building was smashed to rubble.

"Asmodeous! No!"

"Come to me," he instructed as he watched me. When I hesitated, another building was destroyed, and I saw the people of the village run and fall over each other in their bid to escape. These people had never been kind to me, they had never shown me friendship, but as the next building imploded, I screamed when the stone and slate rained down on innocents.

"*Stop it!*" My throat was sore from my screams as tears ran down my face. He winked at me, and Abby's pub blew up like some horrific special effect in a film. Except it wasn't an effect, and I wasn't in a film. This was real life, and I was weeping as I wished it was not my life.

And as I watched the horror unfold in front of me, I felt them.

Finally, I felt the power swelling within me.

When Asmodeous turned to look at his destruction, he laughed at those lying hurt and injured...dead on the streets. He *laughed*.

And the world tilted as I opened my eyes with my powers in my hold. When he turned back to me, his laughter stopped. He stepped forward.

"Well, witch, what have we here?" he asked curiously as he looked me over. "Not a witch, not *just* a witch. Now I see." He vanished, but I could not let go of the power raging inside me. I had no outlet. My powers were here, called to me *for* me to fight that prince of hell, and instead I was alone, while I saw the souls of my neighbours rise from their fallen bodies.

"Witch," Sam called from behind me.

Watchers.

The wind picked up, and those who had ventured out from shelter screamed in fear as a wind that could not be natural howled through the village.

"Witch, control it," Sam bit out as he moved into my vision. I met his hard stare with one of my own. "Ah fuck," he cursed. "Gadreel!"

Der moved in front of me and looked at Sam once before he returned his attention to me. "You levelled up, huh?"

"Have I?" Holy shit, was that me talking? My voice was different, heavier, stronger.

"Pissed for definite, yeah okay, this should be fun." Der nodded, his thick beard bobbing as he scratched his jaw. "Star, I need you to calm down."

"I need you all to fuck off." I was a soul and I had no veins, but the *power*, the sweet power coursing through me, didn't know that, and if it did, it didn't care. "He puts you in front of me, why?" My head tilted. "Where is your *general*?" I scoffed. "And your demon of war."

"Hey, Star." Ros edged into my vision. "Hey, girl, you're looking…freaky and shit, and it's freaking me out."

I was aware that my hair was floating around me. How, I didn't know, nor did I care.

"Help them."

"We can't, Star," Ros said and flinched when I hissed at him.

"She hisses now?" Der asked incredulously.

"Will you shut up and help me calm her the fuck down?" Ros muttered.

And then I saw them.

They walked through my destroyed village—three hellhounds come to carry the souls from this world into the next. Hound was in front, his red stare fixed on mine. I could feel the hellhound's anger, and it matched my own.

The hellhounds paused and gathered the souls of those who had passed, but Hound continued on towards me.

"We letting her go with him?"

My head whipped around searching for the speaker. Zel stood

with his arms crossed as he watched the scene play out in front of him.

"You."

"Whore, you fucked up again."

My arm flung out, and lightning followed it, hitting Zel square in the chest, knocking him backwards. "I am *no* whore."

Zel stood and my brain registered I was fucked because Zel the poison-tongued demon wasn't in front of me. *Azazel the Watcher* loosened his sword with his shorter sword already in his right hand. He advanced and I braced myself.

"You strike me, you better be ready to fight, witch."

"I've been waiting for you." I smiled and I was conscious that my powers had taken control.

"I'm right here," Zel grunted as he struck, and from heck knows where, I had a shield, blocking him.

My powers picked him up and spun him before throwing his body against a headstone, causing him no damage but cracking the headstone in two. But Zel wasn't even slowed, he was charging me, and I braced myself for impact.

As his sword swung down, a hand shot out and grabbed his wrist, somehow stopping the blow. "Enough," Sam growled. "Witch, dial it the fuck back. Zel, stand down."

"Fuck off," Zel spat out.

"*Azazel!*" Sam's voice was rich with authority, and Zel locked his eyes on Sam's before he yelled in frustration and threw his sword from him in temper.

"Star," Pen spoke, and I saw him out of the corner of my eye. "You've been busy."

"He destroyed my village."

"You need to come off the stone."

I looked at my feet. I was still securely on the tombstone. "Why? Demons cannot come on it." I looked towards Hound. "Can you?"

Hound huffed in contempt as he stepped onto the stone beside me. My hand reached out to touch him, and the hellhound did not flinch from my touch.

"He attacked my village," I repeated. "I will destroy him."

"Because you stayed on the stone, getting juiced up by power that you have no right to hold," Zel snarled at me. "You hid like a coward. Again."

"You think I'm a coward?" My lightning raced across the sky.

"Star, this is not the time for your disputes with Azazel," Pen spoke again.

But it wasn't Pen who held my attention as I turned back to look at him. It was the demon *behind* him. With dark hair like Sam's, with the same high cheekbones, with the same full lips, only his were in a permanent sneer, the demon with the blue eyes.

The liar.

The trickster.

The betrayer.

Yeqon.

"You." My hatred for this Watcher powered my anger. "Asmodeous spoke to me of you."

I saw Sam turn to look at Yeqon in surprise. "Why?"

"You have dissension in your ranks, general," I sneered. "This little pig keeps squealing to the prince that holds and tortures your brothers."

"The bitch lies," Yeqon snapped.

"Azazel," I called. "You love to tell me all my flaws; tell me, is lying one of them?"

Zel looked between us and then at Sam. He shook his head once.

"Fuck, Yeqon, what did you do?" Sam demanded.

"He tricked me into bed," I started. "He sided with Asmodeous against you on the clifftops of Dunnottar, he feeds the Prince of Lust information even now. Do I need to continue?"

Sam looked torn, and a horrible, vindictive, malevolent plan formed in my head. "You tell me to trust you, demon." Sam's head snapped to mine in surprise. "You tell me you protect me."

"I do."

"Kill him."

I heard the cacophony of protests as I held the green-eyed stare of the demon who held more than my body in his power. Whose hold I may never be free of, but if I hurt, then by fuck, I would make him hurt too.

"Witch…"

"I do not trust you, and I will never trust you unless you prove that I can." I looked to Yeqon, who looked far too confident for a demon about to be destroyed. "He is not loyal, he is not and you know it. You need me. Do you need *him?*" Sam's jaw clenched. "You need me to stop the torture of your brothers, you need me to help you free Chaz." Sam watched me with hooded eyes, and I saw the tic throbbing in his jaw. "Prove to me that I am safe with you; eradicate our *common* enemy."

"Star." Pen stepped forward. "You ask too much."

I didn't care. Yeqon's actions had almost destroyed me. Sam had almost destroyed me because of what Yeqon did. And even when Sam knew I had been tricked, he had done little to make it right, his brother coming first. The brother that stood with Asmodeous and not with Sam. I was doing him a favour really. It was time for them both to suffer for their betrayals. It was time for him to choose.

"General?" I mocked as Sam hesitated.

Sam's head dipped once, and I saw his lips move, but I didn't hear his words before he turned and faced Yeqon. Sam's twin swords were in his hands, fire licking along the blades.

"Arm yourself," Sam instructed. "She has a shit way of doing it, but she has a point. You have been treacherous and untrue, and now you shall be tried by sword before your final judgement."

Yeqon looked amused at first as Sam spoke, and then the anger replaced the humour. "You will fight me, brother, over a *witch?*"

"I challenge you in the name of the ones who fell," Sam said as he straightened. "You have betrayed your brethren too many times, brother."

"For a witch?" Yeqon demanded again.

Sam stood stoic as he raised his swords. "To the end."

Yeqon looked at him for a moment longer, and the stunned look of disbelief on his face would be one I would happily take to my grave. A long sword appeared in his hand, and he dipped his head in acknowledgement. "To the end."

If I had been in my right mind, I would have stopped them. Had I been in my body, I would not have asked this. I would like to think both were true. In my soul, I knew I was lying. Yeqon deserved to bleed for what he had tried to take from me under pretence, and I was eager for his demise.

I felt Hound's disapproval beside me as the fighting started.

"They are immortal," I said quietly.

A Watcher can fall at the hands of another Watcher.

My head snapped up to look at the two fight. What if Yeqon was stronger? Had I risked Sam for my own revenge?

"Now you see," Zel growled beside me, his voice laced with venom.

"He betrays you all," I bit out. "To kill a snake, you must cut off its head."

"I'll remind you of that when I take *your* head." Zel strode away from me, and my fingers curled into Hound's shoulder.

He probably would. I had no illusion that I had made an enemy of Azazel. As I watched Sam and Yeqon fight, I couldn't help but look at the others and wonder who I had as allies.

Der with his bushy beard, arms like logs, and loud laugh? Ros with his blond Viking braids and quick easy smile? Pen with his thoughtful consideration before he spoke? Chaz whose soft blue eyes only ever showed me kindness; would he still feel kindness when he learned I was the reason he was about to lose a brother?

Yeqon struck Sam, and I saw the blood flow down Sam's arm. I felt my hair settle around my shoulders as the wind died. My worry over the demon in front of me was more than my hold on my powers. If the Watchers were aware that I was losing the hold on my powers, they didn't show it.

They fought savagely. Sam was something to behold as he drove Yeqon into the village.

It is rare to see the general fight.

I glanced at Hound as I chewed my inner cheek. *He will win.*

Hound didn't speak as he watched, and I felt the other two hellhounds settle beside me, which surprised me.

They are here for you should it go wrong.

Thank you.

The battle raged, and I started to get nervous. Yeqon was forcing Sam back, and Sam was letting him. Suddenly Yeqon had lost his sword, and I wasn't even sure how.

"You can yield," Sam said as he breathed heavily.

"Yield? For a bitch and her puppet?" Yeqon sneered as he produced two daggers. "I'd rather burn for eternity."

Sam's eyes met mine once, briefly. But I felt his rage. I swallowed past the lump in my throat, and I held my head high. I could not be weak now.

Sam struck, his sword embedding deep in Yeqon's chest. He thrust further in, and I saw the end of the sword burst free on the other side.

"I am no one's puppet." Sam's eyes were full of sorrow as he pulled his sword out and Yeqon slumped forward. "You have been judged, and you have been found wanting."

CHAPTER 15

I watched breathlessly as the others formed a circle around Yeqon as he bled on the streets of Slate. Their hoods were drawn over their heads, and I counted more than the six who had been here. There were two more.

"You have been judged, and you have been found wanting." They spoke as one, and I felt fear run through me.

Yeqon sat slumped on the ground, his head hanging low.

"You have been judged, and you have been found wanting," the Watchers said again, and I saw them all holding a weapon.

I opened my mouth to speak, but Hound nudged me, and I shut my mouth again.

"You have been judged, and you have been found wanting."

Yeqon raised his head to look at me. Deep blue eyes stared at mine as I stood still on the stone of the tomb. Hatred so raw pierced my skin, and I flinched.

"You're next," he mouthed to me as I saw the blades strike him, and I forced myself to watch as his brothers struck him down as one.

As he fell, they stepped back as his body lay on the cobbled stone of my village. Blood that had run red stopped and seemed to be sucked back into his body. With wild eyes, I saw the golden haze surround him before it turned a deep brown to black.

I heard the collective murmur from his brothers, but I didn't understand it.

When Cross appeared amongst them, I thought I had hallucinated. He was in a black suit with a black button-down shirt, his feet still bare.

"You need to let him go," Cross instructed as he turned his attention to Sam. "He needs to be collected."

Sam nodded, but his head was still bowed, and then I noticed that they were mourning. He may have been a bastard, but he was their bastard, and weirdly I understood that.

"Samyaza, they will come," Cross spoke with a calmness that I envied.

Sam shook his head, and when I thought Cross would need to speak again, Sam raised his head and looked right at me.

"Did it feel as good as you hoped?" he asked me, and I winced at the anger in his stare.

"He was disloyal." Only this time when I spoke, I lacked the power of conviction.

"And my pain, is it as crippling as you hoped?" Sam straightened, and I realised that instead of being in a circle, they were now all facing me.

"Sam—"

"You wanted me to suffer as you had suffered. You wanted me to feel loss the way you have lost. You wanted me to know betrayal as you have felt it."

"Sam—"

"How does revenge taste, witch? Is it everything you hoped?"

"If you knew why I pushed, then why did you do it?" I shouted in frustration.

"Because the only way for me to be able to communicate with you is to make you see how much I would do for you, how much *we* will do for you."

"What?" I didn't understand. "You make no sense."

"I am done proving myself to you. We are not here to entertain you. Learn your craft, learn your control."

Sam was gone.

I noticed that Yeqon and Cross were too.

Six Watchers watched me, and then Zel was gone as was Pen. Bara and Suriel, the ones who had been with Yeqon at Dunnottar also disappeared.

Ros and Der remained, and with a shake of his head, Der was gone too.

"Ros?"

"Yes, Star?"

"The hellhounds have gone."

"They went with their master."

I nodded and looked down at the stone.

"You stuck here?" Ros guessed.

"Yeah."

"Need to go back to Cross and don't know how?"

"Yup, pretty much." I looked back up at him, and he was in front of me, the usual playfulness gone.

"I'm angry at you."

"I know." I couldn't look away from the pain in his eyes.

"He fell just before me. He told me he would check the way for my arrival." Ros rubbed his hand over his beard as he looked at the spot where Yeqon had fallen. "He always went before me, to make sure I was safe."

"He seems like he was nice once."

Ros huffed as he looked back at me. "He was my brother."

"I'm sorry."

"You're not sorry," Ros grumbled. "He did wrong by you, took something that was not meant to be his, he sided with Asmodeous, he knew where he holds Araqiel, and he would not tell us. He knew that Chaz was going to reason with the prince, and he did not stop him." Ros inhaled deeply. "Sam would have stopped him."

"I'm not sorry," I admitted. "But I *am* sorry for your pain."

"Thanks." Ros was staring at the stones again before we both became aware of the sirens. "What a shitshow."

"Yeah."

"Hold onto me, I'll take you back."

I reached out and Ros took my hand. "You may never make this right with Zel," he said as he squeezed my hand.

"I know."

Ros nodded and then we were back in Cross's living room. It was empty, and I was surprised when Ros sat on the couch.

"You're staying?" I asked him as I sat down opposite him, exhaustion washing over me. "How did you get in?"

Ros chuckled as he leaned back. "I taught enchantments; do you think a few wards can lock me out?"

"I guess not."

"Star, you messed up," Ros said after a few minutes of quiet.

"Did I?" I hoped he could hear my sarcasm.

"You've alienated some pretty heavy hitters in my brothers." His head was tipped back against the cushions, his eyes fixed on the ceiling. "You've alerted the Prince of Lust you are more than a pretty witch, you have Cross dancing to your tune, and fuck, I dunno how we're going to heal the rift between Zel and Sam."

"I did all that?" I thought about it—quite productive for one afternoon.

"And we still need to free Chaz and Araqiel, and fuck, that's going to blow up in our faces, because Araqiel was closest to—"

"Yeqon," I stated flatly. "Of course he was."

"How many times do we tell you to think before you act, woman?"

"Look. The fucker came at me, he destroyed my village, and" —I shot to my feet in alarm—"my mum and dad won't know I'm okay!"

"Relax, Pen is there."

"Oh." I sat back down again.

Ros was watching me. Ros who had always been easy, playful and fun. "I need to get to the tree."

Ros's eyebrows rose in surprise, and then his head tilted back again. "Makes sense," he said carefully. "I didn't know you would know." He gave a short laugh. "It makes sense that you would know. Maybe we underestimated you after all."

"Can you take me?"

"Nope." Ros straightened. "Too much shit happening. I need my brothers out of Asmodeous's hold. I'm telling you, Star, it's all I can think of." His hands ran over the shaved sides of his head. "Araqiel, he can be, you know, but Chaz." He shook his head sadly. "Chaz is my boy."

"What do you need me to do?" I asked him quietly.

"You got hold of your powers again?"

"I think so, maybe." I felt for them, and I felt a tingle. "Possibly."

"Then you need to train harder, do more, be stronger."

"Sam distracts me."

Ros winced as he looked at me sadly. "I think you may be Sam-free for a while."

It shouldn't hurt getting the confirmation that I had messed things up with Sam, but it did. "I understand. I pushed him too far."

"Possibly. Truth is, judgement was coming for Yeqon. He just got out of the pit, and you went and ended him completely."

"I didn't."

"You may not have struck the killing blow, but you were the reason for it."

"And you despise me too?" I asked as I stood again and made my way to the window.

"No, I know why you did it, we all do. It will just take some of us longer than others to recover from the loss." I heard Ros stand. "Train hard, Star, we still need you."

"I will."

Alone I stood looking out at the still waters for a long time as I considered my actions of today. He asked me if my revenge was everything I hoped, and I wondered if he knew the answer was no. That I felt like shit, that I felt like I had struck a killing blow to them all.

"Your energy is so low I am surprised you can still stand."

Turning, I looked over at Cross as he sat, a glass of red wine already in his hand. "You're late."

"Watcher collection is always tedious."

"Is his soul on the Plains?"

Cross snorted as he took a drink. "No, the Watchers are returned to their Father for final judgement."

"He does everything that he does, and he gets to go to *heaven?*" I demanded incredulously.

"No, the ones who fell cannot ascend again, even in death. He is in purgatory, where I think he may wait a very long time before his Father calls for him."

I turned back to the window. "I'm a horrible person for hoping he stays there."

"You are still human." I heard Cross get comfortable. "Come, sit, have wine."

Walking over to the couch, I looked at the glass of red wine. "Can I have white zinfandel?"

Cross looked at my glass of red wine. "You always drink red."

"I don't like it."

"Then why drink it?" he asked me, perplexed.

"Because you drink it."

"That makes no sense." He twirled the wine in his glass. "So why change your mind now?"

"Because I'm fed up following others," I told him truthfully. "I'm tired of not feeling *me.*"

"You are concerned for how Samyaza will react."

I saw him change my wine, and I took a tentative sip. "Thank you." It was delicious. "I know he will be angry for some time."

"You fear you broke the bond?" Cross guessed.

"The bond broke the moment he slid his knife between my

ribs." Taking a larger swallow, I tried to drown the grumpiness in me.

"I will not get involved."

"You are already involved," I stated as I watched Cross try to shrug it off. "You have kissed me when he was watching, *only* when he was watching. You push him as much as I have, admit it."

"I push for other reasons."

"What reasons?"

"They are my own." Cross sipped his wine as he watched me with amusement.

"Everyone plays a game."

"And you do not?" Cross asked me casually.

"I'm tired." Standing, I downed my wine. "I need to refill my energy."

As I entered the room, I wished I could put my own night-clothes on. I wanted flannel pj's. I was feeling sorry for myself and wanted comfort. When I looked down and saw the red tartan flannel, I hesitated. Was that me?

Climbing into bed, I decided I didn't need to worry about it. Shutting my eyes tight, I willed sleep to come with no Watchers.

I got my wish. For several nights. Nights that turned into weeks, weeks turned into months. I was a Watcherless zone.

I was alone, and because of that, I was dangerous...because I was restless.

HOUND and I sat in the Void. He was in his weird male form, and I had conjured up a chair from don't even ask me where. I just knew I had done it, and I was happy at my accomplishment.

"You almost had it," Hound spoke to me in his rough guttural voice. He still wasn't happy about being in the humanoid form, but he did it when he wanted to teach me something. At the moment, we were trying to teach me how to conjure the lightning without being in a furious rage.

"Dude, I'm pretty sure that spark was me," I said as I leaned back in my chair.

"The flash? The tiny little spark of nothing?"

The thing about Hound in a human shape was that his sarcasm was sharper. The eye rolls I was used to, which sometimes had attitude, were now expressed using his whole face. I preferred it when he was a hellhound. The dripping disdain with which he looked at me sometimes made me feel like I'd just been publicly flogged.

"You're such a joy in this form."

He huffed, which sounded so much like his usual self that I grinned.

"We do not have much time, why are you dallying?" Hound gruffed at me.

"Because Cross is being odd and keeps vanishing for days on end."

"You miss your Watcher."

"They betrayed me, I got revenge on them, it's done." My words tasted like ash in my mouth, and I wasn't sure if I *was* done.

"Hmm." Hound flexed his shoulders, still not comfortable in the shape he wore. "Again."

With a sigh, I pushed myself up out of my seat. "Fine."

"The prince still seeks you, witch. You are not safe. Your visit to your town merely highlighted to him that you were being shielded. The Watchers do their best to protect you, but they have to be seen searching for you also. You think the princes of hell didn't notice the death of one of the Watchers? You think they aren't waiting for the fallout?"

"I know, I pushed too hard, I said sorry."

Hound gave me the look he had perfected so well. The one that made me feel like two inches tall. "You apologised to Ros."

"You can't say that I didn't say sorry."

"If you paid as much attention to your studies as you do your semantics, we would be better off."

I stood and waited. My powers were stirring inside me, and Hound was lecturing. Hound was usually lecturing. He believed I could be better, quicker, sharper, and I wanted to tell him many times that I was just me. As he droned on, I let my powers loose, and lightning cracked against the Void. Hound stopped talking and looked at me in disbelief.

"I think that was me," I said sheepishly.

"Why I should not march you to the prince now and say *take her*, I do not know." Hound morphed back into his hellhound shape just as six Watchers appeared in front of me.

"Are you serious?" Ros snapped as he grabbed my arm and we all arrived in Cross's living room.

Shirking off Ros's hold, I had eyes only for Sam. "All of you needed to come?"

Zel stepped in front of Sam, blocking my view. Deep hatred exuded from the dark-skinned demon, and I shook my head in defeat. "Why are you all here if you don't want to be?"

"You shook the earth with your power," Pen said quietly. "We thought you were in trouble."

"She *is* in trouble," Cross snapped as he walked through from the bedroom. "Why were you in the Void?"

"I thought I could practice." Even I wasn't buying my act of casual innocence.

"We practice every day, why would you take yourself to the Void?" Cross demanded angrily.

"I like it there," I defended weakly.

"She likes the Void?" Der asked Ros. "She's finally lost it."

"*Have* you finally lost it?" Ros snapped at me. "Why are we trying to save you when you seem intent on killing yourself?"

"What are you talking about? No one has been anywhere near me in weeks, *weeks.*"

"And why do you think that is?" Sam asked coldly as he stepped out from behind Zel. His anger was evident on his face as he looked at me quickly before he looked away.

He was angry again, and I didn't care. He looked good, better than good. His hair was a little shorter, his eyes a little brighter, his jaw clenched in anger. If my heart had been beating, it would have skipped a beat as I met his stare.

"Because you killed Yeqon," I replied quietly.

"Do not pretend to feel *guilt,*" Zel snapped in disgust.

"We have been fighting every demon sent to kill you," Der said as he sat down on one of the couches. "The prince is pissed, and he has sent every demon in hell to fetch you, Star. Dead or alive, he isn't fussy."

"You've been protecting me?" I asked as I took a step towards Sam.

"Yes, you think we want you dead? I'd have tossed your body to the levels of hell and told them to feast if that were the case."

He still wouldn't really look at me, whereas Zel couldn't take his hate-filled gaze off of me.

"I don't need you to protect me."

"Then you're a bigger fool than we thought," Zel growled.

"What are you even protecting me from?" I asked in exasperation. "I already told Ros I would help you free Araqiel."

The room stilled.

Every pair of eyes swung to Ros, who gave me a look that spoke volumes before he turned to look at Sam. "I can explain."

CHAPTER 16

"Then I suggest you be quick, brother," Sam spoke softly, and I felt bad for poor Ros.

"It's my fault," I spoke up. "I don't want Chaz to suffer. I know he went to save me, and I can't rest knowing he is in pain."

"Everyone out."

I looked at Cross in surprise as he looked around the room. "This is *my* domain, and you are not welcome."

I didn't see what he did, but I felt it. It was as if he *pushed* them out, and I even felt the pressure on my soul. Was I supposed to go? Forcing myself to stay there, when I felt the pressure easing, I opened my eyes and saw only Cross and Sam remained.

"Was I supposed to go?" I asked in a light tone as I stood there trapped between both of their heavy stares.

Cross grunted as he took his usual seat, and Sam said nothing while he watched me with hooded eyes as I made my way to the couch.

"When did you speak to Ros?" Cross asked me as a glass of wine appeared in his hand.

"When Asmodeous tried to destroy my village." The Watchers had done their best to restore the damage, but they were not infallible, and the belief was that there had been an earthquake. Which was uncommon for Scotland, and last time Cross updated me, he said they were blaming global warming. They may as well have said a hoard of pink elephants had paraded through the village because the locals would have believed it more. Adding on the fact that I was missing in action, I just knew I would be getting the blame.

"He didn't try to destroy your village, he tried to *destroy* you," Sam growled. "Why do you insist on being so stubborn?"

"I don't know what I did wrong," I protested. "The Void is peaceful."

"Peaceful?" Sam looked at me in disbelief.

"She hasn't experienced it as we have," Cross murmured.

"How?" Sam turned to look at him.

"It seems to welcome her," Cross answered as he studied his wine. "Like it does the hellhounds."

Sam looked at me and then Hound and back to me again. "Well, that can't be good."

"Why?" I asked from where I sat. Sam was in his tunic and leathers, and Cross was in dark formal trousers with a black shirt, whereas I sat on my couch with yoga pants and a loose black T-shirt.

"I think I need to start wearing better clothes," I said to no one as I picked at my yoga pants. My hair was in a loose plait, and I just felt scrubby compared to the males in the room. "I need to look better. Maybe I got too comfortable here."

"I don't mind that you're comfortable here," Cross said to me with a warm smile.

"It's time to remember you *don't* belong here," Sam growled at me as he looked me over. "What are you actually wearing? Tights?"

"Leggings. They're for exercise," I snapped back.

"You? Exercise?" Sam laughed harshly. "Fuck, the only thing you exercise is your mouth."

"Never heard you complain about my mouth before," I bit back and then realised what I'd said and that we weren't alone.

Sam looked smug.

Bastard.

"How is her training?" Sam asked Cross.

"Her inner peace is in turmoil, no matter how much we meditate. She is distracted easily." Cross sipped his wine. "Usually by her own thoughts."

"*She* is right here in the room," I drawled sarcastically.

"The witch has always been flighty," Sam said thoughtfully. "She felt calm in the Void." I could hear the question in his voice.

"She seems at peace there."

I stood up from the couch. "Seriously, I am right *here.*"

"Why the Void?" Sam asked as he gave me his full attention. It was the first time since Slate. "Talk to me."

"Like you talk to me?"

"Witch."

"Demon."

Sam gave me a tight smile and then reached out, clasping my arm. We were in the Void.

Instantly, I felt the calm wash over me, even with Sam touching me, the male who had broken so much between us, but in here, I didn't move out of his hold.

"I can feel you settle as you're here." Sam looked around at the dark ground, the darker surroundings, the small light that was illuminating the space, coming from…me. "Why are you in tune here? I know of nothing that seeks here."

Three hellhounds walked out of the darkness and surrounded me. Hound to my right, one to the left and one protected my rear.

Sam watched us through narrowed eyes, and I saw his green eyes linger on Hound. "Morax," he greeted. "You really have come into play?"

Hound said nothing, merely stared at the Watcher. I knew that Hound said nothing, but I kept my face blank.

"You bonded with the hellhounds," Sam said in wonder. "They are Cross's reapers."

I could deny it, or I could own it. "They are with me," I said clearly, proud that my voice remained steady.

He said nothing as he watched me. "Well, shit just got interesting," Sam said eventually. As he looked between the four of us,

I could almost hear his brain working. "You never cease to amaze me."

I wet my lips as I shared a look with Hound. "In a good way?"

Sam smirked as he shook his head. "Yes, witch," he said ruefully, "in a good way."

We looked at each other, a mountain of unsaid things between us, and I didn't know how to fix it. I was still so angry with him, and I knew it would be a long time before I would ever trust this demon, but he was *Sam*. He may have used me more than I would like and kept things from me more than he should, but too much had happened between us in too short a time for me to turn away from any assistance he may give me.

"Are you okay?" It was a lame attempt to start a conversation with this guy who would rather kiss me than talk to me, but those days were gone.

"I'm fine."

"Have you been able to see him?" I asked as I stared into the dull grey.

"Him? You mean Chazaquel?"

"Yes."

"You are angry at Chaz."

My eyes flashed angrily towards Sam. "Yes."

Sam looked around us. "Witch, have you been experimenting here?" he asked me cautiously.

"No."

"Witch?"

"A little."

"You have no idea what you do here." Sam shook his head as he walked towards me. Hands tangled into my hair as he tilted my head back and stared deep into my eyes. "You are going to cause trouble."

"Is that bad?"

His mouth captured mine, and my fingers slipped up over his chest and into the thick hair at the back of his neck.

Is this really the time?

I heeded Hound's dry question, and reluctantly I stepped back. "This is probably not wise, for us." I didn't meet Sam's eyes as I turned away.

"Right."

I heard the derision and knew Sam was on the same page as me. I had, after all, made him kill his brother. Why would he want to kiss me? And he stabbed me, why would I want to kiss *him?*

"Why is me being here so wrong?"

"The Void is dangerous," Sam said easily. "The word itself should warn you. Hollowness, emptiness, nothingness."

"Nothingness," I interrupted. "It was what I called it when I came here for the first time." I turned slightly. "It doesn't feel empty anymore."

"Because it never has been."

"But I see nothing."

"But you feel it."

Nodding, I looked at him. "I do."

"Then that alone should tell you to be wary." He glanced at me once. "I thought you especially would be more untrusting now."

"Since you betrayed me in the worst way possible, you mean?"

"We explained why we did what we did," Sam said patiently.

"You had *just* had sex with me."

Sam barked out a laugh. "Is that why you're pissed?"

"No, Sam, I'm all happy and bouncy with everything that's happened to me since you grabbed me off the streets of Slate that very first night."

"You are so much more than that now."

"Am I?" My challenging stare met his. "I didn't change."

"Your power is changing you as we speak," he said quietly. "You think you are the same, but you are not."

"I don't understand."

"You never do." Sam gave me an almost sad smile, and then he was gone.

Well, that was rude.

THE NEXT FEW DAYS, there was no sign of any Watcher. No pop-ins from those who usually disregarded anybody's feelings or considerations.

Not bitter at all, are you? I mocked myself as I grappled with the punching bag and beat out my routine training shots as Cross had taught me. Since Sam had shown me that I was more than my body, which was a good thing as I currently floated around in just my soul, I had improved in speed and precision. My worry was that when I was finally reunited with *myself*, my poor unexercised lump-of-meat body would not keep up with the toned soul that I now was.

Actually–how did that work? I looked at Hound, who was judging me, I could feel it, even though he was being quiet.

"If my soul is the better, stronger me that I can be, what happens when I meld back into my body?"

Hound stared at me impassively.

"You know what I mean, how do I get back in? Do I wiggle in through an opening?" I instantly felt awkward. "Oh gosh, please tell me it's my mouth, and I like...swallow myself." My stomach turned. "No, ick, yuck, *no*." I swear this hellhound had eyebrows. "Don't judge me, mutt," I muttered as Hound gave me a low growl at the less than flattering term.

Mutt?

"Too harsh?" I tried a side kick that Cross had been trying to teach me, and it was, frankly, embarrassing. "You didn't see that? Did you?"

No.

"Good." I tried again and had more impact but still nothing to rival Bruce Lee.

I didn't see that either.

"Comedian." Declaring myself the ultimate winner against the bag, I went and lay on the couch. "How do I get back into me?"

You'll know what to do when it comes.

I eyed Hound. "Have you met me?" I gestured along my prone body. "I need a map and a compass to put my shoes on some days. Knowing how to merge my soul into my body? I think I'm going to need a shaman."

Utterly ridiculous. Charlatans.

I lay on the couch, contemplating all the ways a soul could re-enter. I wondered if I needed an apology card for having left in the first place?

"You're not shielding your thoughts?" Cross said from the window.

Perching up from my prone position, I grinned at him. "When did you get back?"

"Just now." He was thoughtful as he stared outwards. "I want to talk to you."

"What did I do this time?"

"It's not what you *did*, it's what you offered to *do*."

"Ah, I've been waiting for this," I told him as I sat up straighter. "You don't agree?"

"Agree? With the idea of you walking into the domain of lust, intent on stealing from its prince?" He turned to look at me once before looking back out the window. "I don't know why you would think I had no reservations."

"Is it sarcasm day?" I mumbled as I stood. First Hound, now

Cross. "What's wrong?" I joined him at the window and saw what I usually saw, sea and sky.

Unexpectedly, Cross dropped the illusion, and I stared at the scene from before. Downtrodden souls marching downwards, the wraiths, or reapers, fluttering amongst them. The walls were no less red, the fire still burned, and the walls still oozed.

"Why show me this?"

"Do you see it?" His voice was a soft caress against my stretched senses as I struggled to take in all that I saw.

I was close to saying no, and then I saw. Cool glass touched my forehead as I pressed against it, peering down the path the souls walked.

It wasn't round. It was more a square, dug deep, as coals burned brightly from beneath, illuminating everything. Not coal, I realised. Crust. The blackened crust of cooled lava, but how could it cool here?

As my vision sharpened, I saw the chains, the spikes, the burning vats of...oil?

He was spread-eagled over the lava, his skin burned, weeping and blistered. My stomach turned as I saw his eyes had melted right in his face, but some flesh still hung on loose cheeks, enabling me to identify him still. White snow fell onto his broken body, and the scream was inhuman, driving me to my knees.

"What is that?" I whispered in horror.

"Salt." Cross sniffed disdainfully.

I felt the wetness on my cheeks as I scratched futilely at the window, trying to break the glass partition keeping me from running down to the pit, keeping me from freeing the male who hung suspended as if on a spit while his flesh dripped from his bones. Keeping me from saving Chaz.

"Look at you," Cross chided as he watched me. The scene was gone, the sky and sea replaced.

"Cross, I…" I sobbed and felt sick at the same time. I was on the ground, the sight of him burned into my mind, completely immobilising me.

"And this is why you cannot be part of their plan."

CHAPTER 17

C ROSS ALWAYS TRIED TO TELL ME THAT I NEEDED TO SLEEP TO recharge. But I didn't *actually* need to sleep in this state, something I realised as I lay wide awake for days. All I could see was Chaz burning on the surface of the pit, all I could hear was his scream when the salt was poured over his burnt, peeling flesh.

All I could see and hear was the Watcher who went to the prince of hell in my place.

I felt him come into the room. Hound had left me a while ago, as my unresponsiveness was annoying him.

"How long do you plan to wallow?" Sam's voice was sharp, his anger evident.

"I'm in limbo, I have eternity."

"You have five minutes to get up."

"Or what?"

"Or I'm getting into bed with you, and I'm going to remind you why you're mine."

I rolled my head to the side. "Seriously? *Sex?*" I felt my anger rising. "You think you can just climb into bed, and I'll just spread 'em and say jump on."

"No. I expect you to beg first."

Swinging my legs over the side of the bed, I stood, glaring at him. "You are such a pain in my arse, do you know that?"

"Told you I would get her out of bed," Sam spoke casually, and Cross appeared beside him.

"I didn't think the idea of having sex with you being so repulsive to her was something you would want to broadcast." Cross looked at me as he spoke and gave me a wink.

That was actually funny, and I grinned as Sam's jaw tightened, biting back his response.

"Why are you both in my bedroom?" I asked as I stretched the kinks out.

"Your muscles aren't even sore," Sam muttered. "You need to stop thinking that you're human."

"I am human." I thought about it. My body was elsewhere. "Aren't I?" Turning to Cross, I felt anxious. "When I go back, I'll be human?"

"Possibly."

"Possibly? Are you serious?" I looked between them both. "Possibly? Define possibly."

"You've been here for a while." Sam sounded hesitant. Why would this demon, who probably invented the word "confidence," be hesitant?

I kept my attention trained on him as I spoke to Cross. "What's the Watcher saying?" Sam raised an eyebrow at my terminology but said nothing. Cross was silent for too long, but I knew he was still in the room. "The fact both of you are thinking of how to tell me this, worries me."

"It makes sense if you are a demon," Cross started, and my gaze snapped to his. "Only because they were never human," he added on hurriedly.

"You're not demon or human. Make it make sense."

"You have too much power," Sam broke in. "You think that you have lost it, but you haven't, we all feel it. Since your experiments in the Void, it's increased." His dead stare made me swallow my protestations about the "experiments." "Some of it seems to be blocked to you, but when you went topside and met with Asmodeous, you actually uncovered a lot of that which you had hidden."

"Okay…" I had my powers, but I was blocked from them? By myself? I could come back to this; I had more important things to consider. "And this stops me being in my body and human how?"

"You've changed." Sam folded his arms across his chest, and I knew he was buckling down for an argument. This was his bossy bastard pose.

"No, I'm exactly who I always was," I countered. "I'd say you changed, but more like you were unveiled."

"I will not apologise and will never apologise for keeping you safe."

"When you're the reason I was in danger, I think you should be begging for forgiveness."

We stared at each other across the room, both ready to fight, both conscious of Cross. I saw the look in Sam's eyes, and it thrilled me as much as it scared me, which clarified for any doubters in my subconscious that I would always be drawn to him. I just didn't want to be. They could tell me until the cows came home, that they were protecting me from Asmodeous, but they went about it a shitty way, and my trust levels were so low with any of them I would never be the same.

He had to know that? He was many things, but stupid wasn't one of them. I saw Sam's eyes narrow as my thoughts ran through my head, and I returned his calculating look with one of indifference. The small smile that played around his full lips pissed me off, but I'd be damned if I reacted to him again.

"Are you both done?" Cross asked, and his dry tone snapped my attention away from the demon next to him.

"I'm so done." I nodded enthusiastically. "But you still need to tell me about the *possibly*."

"The living room is better, no?" Cross turned and disappeared, and I followed, the thought of walking through a wall no longer holding me back. As I made my way to the sofa, I stopped and looked at the wall.

"Just got it?" Sam asked coolly as he sat on the sofa, his long legs crossed in front of him as his arm draped along the back of the cushions.

"I winked."

"*Travelled,*" he corrected with slight emphasis.

"I thought I was unable," I replied as I eyed the wall before turning slowly to the sofa and sitting down beside Cross. I saw Sam's triumphant smile that I had chosen not to sit beside him and cursed myself for being obvious.

"It's all in your mind, your limitations." Cross leaned forward and picked up his coffee cup. I still had no idea where all the wine and coffee came from, but it was coffee, and only lunatics refused the black nectar.

"Pretty sure my body has a lot to do with it too," I muttered as I scooped up a Danish pastry from the tray.

"Your body isn't here. This is what we mean." Sam refrained from eating or drinking, and now that I was across from him, I realised another reason why I shouldn't have sat across from him was because I had no choice but to look at him. Not that I was complaining really, he was absolutely striking in his looks. I just didn't want to look at him all the time and see him looking back.

"Put me back in then." I turned to look at Cross as I happily ate my breakfast.

"If we put you back into the body, you are tied to earth. If you are tied to earth, Asmodeous will find you. If Asmodeous finds you, then there will be a war of dire consequences because I will tear the very fabric of the world apart if he harms you."

My cup was frozen halfway to my lips as I felt the seriousness of Sam's words. His look was one of conviction, and even though I trusted him not one ounce, I believed him absolutely.

"I'm just a clairvoyant."

His response was a snort and a small frustrated shake of his head. "You try," he directed at Cross.

"Star, what am I?" Cross asked me as he turned his attention to me.

"My caffeine provider?"

"Star." His admonishment was real, and I giggled as he gave me his headteacher look.

"You're Death." Still blew my mind when I said it out loud.

"And what are you?"

"A pain in the arse?" I heard Sam murmur his agreement, and I refused to look at him. Cross's expression was one of tolerance, and I sighed. "You say I'm a necromancer."

"I don't say, you *are*. You are a very powerful one too. But you are untrained and unskilled. We've been working on it, and you have improved, but you hold yourself back. Because you think like a human."

"I am human."

"No. You were." Cross placed his coffee cup back and turned to look at me, his soft jersey trousers allowing him to face me as he crossed his legs on the couch. Reaching over, he took my hands in his, capturing my whole attention. "As a necromancer, you belong to me. Not as a chattel but as a disciple of Death."

"Disciple of Death?" My voice was high, and I'm sure only dolphins could hear me. "That's a little OTT, no?"

"You deal with the dead, with spirits. Necromancy is not a negative thing. You've proven this ever since you felt your first elbow itch. You help the living move on, knowing their loved ones are in a better place. That's not a negative thing," he repeated. "Your work as a *clairvoyant*"—I frowned as he air-quoted the word *clairvoyant*—"is not harmful. The modern world depicts death and spirits as negative and dark. But what is more loving than a spirit being able to tell a loved one their final message?"

"I like that," I told him shyly as I felt the lump in my throat.

"As I have tried to teach you with all things, where there is a positive, there is always a negative. What I just shared is one of the positives, but there is always a balance, and the negative is just as powerful. You can command the dead to do your will, as you have proven that night in Kansas when you called them forth to fight your Watchers."

"They're not my Watchers," I mumbled with a glance at Sam.

"Pay attention," Cross chided. "You remember calling them forward, you remember the scenes, and you remember the carnage. That's a negative. That you had the power to do that, as untrained as you were, told me then the extent of your powers."

"Okay, so…if this pep talk ends with me having to stay out of my body forever, I'm not going to be happy." I felt him squeeze my fingers, and I wasn't entirely sure it was in consolation.

"You are a disciple of Death. Just as the Watchers were once warriors of God, you are a warrior of mine."

"Huh?"

"Once you learn your craft, really learn your craft, you will be immortal."

"Say what?"

"When you are trained, you will be invincible."

"Excuse me?" I was on my feet. My heart, which wasn't anywhere near me, was racing. "Sam?" Turning to him, I saw his sympathy before he stood and stepped towards me.

Sam reached out as if to touch me, but his hand dropped to his side. "You had a choice. You didn't know it at the time, but you did. You could have lived your life, with your weekend tricks, or you could have taken the bull by the horns and learned your craft. Really learned your craft. Your ignorance chose for you."

"There are so many things wrong with that statement." I rubbed my forehead as my brain threatened to break. "One, 'weekend tricks' makes me sound like a prostitute; two, you are the reason I'm in this mess. You came to me. I didn't go searching for bones of Druids and spells on my own."

"I know. But if it wasn't us, it would have been others. Asmodeous was getting desperate, so be glad it was me."

"Glad?" I laughed. "You're the reason I am being hunted and I am in the pit of hell, missing my body, being sculpted into some disciple of Death."

"No, you made the choice to destroy the spell. You made the choice to say no to a prince of hell, you made the choice to work with us. Everything you did was your choice."

"You stole me off the graveyard!"

"Yes, I know."

"You gave me the spell to learn."

"I know."

"You slept with me, many times, so you could always know where I was!"

"No, I slept with you many times because you taste delicious, and I'm getting close to tattooing it on your forehead until you accept it. You…are…mine."

"I hate you."

"You want to, but you don't."

"Nope, I really do." I walked away from him and stared out through the window. "We need to get Chaz," I whispered quietly. I felt Sam as he stood close behind me, and despite everything between us, I felt his pain too. "Why would he do this?" I whispered as I felt my tears flow.

"Because he hated the choice we made," Sam answered gruffly.

"You said it was his idea." I pressed my forehead against the glass as I looked down, down to the Watcher I had trusted the most and whose betrayal had cut the deepest.

"It was the only way he knew how to save you from him." Sam sighed as his arm circled my waist, pulling me slightly into him as I felt his head bury into the crook of my neck. "We had so little time, and not everything is always as it seems, witch."

My eyes stayed trained on the Watcher before me as I accepted Sam's words. "Cross says I can't help you because I care too much," I admitted softly. "Why have none of you gone to him?"

"Because I won't allow it." Sam dropped his arm and stepped back.

As I turned to him, he saw my confusion. "You're punishing Chaz?"

"I'm protecting you." His jaw clenched as he looked away.

"You're all powerful. I've been told before that you answer to no prince of hell." Quickly I looked to Cross, who sat calmly on the couch. "If you're all *that*, and for once, I accept you may be, why have you never gone and taken your brothers from Asmodeous before?"

"It's complicated." Sam turned and went back to the couch, and then he was on his feet again. "Cross, keep your hands off what is mine… She needs more time."

Cross nodded and then Sam was gone.

"I need more time for what? Why is it complicated? How does Chaz suffering protect me? Where did he go? Why aren't they saving him? No one has answered why I'm not human!"

Cross smiled widely. "Your questions will always be a source of delight," he told me as he looked me over.

"Why am I possibly not human?" I demanded.

"Your soul has evolved, you will be immortal, and your human body may not sustain you as it should."

"Do I have a choice?"

"Not really, the process began the moment your soul came across the veil."

Well, that was quite possibly the most depressing thing I'd ever heard. "And the rest?"

"The rest?"

"Cross…don't make me cross!"

"Asmodeous believes the Watchers are hunting you. He does not know that they know where you are and that for months, they have been protecting you. Chazaquel was rash in his decision to barter for your life, and although his suffering is great, he knows that his brothers have you and continue to keep you safe."

"He's suffering that willingly?"

"In parts. His pain is very real, the pit is…difficult. When he is lucid, he sometimes remembers, but time is warped here. I control our time, but Chazaquel has been enduring his torment for many more months than you."

"Is he there?" I asked Cross as I turned to look out the window one more time. The illusion of sky and sea fell away, and I forced myself to look down. The scene was the same, the burning, the melting, the horror and the pain, and it was more horrific because I knew it wasn't an illusion. I knew it wasn't a scary scene that they were using against me. "Why can you not help him?"

"I cannot play my hand, as then Asmodeous will know exactly where you are."

"But he knows. He saw me in Slate, he said to me that I was not just a witch. He knows I'm a necromancer." I flinched at the word, but Cross was not fazed.

"He knows you are more than a witch, he does not know more what exactly. I have taken meticulous measures to ensure your ability and my association with you is non-existent."

"Oh."

"But you vex me when you go into the Void and play with my hellhounds and create lightning because you can."

I bit my lip as I heard his annoyance. "Oops?"

"Not oops," Cross scolded. "I need you to stop. Please. I can only do so much, and when our hands are revealed, we will need every surprise we have."

"They want me to go to Satan."

"And now, I think you should. You are better prepared than you were."

"He's Satan!"

"He's also the only one who may be able to save you from Araqiel."

"Because of Yeqon?" I asked with trepidation.

"Because you are still a witch, and he hates them more than Asmodeous does." Cross looked me over. "The fact you have bewitched Samyaza will not sit well with his brother."

"I didn't bewitch him!" I protested vehemently. Cross chuckled, and I flopped down on the couch. "It's just like being on earth, a bunch of political, racist bullshit that's fucked up."

"That's life."

I snorted in a very unladylike fashion. "Says the guy who's Death."

CHAPTER 18

CROSS LEFT ME ALONE FOR A WHILE, AND I WOULD BE A LIAR IF I didn't say I was completely freaked out. Did Mum know I was a necromancer, like a proper *disciple of Death* necromancer? Disciple of Death, I rolled the words around on my tongue a few times. Nope, it would never feel comfortable saying I was a disciple of anything to be honest.

"What is a disciple anyway?" I asked Hound, who sat staring out the window. We were back to sky and sea, a stormy looking day, the kind that at home would have had me reaching for my cosy loungewear, a blanket and a book. I missed books. All of Cross's library was some kind of weird ancient collection of gibberish, and several gave me the heebie jeebies when I went near them.

"A servant, a messenger, a follower."

I jumped up from my position on the floor to look at Ros. "Why are you here?" Now I knew why Hound hadn't answered me.

"You could also call them pupils, believers," Ros continued as he sat himself down on my seat of the couch. "And I'm here because I saw your guy leave, and he's currently off doing his thing."

"Right." I looked at him. "So...you're visiting against his wishes, or I'm being babysat?"

"Both." His feet rested on the coffee table, and I saw several of the carvings stop their carnal pursuits and stare up at him.

"You'll upset the coffee table." I nodded to his feet, and Ros grinned.

"Another one of the things you never thought you would say?" he asked as he leaned back.

"I'm having more and more of those moments the longer I'm here," I admitted as I joined him on the sofa.

"What were you doing?"

"Meditating."

Ros laughed and I realised my tone and my expression did not hide my thoughts on "meditation."

"You're one of the most hectic females I have met. Disaster follows you, and it has nothing to do with the demons in your life; you and calm…I just can't see it, little witch."

I rolled my eyes as I nodded in agreement. "Truth," I said with conviction. "Maybe not about being a disaster, but unable to achieve calm, definite word."

"Word?" Ros's head tipped back, and he bellowed. "Did you go back in time?"

"I don't know," I said good-naturedly. "Time is weird here, and I have been here for so long there's no way my mum hasn't confessed all to my dad." I lost my easy smile.

"Pen has it under control. He even met your dad." Ros watched my jaw drop, and he grinned at me as he leaned forward. "I stayed hidden, but girl, honestly, his reaction was so fucking *you*, I split my sides."

"He hit him. Didn't he?" I asked as I screwed my eyes shut.

"Yup."

"Oh, Daddy…" I sighed as I fought the smile. "I miss them."

"They miss you too."

"How much longer must I hide?" I asked softly.

"You ready to don your cape and scythe?" Ros asked me seriously.

My eyes widened in alarm. "What?"

He burst out laughing again, and I leaped over the table and tackled him. As we wrestled on the couch, me with intent to harm and Ros with intent to piss me off more by laughing so hard he choked, we ended up in a tangle of limbs on the floor.

"If I were human right now, you would be super heavy," I mused as Ros manoeuvred us around.

"You still fight like a girl," he said as he planted a chaste kiss on my head and then pushed himself off me. "I thought you were being trained?"

"I am. I'm just slow."

"You're a soul collector, you're the shit, own it."

"You're a six-foot something demon that looks like you're a descendant of Ragnar Lothbrok. Don't *own it* with me, it's in your genes to be a killing machine."

"I don't know who he is, but thanks, I think. Also size doesn't matter," he teased as he wiggled his eyebrows. "I thought you would know that, and finally I *am* a killing machine, I'm a warrior as well as a soldier of heaven. Well, formerly of heaven, but my nature is to kill. You're a fucking necromancer, babe, we're fucking matched."

"Do you miss heaven?"

"The rules, the orders, the sanctimonious bullshit, the sterileness? No."

"But it's heaven."

Ros turned serious. "For those of us who fell, earth was heaven. Earth was the promise of a better life. Just as humans envisage a holy land, those of us who looked down saw that holy land on earth."

"The grass was greener," I mused.

"Hell yes, so lush, so much green, so much *life*."

We watched each other for a moment, a moment of pure honesty. "How are we matched?"

"I'm a warrior, you're a warrior, we fit."

"You're a fallen angel, I'm a twenty-four-year-old woman."

"And this is why you fail." Ros was on his feet. "Where are you allowed to go?"

"Nowhere."

"Void?"

"Banned."

Ros snorted and then eyed me speculatively. "You up for an adventure?"

I was on my feet so fast my eagerness surprised even me. "Where?"

"We can't go to the Land of the Souls, no to earth, and apparently you aren't allowed to go to the Void."

"Stop telling me what I know." I punched his arm, and he hooked his arm around my shoulders.

"You tell, we're both fucked."

"You have my word."

The scene changed. I was in a…castle? Turning in a circle, I looked at the room, large and empty except for the weapons on the wall. High windows let light in, but I was too small to see out. What I could see was that the sky was dark.

"It's nighttime?" I asked as I turned back to face Ros and almost swallowed my tongue when I saw he was now in grey sweatpants and nothing else. "Whoa."

He winked as he advanced. "Did I not tell you that I would teach you to fight?"

"Yes," I said to him as I took in all his flesh. Abs that looked painful, they were so hard and cut. Biceps that went on for days, and holy baby Jesus, he was everything yummy and nothing bad at all.

"When you stop looking at me like I'm a steak and you're a hungry Rottweiler, can we train?"

Hiding behind my hands, I laughed. "I was objectifying you," I wailed. "I'm sorry!"

"Meh, I look the shit, you *should* be speechless," Ros joked as he nudged me with his shoulder. "But focus."

Nodding, I straightened my T-shirt. "I'm ready."

"You're not, and that's the problem." Stepping away from me, he started to swing his arms in circles as he loosened up. "Follow me," he instructed and waited until I did. "Now, you know, and we all know you know, that you aren't in your body. You're in non-corporeal form because your soul was taken over the veil. So although you are not dead, you're not alive. Your soul does not need to be nourished with food and water, you have no lungs to draw breath, you have no heart to pump blood around your body. In *this* form." I was caught up in his words. Ros was telling me what I knew but in a way that I accepted his truth. "You with me?" When I nodded, he slapped my shoulder. "Good, now, you are still alive because your lungs are still breathing, your heart is still beating, and we are still feeding you. However, as your body stays in stasis, your soul, it's evolved. You have encapsulated all that you were, and your potential to be more is mind-blowing." Ros looked at me in admiration. "Honestly, your raw power, it's fucking something."

"Really?"

"Absolutely, but as with any being, there are limits. Presently, your limitation is quite frankly...you."

"Always a catch," I tried to be funny, and he smiled as we moved onto leg stretches.

"Your consciousness believes you're human, and you are, when you are in your body, but now, right now, your soul is... more. You can be more, Star. You *are* more, you just need to accept that somewhere your body rests, but your body *and* your soul are alive. Alive and powerful. You're five seven in height, but your reach in this form doesn't stop at your fingertips. Reach for what you want. Take what you need. You are a witch and a necromancer, *own* your shit."

I stopped stretching. "Do I really need to exercise?" I asked suspiciously.

"No, but while you still think you're only a human, doing human things makes you a better listener."

"I can kick your ass?"

His laughter echoed in the large room. "No, little witch, but we're going to try to change that."

"Where am I?"

"Home."

"Your home?"

"Yes."

"It lacks character."

"Says the woman living in the pit of hell." We shared a grin as he stopped stretching.

"Do you hate me? For Yeqon? For Chaz?"

He thought about it, and I respected that he did. The Viking warrior was who he had always been with me, casual, easy and less than serious. "I don't hate you. We had little choice and no time to execute." When I flinched at the terminology, he grimaced in apology. "We had to do it the way it was done. Hound was not supposed to interfere. Of course, at the time, we never knew that Cross had been watching."

"Hound acted on his own."

"We know that now." Ros nodded. "But fuck, when you vanished completely, it was really, *really* tense."

"One should be more careful where they stick their daggers."

"Stop being salty, you know why we acted that way. You know Asmodeous will hunt you, and you know when we acted, you were no match for him."

"And I am now?"

"Not yet, but you will be." Ros plucked a short sword off the wall and tossed it to me, which I caught without killing myself. "We will practice with this."

Turning the sword over in my hands, I studied it. "You never answered my question."

"I do not hate you. I am…upset at the loss of my brother, but we fight a war, and in war, soldiers fall."

I waited as he looked at me, and then Ros rubbed his hand over his plaited hair. "Chaz made his own choice. We all told him not to act in haste, but he cares for you."

My sword was heavy in my hands, and had my heart been inside me, it would have felt the same. "Have you seen him?"

Ros's eyes tightened in anger. "I have, it burns to see him suffer so."

"We need to get him out."

"Which is why we are here, little witch. Now. Enough bonding, let's teach your soul how to be a badass necromancer."

As Sam had done, Ros helped me accept that my strength was more than I thought. As he stood behind me and worked through my punches and kicks, I felt the change. It was as if an inner awareness opened.

I became more fluid, my movements were swifter with more strength, and soon we were sparring with swords. Honestly, I would have made an epic Disney montage right now, which had I not actually been enjoying myself with Ros, I would have questioned.

Ducking the Watcher's attack, I spun and kicked out, hitting him in the chest. It was the first time I had actually struck him, and I jumped up and down with glee. Ros laughed as he tackled me, and we both fell to the floor in a heap as we lay side by side in easy companionship.

"That was fun!" I turned my head to look at Ros, who was staring at the roof with a smile on his face.

"It was. I could actually see your transition, you did good."

We lay like that for a moment more before I felt Ros stiffen beside me. "Ah shit," he muttered before he was on his feet. "Brother."

"Why is the whore here?"

"Azazel," I grumbled as I stood. "I haven't missed you either."

"Like I care?" His look was as heavy as one of Ros's punches.

"Get it out of my home."

When Ros opened his mouth to protest, I tugged on his arm. "Leave it, let's not ruin our day."

As he dipped his head in acknowledgement, Ros entwined our fingers, and I was back in Cross's living room. Hound sat in one corner of the room. He looked to be half asleep, and Cross was not there.

"He could always come around," Ros suggested half-heartedly.

"Yeah, or I may as well accept that I made an enemy out of him a long time ago."

Ros started to protest and then half shrugged. "Or that." As he pulled at his long blond hair, his clothes changed back to leathers and a tunic.

"Why can't I clothe myself?"

"Different skill set," Ros answered as he reached for a glass on the coffee table.

"Teach me."

He snorted in amusement. "Teach you? No. That takes too many years. You will get it; as you open to all of your powers, that will come." I noticed when he sat up straighter slightly, and then Sam was there. "Brother."

"Ros," Sam greeted as he walked towards me. His arms circled me as he buried his nose in my hair and inhaled deeply. "You've been in the ether."

"Space?" I asked, my question muffled against his broad chest, but I felt his laughter as he pulled me tighter.

"Why are you trying to suffocate me?" I asked as I pushed against him.

"He is trying to hide your scent," Cross spoke from behind us. "Was it wise to take her there?" His question was for Sam, but it was Ros who answered.

"She came on months in ability in one training session. You all forget one very simple thing," he said as he stood.

"And what's that?" Sam asked dryly as he pulled away from me, his arms holding me loosely still as he looked at his brother.

"She's only twenty-five years old. She needs nourished, she needs fun, she needs to be told she missed her birthday. She needs to mourn the loss of her humanity the longer she stays here."

"I missed my birthday?" I asked in anguish as I stepped out of Sam's hold. Of course I would have, I had been here for months. "Dammit. I had a weekend booked to Germany. It was completely non-refundable."

Ros grinned. "Body snatching not in the small print?"

"Goofball."

"Next time, I'll bring cake." He winked and was gone.

"Cross leave us," Sam commanded, and to my surprise, Cross did. Which left me alone with the demon I had been avoiding being alone with.

"Hey."

"Hey." He advanced towards me, and I took a step back.

"Sam," I warned as I held a hand up. "I can kick your ass now," I reminded him.

"No, witch, you can't, but it is adorable that you think you can."

"I swear to Christ, you kiss me or do anything else dodgy, I will cut your balls off."

Strong fingers caught my chin and tilted my head back. "You smell of my dimension, you smell of my home, you're like fucking catnip right now."

I may as well have spoken to the wall, because his lips were covering mine, and I was letting him. I had been angry for so long, I had been hurt for so long, I had been alone for so long. I had missed him for so long.

My last defence against the Watcher crumbled as my arms slipped around him, and I kissed him back.

CHAPTER 19

Sitting in my meditation pose, I could feel Cross's disapproval washing over me.

"Just say it," I sighed as I opened my eyes.

"You wish to be intimate with the Watcher."

He really just said it. "I kissed him," I corrected. "Once." For a long time. A *really* long time. *Focus!*

"You forgive so quickly."

"You verified that they acted in my best interest." I studied Cross's beautiful face. "Are you saying that it isn't true, which then means that you lied to me?"

"They did what was best for you at the time."

"And now?" I gestured along my body, my brain glitching at the fact that it wasn't my actual body. "Is it still what was best for me?"

"Now is not then."

"Okay, I'm so glad we cleared that up."

"Star, they are still your enemy. You are still hunted by a prince of hell, and I am still doing everything possible to keep him from you." Cross stood with a heavy sigh. "And you want to go into his very domain and steal a Watcher from under his nose."

"Two Watchers," I corrected. "I cannot leave Araqiel there."

"You are not ready."

"Then help me be ready!" I cried in frustration. "The quicker I get the Watchers, the quicker they can then deal with Asmodeous, and then I get to return home."

"Star." Cross turned away from me, and I studied his back as I waited for him to continue. "Nothing will be the same."

"I know that I'm different, so different, but I want to go home,

Toto." I saw his confused look and hurried on. "Don't worry about it. Can you help me?"

I knew he wanted to say something. I knew it, and I was scared to push, but Cross was done being patient. "When you free Araqiel, he will turn them against you. What you have now will be gone."

"They can think for themselves." I thought about it. "Most of them can. I think Bara and Zel may be dangerous if they tried original thought."

"You seek the tree."

I was at a loss for words. Had I told him? I told Hound, I never told Cross. Did I? "I was advised it would help me," I explained truthfully. Cross had never lied to me, and I wasn't about to start lying to him. But as I thought that, I reminded myself he hadn't always been forthcoming.

"The tree is the root of many things," he said thoughtfully.

Was I supposed to have appreciated the pun? I did, but I fought the smile. Death was in a pensive mood, and I was edgy. "Do you know where it is?"

"Yes."

"Can you take me there?"

"No. Only a Watcher can." It's what Hound had said. I carefully avoided looking at the hellhound.

"Will it help me against Asmodeous?"

Cross blinked. "The prince? It is immaterial."

Immaterial? I recalled my gran's words. *Only the tree can save you from him now.* Who was *him* if not Asmodeous? "I was told the tree can save me from him?"

Cross's brown eyes full of infinite wisdom beheld me with sadness. "It is not the prince you need saved from."

"Is this about Sam?"

"Perhaps."

"A Watcher then?"

"Ding ding ding, and we have a winner."

"You don't know classic films, but you know that?" I asked him in exasperation.

"You don't always shield your mind from me."

Oh. "Oh." What had I thought today? Oh lord, I had carried out a whole inner monologue at breakfast over the sexiness of his feet. Not his feet really, the sexy fact they were attached to him and he was sexy! I was doing it again. Oh Christ, could he hear me? I saw Hound turn to me and make eye contact. Okay, someone could hear me right now.

"Paranoia over?" Cross asked me casually.

"Yup, all done."

"Wonderful."

We sat in silence until I began to fidget as Cross lost himself to his own thoughts. I kept looking at Hound, who watched Cross without blinking, which was creepy but so completely Hound I was used to him.

As the sky darkened outside, I decided to speak. "Cross?"

"Hmm?"

"Where are you?"

"Deep in my thoughts," he said as he brought me into focus. "Are you ready for a very brief visitation?" he asked as he stood.

"What?" I scrambled to my feet, preparing for an attack when the world turned white and I was in the Land of the Souls. I couldn't even ask, because she stood in front of me, a wee bit more tired than last time I had seen her, but she was here.

"Gran?"

"Starlight!" I fell into her embrace, and I felt her crying as I cried. "My girl, how are you here? I can see you, but I know you're shielded."

I was? I could feel Cross behind me, and I knew it was him. I also knew I couldn't admit who my protector was here. "He let you go?" I asked as I squeezed her tightly.

"Someone bartered for me. I don't know who, and I know there will be a price to pay, but I am free from punishment."

"For now," Cross murmured behind me, causing me to clutch her tighter.

"Why aren't you a necromancer, Gran?" I blurted out.

"I dealt with the living, lass. The dead held no sway for me. I was content to help those who could live to tell the tale."

"Why am I one?"

"Your power chooses you, not the other way around."

"Not much time, Star," Cross warned me.

"You told me I needed to get to the tree, how?"

"The Watchers will hunt you," Gran told me as she drew back. "They are no longer the ones who fell for the desire to live, they want to return."

Sam didn't seem to. Ros had said they were at war, so was this what he meant?

"Did Asmodeous want to return?"

"The seven princes are each different. Wrath has too much to keep him entertained here. Sloth, he is and always was lazy. Gluttony wanted it all, but he was destroyed many years ago. Pride, he most surely would return. Lust, I am unsure. Envy would of course, because well, it's in his name. And Greed, Mammon has been gone for many years."

"You know their names."

"I know the names, not the faces." She looked behind me. "Who shields you, lass?"

"A friend," I answered truthfully. "Who will the tree save me from, Gran?"

"The Watcher."

Every part of me stilled in shock. "The Watcher? Which one?"

"Why do you think there is only one who will strike you down?"

Did she know I was already struck? As I opened my mouth to

tell her, I felt Cross touch me softly. Heeding his warning, I hugged my gran one more time. "Be safe, I'll be back."

Back in his living room, I turned to Cross, the question already answered when I saw his face. "I can't believe he would do that for me."

"Chazaquel felt your sense of betrayal the hardest."

"So he has suffered so my gran doesn't have to?" I asked as I wrapped my arms around myself.

"It is a sacrifice he is content to make," Cross shrugged slightly.

"Would you?"

"Would I what? Endure excruciating pain so one of your loved ones can be free from the very pain that is taken on for them? For you? No."

"Wow." I sat gingerly as I felt the weight of his words settle on my shoulders. "Brutal."

"I am Death."

"You're being a dick."

"And yet again you are deflecting the obvious. It is a Watcher who will tear you down, Star. Why will you not accept that?"

"Have they not already struck me down?"

"You think it's a one-time only occurrence?" Cross asked incredulously.

"I don't understand! You let them in here, you let them train me, why are you now saying I can't trust them? How do I know I can trust you?"

"You don't. And you should never trust me, I never asked you to."

"Wow." Shaking my head as if to clear it, I looked at him in astonishment. "And yes, I know, I said wow twice."

"The Watchers seek the tree. The tree can take them back. They are planning a war."

"With who?"

"Heaven."

"Quite dramatic," Sam spoke as he rounded the couch and sat beside me, his eyes on Cross. "Some Watchers seek the tree, some Watchers will do everything they can to stop them from reaching it."

"Are you a seeker or a stopper?" I asked tentatively.

"We made our choice, we live with our choice." Sam's eyes were hard as he considered Cross. "Why are you telling her this now?"

"She needs to know."

"This is not new information to you, why not tell her immediately?"

"You know I need the tree?" I asked Sam, and he nodded. "Ros told you?"

"Of course, he is loyal."

"Is Zel?"

Sam turned to look at me. "Azazel does not seek the heights of heaven, witch."

"You know my name is Star. I mean, I've heard you use it."

"Shh. The adults are arguing." He had the audacity to pat my hand as he turned back to Cross.

Was he freaking kidding me? "Are you serious?" I asked as I jumped to my feet.

"She always stands when she is put out," Cross commented as if I was a strange experiment he enjoyed watching.

"Everyone stop," I demanded. "You, don't start talking about me as if I'm not here, I've been with you for months. *Months.*" Then I turned to Sam. "You, do not even dare, I mean it, do not *dare.*"

"Witch." Sam gave me a slow smile. "Sit down, shut up. I need to hear this, and then you can squawk all night."

"Squawk!"

"Exactly like that." He tugged me down beside him. "Now, Cross, explain yourself."

"She needs to know who you ask her to free. She needs to know the consequences."

"With my brothers free, Asmodeous is vulnerable. He holds no power over me. Over any of us." Sam's voice was hard. "You refuse to assist."

"Your squabbles with the princes of hell are inconsequential to me."

"Had you ever been a being that felt emotion, you would understand." Sam's voice was hard and cold, and Cross merely shrugged. "I leave her here with you, for her protection. You agreed, she is your disciple, you are responsible for her honing her craft. Why are you now choosing to interfere?"

A lot was going over my head, but a lot wasn't. "Hound took me here, but it is Sam that makes you keep me here?" I looked at Hound and remembered when Cross told me that Hound acted on his own. "You would never have gotten involved."

"You are interesting, I like to watch you."

"I'm glad I can entertain you; may I suggest you get Netflix instead?"

Sam actually huffed out a laugh. "What is your angle?" he asked Cross.

"I was never human." Cross looked at me, and he had my full attention. "I was never an angel, despite what religious texts say; the angel of death is not me. I am and always will be Death. As there is Life, there is me."

"Balance," I spoke softly, and he nodded.

"I am the counter to the other."

"God?"

"Call it what you will. Do not call it a creator, as to have creation, you have to have destruction. A creator cannot create its opposite."

"So how are you here?"

"How are any of us here?" Sam interrupted.

I turned to Sam. "Really, philosophy? Now? As I sit beside an *angel*?" His smile infuriated me. "Carry on," I encouraged Cross.

"I am the counterbalance. I am Death. I am the *final* Death. The bid to ascend for the ones who fell interests me not. What interests me is the collection of their soul when they fall to their final death."

"But that's changed," I realised. "Did I change that? I piqued your interest."

"You are one of mine. Very few throughout time have been gifted with the ability such as yours. I did not interfere when you were struck, as it is not for me to become involved. Nothing has been or ever will be a life-or-death situation that actually *requires* life or death to stop it."

"But when Hound took me here, you were involved."

"I was. I pick no sides. Let the princes burn who they want. Let the Watchers covet once more. But you, you are like *me*. You can be so much more, but you are still so human."

"I don't understand."

"To free Araqiel, the Watchers know they need death on their side. They need the dead. The souls. Only with souls can they enter a level of hell undetected."

My eyes flew to Sam, who looked completely complacent that this had been revealed.

"They plan to steal under the guise of one who can shield them all." Cross waited. He didn't need to wait long.

"You're using me?" I was on my feet again. Far away from the Watcher who sat and watched me. "Again. *Again*? I'm just a pawn for you?"

"You know you are more."

"Do I?" When he didn't answer, I turned back to Cross. "What is the danger to me? If I get them in, what am I losing?"

"Araqiel will be free." Cross turned to Sam. "Tell her what she loses."

I could practically hear his teeth grind. Sam hated being forced into anything. "It is possible that my brother may seek vengeance for Yeqon."

"But you can tell him no. You're the general."

"Araqiel holds the same authority as I do."

"Then we save Chaz and leave the murdering bastard behind."

Sam's lips twitched. "Araqiel is key to stopping those who seek the tree."

"*I* seek the tree," I reminded him. And then it hit me. "Only the tree can save me from him, it's Araqiel I need to be saved from? Not Asmodeous?"

"Technically both."

"Sam!"

"I can handle my brother."

"Can you? Can you take on a prince of hell and a Watcher *and* Zel? All of these for me? Maybe you can, but you stabbed me already, demon, so now tell me, why do you save me next time?"

"You should trust that I want to."

"My trust shattered the day you pierced it with your dagger." I turned my back on him. "You can go."

I felt him leave, and I looked over at Cross. "Is that all?"

"You cling to your humanity, or the idea of your humanity. If you free Araqiel, you lose either one or the other."

"What? How!"

"A necromancer commands the dead. A full necromancer. Your humanity weighs you down."

"Cross…" I was wringing my hands together in anxiety. "Speak to me in simple plain English."

"You want to return to your body, you want to live your life, you give that chance up if you free either Watcher. As you have clung to the idea that you can return to humanity, the Watchers have kept your body alive. If you act for them, you need to lose either your life or your soul. Asmodeous cannot kill your body if you are soulless. The Watchers cannot be free if you are human."

"I can't make this choice."

"Which is why I told you, you cannot free them. Let them burn."

"I can't."

"Then die." He watched me closely. "It's one or the other, Star. There is no happy ending for you in this story. And you already know, if you choose the Watchers, Araqiel will demand your death for Yeqon."

I turned away, and sensing he had finished with his shell shocking news, I retired to my room. Well, his room, but whatever.

Hound followed me, his head nudging under my hand until I scratched his ear. "I feel cheated."

Red eyes burned into mine. *There is another way.*

"How?" I felt hope rise within me as I stared at the hellhound.

You kill them all.

CHAPTER 20

The hellhound's words reverberated around my head as he stared at me, and I stared back.

Kill them all? I was a necromancer; I wasn't Death, and I wasn't a murderer. Is this what I would become? "Hound?"

It can be done, I will aid you.

"Am I shielding?" I whispered furiously.

Yes. I block you when you cannot block yourself.

That was new information. "I didn't know that was a thing," I admitted. I swear that the hellhound shrugged. Which was all very well and normal when he was in his humanoid shape, but seeing a giant dog shrug was something I had only seen in *Scooby Doo* cartoons.

Focus.

"I *am* focused," I snapped at him as I lay back on the bed, away from his prying eyes, eyes that saw too much. Taking a deep breath, I closed my eyes. "Tell me who and how."

In your soul form, you can command the dead as well as you did when you were in your body. If not better. Your powers are there, you just have an unhealthy fear of them.

"Not entirely true," I muttered sullenly.

We need to go back to the Void but disguise it. The Void has a certain...fragrance. As they can tell when you are in the ether or the Land of the Souls, they know when you are in the Void. You need one of the Watchers to vouch for you.

"Ros," I suggested.

I agree. He is more gullible than his brothers.

"Ouch."

He also admires your form. Interact with him.

I hesitated. Interact with him…no. "Are you suggesting I have sex with him?"

Whatever you need to do so he will cover your scent.

"As he covers my scent from the Void, Sam kills us both for me sleeping with his brother."

Hmm.

I was propped up on my elbows as I looked down at the hellhound. "Hmm? That's it?"

There is a swamp at the edges of the pit. It would disguise you, but I fear we can only use that reason once, and plus, Asmodeous would know immediately if you walked into the pit.

"I hate that plan." Lying back down again, I stared out my skylight. "Say more words where I get out of this."

We train in the Void. You actually pay attention. You protect yourself with the dead, and then when the time comes, the dead will get you close to the pit. As the Watchers free Chazaquel, you will kill Asmodeous.

"How?"

I can work out the specifics later, but I know it can be done. When he is dead, I will be waiting. You need to strike Araqiel, swift and sure. There are Watchers who are loyal to him.

"Bara and Suriel, the uptight one." I thought of them both. "They were Yeqon's."

Yes. And you need to prepare to fight Azazel. He was not close to Yeqon, loyal always to Samyaza, but he harbours great dislike for you.

"It's called hate, my friend."

Hound grunted, and I lay in silence for a while. "Can this be done?"

If you resume training in the Void and listen, yes. I can aid you.

"And when it's over?"

You return to your body; I can show you.

Chewing my lip, I thought about it. "Why has Cross not suggested this to me?"

He wants a necromancer, but the form you are in when you become his fully, matters not.

It made sense. I mean, he was Death. The final one. The one you didn't come back from. When Cross collected your soul, it wasn't the Land of the Souls you were heading to. It was purgatory. To be judged. The final judgement.

"Why is there no devil?"

There are seven princes of hell. Don't you think that's enough?

I smiled at the hellhound's dry sarcasm. In a world of upheaval, who would have thought that it was the hellhound who took me here who would be my source of normality?

"Is Ruairidh okay?"

Hound snuffed, and it was amazing how much could be said without being said.

"Hound?"

I would have preferred they stuck to the original plan. I like that human not.

It was on the tip of my tongue to defend my best friend when Hound's grumbling penetrated my brain. "Original plan?" Sitting up, I looked at Hound. "I wasn't meant to be the sacrifice… They changed the plan when I didn't do the spell…" Cold horror washed over me. "Ruairidh."

I winked.

I hadn't travelled so easily ever before, and had white hot rage not been coursing through my body, I would have stopped to consider that. Instead, I was in the castle training room, and two Watchers were staring at me in surprise and fear.

You better fear me.

"Where is he?" I demanded of Der.

"How the fuck are you here?" he asked me as he looked at Ros in accusation.

"Where is that fucking demon?" I demanded as I started to walk to the doors. "I'll take his head," I seethed. The doors flew open, and I tucked the nugget of information in my memory for later consideration. I had control of the elements? *Well, here I come.*

Thunder rattled the castle as I strode angrily through the halls. I could feel him pulling me to him, and I wasn't sure if it was Sam pulling *me,* or my anger seeking *him* out.

I found him in the room I had seen in my vision. Sitting on that fake throne. He had a woman at his feet.

At his feet.

His eyes met mine, and he smiled. I knew right then that I had made a mistake coming here.

"Witch."

"Demon." I strode towards him, willing myself not to look at the tart on her knees in front of him.

"What brings you to my home?"

"Betrayal. Duplicity. Treachery."

"They are one and the same, no?" Sam's hand cupped his jaw as he watched me in relaxed amusement.

"You backstabbing fucker, you were going to kill Ruairidh."

"Ah, you figured it out. And I stabbed you while I looked into your eyes. Not a lot of people can say that."

I was ignoring all that. Psycho. "He's my best friend!"

"He is disloyal, treacherous, and betrays you on a regular basis." Sam smiled. It was not friendly. "There was not one of us who disagreed that he was a fitting sacrifice."

Lightning struck across the sky as thunder crashed in haste after it. Rain pounded on windowpanes so hard it sounded as if the glass was shattering.

"Witch, your temper is making me want to fuck you."

The whole room was lit with my anger as the lightning crackled outside.

"You touch me, you die."

"Why does her hair float?" Ros asked Der in a loud whisper.

"Because I am living electricity," I snapped at him. "You wanted a necromancer, Watcher. Here I am."

Sam got off his chair as the woman cowered in fear. She reached out to touch his leg, and my lightning was loud in the hall. "Do not *touch* him."

"Go," Sam commanded her softly. "I will call on you later when I have need of you."

What need? What did he *need* her for? Sex? Several window-panes broke, and the storm was fully inside.

"Look at you," Sam spoke in admiration. "So much power, so much anger." He walked towards me. "Your soul is breathtaking."

"I don't think you should touch her," Pen warned from the side of the room where he and Zel had just burst through the doors, weapons drawn, ready to defend an attack, and looking at them, I realised that they were still unsure as to whether the threat in the hall was me.

"Touch her? I want to bury myself so deep inside her, her heartbeat becomes mine," Sam answered him softly as his gaze raked over me.

There was something strangely erotic about his words, but somewhere, the old Star Elizabeth Archer flushed in embarrassment at his language.

"Where is he?" I asked as I looked around at the Watchers.

"Who?" Pen walked forward as he stared intently at me. "You've changed, Star."

"So everyone keeps telling me." I locked eyes with Zel as the ice-blue-eyed devil stalked towards me. "Except you," I sneered.

"You will always be a whore."

"And you will always be a jumped up, bigoted racist. You hate me for my craft, I hate you for yours."

"Would you like to see your body?" Sam asked comfortably as if I wasn't causing hail, yes, actual hail, to fall within his hall.

"What?" I turned and looked at Ros, who nodded. "It's here?"

"You're here, witch." Sam walked past me, his hand stretched out as his fingers traced the air in front of me. "Come."

"Is Ruairidh safe?"

"Well, he's still bumbling through Slate, using the only brain cell he seems to possess, so I would say no."

"It's so easy to hate you," I told Sam as I followed him out of the room.

"Are you bringing your pet storm?"

Arsehole. Absolute arsehole.

However, my storm did come because I was still furious, and he was still a dick. It died down slightly, but it followed.

As we climbed stairs, I looked outside when I could, but my storm had brought fog, or maybe they lived in fog. They probably did. Shady fuckers probably enjoyed living in the shadows.

At the top of the stairs, he stopped outside a door and then looked at me. "Are you ready?"

A curt jerk of my head, and he swung the door open.

With no regard for safety, I walked into the room. I was on the bed. My hair was no longer golden honey blonde, more whitish blonde, although it had varying tones to it. It was as if I had put a colour wash through it to tone the golden down. My skin was paler than normal, a weird red blush tinted my cheeks, and my eyes were open and staring at nothing. As I neared, I saw the colours changing in my eyes, light to dark then light again, and the silver flecks that framed my pupils seemed to crackle like lightning across a dark sky. My eyes were reflecting the storm I'd created. Which wasn't freaky at all. Much.

"I look weird."

"Your body is adapting to the lack of your soul," Sam spoke from the doorway. "Do not get too far; I can't be bothered with the fallout if I have to stab you again."

That earned him a scathing look, but the pull to my body, it was as if I had been lassoed around the middle and I couldn't fight the beckoning call of my flesh and blood.

"Witch!" Sam called in warning just as I fell downwards, and blackness swamped my vision.

Everything was dark, and what was this pain? This pain was real. My whole body was a giant knot of pain. What was that sound? That thumping.

Thump.

Thump.

Thump.

It was almost rhythmic. I felt panic wash over me until I realised it was my heart.

My heart.

I tried to move, but the pain was everywhere.

"Stop."

Thunder bellowed around me. Not thunder. Voices. Slowly, I opened my eyes.

Sam and Zel stared down at me, one in relief, one in disgust.

"Everything hurts," I croaked.

"Imagine," Zel grunted as he held his hand out. "Which part?"

"All parts."

His look was withering, like my suffering was an inconvenience to him. As his hands traced lightly over my body, I felt better. He was healing me. I knew that he was doing it only because Sam stood beside him.

When he stepped back, I sat up. "You really do have a little piece of magic in you," I said quietly as I moved my limbs with no pain.

"Shut up," he snapped as he turned and left me again.

Left me alone...with Sam. "I'm back."

"You're in trouble."

"Must be a day ending in a *y*."

"How do you feel?"

"Good, better than good." I pushed the covers back and stood. Then I realised I was naked. With a yelp, I grabbed the sheet. "People have to stop putting me to bed in no clothes."

"I don't want to know. If I kill him, it causes problems."

"Huh?" I was wrapping the sheet around my body.

"How do you feel?" Sam asked again as he stood.

"Good." I smiled at him brightly, and then I felt it, the ache, the longing, the *need*. "Whoa, what the hell is happening?"

Sam grinned as he pulled his shirt over his head. "It's going to ratchet up the longer you're in that body."

"What is?"

"You need sex."

"I need what?"

"Sex. With me."

"Is this a weird pick-up line? I definitely do not want sex with you." But my body was telling me something *very* different. "Sam…" Even that came out as a groan. "Why is this happening?"

"I know it's strange, but it's common, especially in the untrained. You used so much energy your body knows it needs filled." When I glared at him for the salacious wink he sent my way, he carried on, "Your soul is seeking a vitality boost." He was unbuckling his belt.

"You're my *energy drink?*" I asked him incredulously. "Absolutely not. No." He dropped his trousers, and my breathing was becoming more laboured as I drank in his masculine perfection —I didn't even care that was so cliché. Sam, naked? It was a work of art. The ache inside, the ache *there* where it mattered, was throbbing. "Holy shit, I'm horny." My whole body was pulsating. "Get Ros," I demanded as I clenched my thighs together.

Sam paused briefly, the heat in his eyes changing to reflect his anger. "Never."

In moments, I was picked up and flat on my back. "Sam—"

"Don't overthink it, just go with the flow."

His mouth took mine as he covered me with his body. Fingers too clever and familiar with my flesh teased me relentlessly as I clutched at his shoulders.

"This means nothing," I whispered urgently while I clung to hold onto my sanity as Sam expertly manoeuvred his way around my body, stroking, teasing, playing with my pleasure like the master of my need that he was.

Teeth nipped at my breast before his tongue stroked over it, soothing the sting. "It means what it's always meant, this body is mine."

My protest died on my lips as he spread my legs wide and then slid inside me. The stretch was painful but welcome. He paused to let me adjust, and when I nodded, he moved until he was fully sheathed inside. My legs curled around his waist as if I was welcoming him home.

"My body may be yours, but my soul is not." *What a time to have a revelation, Star.*

As his hips picked up in a delicious rhythm, he smiled down at me with amusement. "All of you is mine," he whispered as his fingers tangled in my too blonde hair. "Now shut up and let me fuck you."

His mouth covered mine, and his tongue silenced anything else I could say. His hands were everywhere, his pace was relentless, and I was overwhelmed but hungry for everything he gave me. As he moved inside me, I felt that my energy was building, my orgasm rising with it. As he flipped me effortlessly onto my hands and knees, his hand pressed between my shoulder blades, lowering me to the bed, leaving my hips raised.

"That's it," he encouraged as his fingers dug into my hips. "I can feel you're close. We're not done yet, but you can have this one."

My sharp retort died when he reached around and stroked me in rhythm, causing my fingers to clutch and twist the bedsheet. My mouth opened wide as exquisite pain pulsed to an uncomfortable pressure, and then I was falling over the precipice. The room turned a brilliant white as I screamed my release. I was dimly aware that I heard his answering roar as he pounded into me erratically, and then I felt him slow. Smoothly he brought me back to reality as his lazy, languid pace slackened completely.

As he moved off of me, I felt him settle down beside me, fingers trailing over my spine. "How do you feel?" Sam asked as he pushed his dark hair out of his eyes.

I felt sensational. I couldn't move. My body was jelly. I couldn't tell him that though, he was already a conceited bastard. "Energised and exhausted."

I didn't need to see his face to know he wore a smug grin.

Wanker. How the fuck did I explain *this* to Cross?

CHAPTER 21

Food.

There is nothing better in this world or the next than food. My pathetic attempt to cling to humanity as I ate pastries in my soul form was laughable as I ate my way through the Watchers' pantry. I'd had great sex in the past, trust me, and my body was currently delightfully sore from great sex, but this white bread with thick butter and wafer-thin ham was replacing my last orgasm as the best thing to have happened to me today.

I sat cross-legged in the middle of the bed, wearing a Watcher tunic and the sheet tucked around me to protect my modesty. I had several plates and trays around me, holding a range of cold meats, cheese, grapes and apple slices along with pastries, biscuits, and shortbread, and when Ros walked in with a large chocolate cake and candles, I was quite sure that this was heaven.

Sam, Ros, Der and Pen were in the room with me. Zel refused birthday cake, arsehole, and Bara and Suriel I didn't know that well, and I could sense their resentment from the other room. Their resentment coupled with Zel's judgement almost, but not quite, took the happy edge off my food fest.

"I've never seen anyone so small eat so much," Ros said affectionately as he prepared oatcakes and cheese for me.

"I never knew I could be so hungry," I admitted as I munched through some apple slices. "It's like I can't remember how to feel full."

"Pretty sure I filled you earlier."

While Ros and Der chuckled at Sam's joke, I threw my knife at him and was delighted when it struck the crass wanker right in his upper shoulder. It was my turn to laugh, and Pen joined me.

"Aim's pretty good," Der praised me, and I beamed at him as I watched Sam pluck the knife from his shoulder like he had just flicked a fly off of him.

"I had a nice teacher," I said with a quick smile to Ros, who bowed in his seat in acknowledgement. Looking at them, I sobered a little. "He should be here," I said as I placed my apple down.

"We will retrieve him," Der assured me.

Remembering Hound's words, I nodded but said nothing. They hadn't told me their plan, and I didn't want them to know what I was toying with. I had little doubt that I would be met with resistance if I told them I was working on a way to kill another one of their brothers.

"Will Cross be mad?" I asked them as I bit into a crumbly oatcake with rich mature cheddar atop it.

"He will." Sam looked pleased at the fact.

"I'm human again." I watched him watch me, and I saw the realisation as soon as he knew I knew.

"Which one told you?"

"Who says either of them did?"

"Witch…" he warned.

"Demon?"

"Is this their foreplay?" Ros asked Pen in a whisper. "I mean, it's hot, the tension is making me want to go find a woman, but we're still in the room."

"Maybe that's their thing?" Der contributed.

"Or Star knows we need her in her soul form to save our brothers," Pen added drily.

"Winner winner, chicken dinner." I raised my glass of white wine to him. "Who gets to stab me this time?" I took a long drink of wine, trying to hide my fear.

Sam watched me with hooded eyes, and I knew that I wasn't going to like what would come next. "Everyone out."

Obediently his Watchers left him, and much to my dismay,

they took my food, but not before I grabbed a handful of grapes and the bottle of wine.

"I don't even care if you judge me," I told him as I dropped my grapes into my glass of wine. "It's poetic…in some way."

"You get stranger."

"Yup." I refused to look at him. "You may as well tell me."

"Can you travel?" I wasn't expecting him to ask me that, and I looked at him in surprise.

"I don't know."

"From where you are to beside me."

"I can walk to you," I protested. *Who travels three feet?*

"Which is how I will know if you can or cannot travel."

Fine. I winked. I was on his lap, and as I went to speak, he silenced me with a kiss. My body, which had been sated, was suddenly alert and wanting. Straddling his thighs, I laced my fingers in his hair as he kissed me. Hands slipped under my tunic and pushed it up as he caressed my sensitive skin. I was rocking over the growing hardness beneath me, and my hands were loosening his trousers as my core urged me onwards. As I held his thick length in my hand, I relished his groan as I began to stroke him.

"Witch," Sam murmured as he lifted me up and onto him. My head lolled back as I took him inside, and I began to meet him thrust for thrust.

"Demon," I groaned as he moved me over him at a faster pace. "It feels…"

"Amazing," he growled as he suddenly stood with me wrapped around him. I was slammed against the wall as Sam drove into me deeper. His head was buried in my neck, and I felt his lips and tongue kiss and bite as he fucked me harder. As he got rougher, I became wilder, reckless.

My own hands were under his shirt, and my nails were digging deep into his back as we both chased our ecstasy. My head was tipped back against the wall as I hung on to the demon who claimed me. And when it came to sex, he *did* own my body. No one would ever make me feel like this, I knew that. No one else had ever come close to giving me the euphoria that Sam did. When he was inside me, fucking me like I was his oxygen, I didn't want to be anywhere else. I didn't *want* anyone else.

I wanted him.

He said I was his?

Well, he was *mine*.

Everything else, all the lies, the deceit, the mistrust faded to nothing when we were joined together like this.

My breath caught as his teeth sank into my shoulder, and I knew he had drawn blood. Not one to be outdone, I bit him back, and my cry of ecstasy was muffled when he responded by taking me faster, harder.

Our relationship wasn't healthy, I knew that. But in this moment, as he pulled back slightly to look down at where we joined as his hips moved against me, my pleasure peaked as green eyes filled with power met mine.

"Harder," I rasped as I watched him.

I was on my back as his control slipped a little more. The whole bed rocked as Sam lifted my leg over his shoulder. I never knew he could go deeper. My insides felt like they were being bruised, but it was worth it.

Sam was close to losing complete control. Did I push him?

"Fuck me harder," I whispered. "Deeper."

The growl wasn't human, but the man wasn't either. As he tore himself away from me, his clothes came off, and he ripped my tunic open. I was on top, but I was not in control because all I could do was feel.

Feel the pleasure.

Feel the pain.

Feel the power that surrounded us both.

Shadows darkened the room, and I looked down at him, trying to see past his power and see *him*. He turned me so that I was on my knees as he fucked me relentlessly from behind. One hand tangled in my hair as he pulled my head back, lifting my body until my back was against his chest.

"Sam," I gasped as I bounced off of him. "Harder."

The hand in my hair tightened until the pain almost overrode the pleasure. His other hand circled my neck and squeezed. My pleasure peaked as he flexed his fingers.

"Oh fuck," I whispered as I felt my orgasm hurtling towards me. "Oh fuck, I can't, it's too much, I can't."

"You can." His voice was thick with lust, and as I felt the crash coming, he bit my neck, drawing blood. I felt him drink from my neck as my entire being erupted into a million fragments of joy, and I lost consciousness.

When I came to, I was alone.

Face down on the bed, I knew I was alone and that I was uncomfortable. My legs were at an awkward angle as they twisted in the opposite direction from my hips. One arm was under me with the other flung above my head. My hair covered me, making it hard to breathe. When I rolled over, every part of me hurt.

Sitting up, my lower body protested as I felt the dull throb of pain pulsate from within me. I saw the marks and the bruises on my skin before I noticed the blood on the sheets. My hand flew to my neck as I checked to ensure the bleeding had stopped. As my hand came away showing flakes of dried blood, I knew it had. On my feet, shaky legs held me up when I spotted the bowl of water and the washcloths. Gingerly, I cleaned myself, wincing when my poor broken vagina protested at the rough touch of the washcloth.

Gently I lay down again and closed my eyes, taking stock of...everything.

"Fucking hell," I whispered to the empty room, that was possibly the best sex I would ever have.

"How bad is it?"

Opening my eyes, I saw him above me, shirtless, wearing only dark sweatpants, his own body showing signs of my lust on him.

"I feel…satisfied."

His harsh, closed-off stare was gone as he blinked his shock. I saw the tension leave him as he checked me over. "Satisfied?"

"I don't think I'll survive if we do that regularly, but wow." I smiled as my back arched while I stretched.

"I bit you."

"Mm-hmm, I liked it." I grinned.

"I fucked you so hard you passed out."

"I couldn't help it! I think it was when you squeezed my throat too hard."

"Because I choked you."

I sat up, wincing as I did so, and pushed my hair out of my eyes. "I never saw the attraction with that to be honest, but if it's like that? Consider me converted."

"Witch?"

"Yes, demon," I answered, and I saw he still looked tense. "You okay?"

"No."

"What's wrong? Oh, was it me? Was I not…good?"

Sam looked at me, and I couldn't tell what he was thinking. It was a common thing for us—the guy had more layers than an onion—but when it came to sex, I was usually on the same page with him. Sex, we never struggled with.

As he sat on the bed and reached for me, I prepared myself for the worst. Gently I was lifted onto his lap, naked, but all I could see was the emotion in his eyes. Slowly, as if he would hurt me, he lowered his head and burrowed into my neck as his arms slipped around me, and he held me as if I were glass.

"Were you not *good*?" he muttered. "You were perfect."

Oh. I felt the smile slip free, and with confidence, I stroked his hair. "Then what is it?"

"I thought I hurt you."

"You did." I felt him stiffen. "At the time, I loved it. It was exactly right for what we were feeling, and it felt fantastic. Trust me, I was there."

He drew back from me, and his lips brushed mine. "You're okay?"

"I don't have the same experience as you, but I can tell you that it was"—I shook my head—"wow."

"Wow?" His arrogance was coming back. Darn it.

"Don't be too smug; I still made a mess of the bed, because apparently you're also a vampire."

His rich laughter made me relax completely as he held me close. "It's very rare that one of my kind is driven to bloodlust," he told me as he pushed my hair away to study my neck, "but you felt so perfect that I needed to taste you. All of you."

"I made you lose control?" I asked him, feeling shy, which was ridiculous as I was naked as the day I was born, curled up in the arms of the male who had detailed carnal knowledge of my entire being, and making him lose control had been my intent.

"I almost forgot you were human," he said as he nuzzled my cheek.

We sat wrapped up in each other until I realised that I was entirely comfortable with him. How could I be, someone may ask, but I was. I didn't understand it either, and I wasn't about to try. Not here. Not now. But still I had to ruin the moment. "Me being human is a problem for you though." I broke the feeling of contentment as I raised the question.

"How so?"

"You need me to be a soul, not a human, to command the dead for what you need."

Sam nodded. "I do, but you hold the power in both forms, more power than I thought. If we can keep you in this form and if your power develops more, we may manage."

"Lots of *ifs* and *may*s in there," I said gravely as I slipped off his lap and realised that I had no clothes to wear. Also, I ached, I needed a painkiller. I wondered if they had ibuprofen here.

"Sore?"

"Really sore," I admitted. "It was tremendous at the time, but I think my insides may be more bruised than my outsides."

"Lie down."

"No." I looked at him in alarm. "Keep that thing away from me! I can't, Sam, you'll break me!"

Sam snickered as he picked me up and laid me on the bed. Gently he traced my bruises as his head dipped and kissed along the marks on my body.

"Sam," I sighed as I felt his tongue trace over my nipple.

"Shh," he commanded. Wicked green eyes locked with mine. "It's not only Azazel who can heal."

Large hands spread my legs as his body moved lower. When I felt the gentle stroke of his tongue over my core, I closed my eyes and sighed in contentment as I felt his gentle soothing power pulse over me.

"Still want me to stop?" he asked, and I could hear his amusement.

"Shut up and get back to healing me." He'd turned me back into an insatiable, wanton harlot. As I felt my body heal and my insides tighten in anticipation of yet another orgasm, I realised that I was okay with that.

I also knew I was completely fucked, because once again, I had fallen for a demon. This demon. *My* demon.

AFTER A DAY IN BED WITH SAM AND BEING FED SO MUCH FOOD that I had missed, I knew I had to return to Cross. I was in my human body, but I knew that I could not return to hell in this form. Pen had explained that Asmodeous was not able to enter this realm, but that he would know I had been here if I left as a human.

I also knew Cross would more or less self-extinguish if I turned up in his living room as a living and breathing Star. As my brain refused to accept the method in which I would be "split," Pen caught me up-to-date with my parents.

Pen was a wonderful storyteller, and it made so much sense to me that his sin against heaven had been to teach the art of writing to humankind. As he regaled me with the story of my dad's reaction to Watchers, even though my heart was sad that I hadn't been there to ease his worry, my sides were splitting from laughing so hard as Pen retold the afternoon when my mum confessed everything to Dad.

Dad, and I quoted the Watcher Penemue when I said this, "didn't give a fuck if I was God himself, I would return his daughter right now." I missed my dad. He was my solid foundation on which I built myself. Yes, I was flighty; yes, I was impulsive, but I was also loyal, steadfast and true. My mum had flair, she had presence, she embraced fun, but both my parents had a strong moral compass, and I had never lost my way with them by my side.

I missed my family. I wanted to go home. I wanted my parents. I wanted to sit down at the table and eat mince and potatoes as my mum complained that she hadn't made it in so long that she hadn't made it right, and Dad would nod and tell her how he mashed the potatoes, adding butter and milk. Both would watch me try to avoid the gravy of the mince touching my potatoes, and neither would judge me as I ate the mince first to avoid food contamination on my plate.

"Will I stay here?" I asked Pen when I knew he had sensed my mood.

"Your body?"

"Yes."

"Yes, one of the servants will change the sheets, *again*, and then we can perform the ritual."

I ignored the jibe. Sam and I had been in bed most of the day; my body had never had such a rigorous workout. The demon had been hungry for his witch, and his witch had happily fed his appetite.

"What's the ritual? Please don't tell me it involves me being stabbed in the heart…I can't handle it."

"No blood need be shed," Pen assured me. "It needed to be done on the blood moon, but here, in our domain, it is painless and less messy."

"Do I need Hound?"

"No. Why?"

"He's a soul carrier."

Pen tried to hide his smile as he patted my hand. "Never change, Star, for me, always be this person."

"Did I say something silly?" I looked up at him as he rose.

"Any one of us can carry you across the veil."

I recalled what Cross had said. "Of course, you were angels, you are soul carriers."

"We are. Although the reapers serve their master well."

I nodded at his words, but I hid my thoughts. If he knew how much loyalty Hound and the other two hellhounds showed me, he would doubt the service of the reapers to Cross.

"How many hellhounds are there?" I asked curiously.

"Three." Pen raised an eyebrow. "Are you surprised?"

They come in threes. "No." I watched as Pen fixed his daggers in their holsters. "Do you seek the tree?"

His hands stilled in their movements, and I clenched my teeth to stop my reaction as Penemue the Watcher looked back at me.

"The tree is poison."

"It is the tree of life."

"I would fell it in a heartbeat."

"What happens if it falls?" I asked him carefully.

"Everything falls."

"Everything?" I felt real fear as I waited for his answer.

"Heaven falls, hell rises, and the world ends."

"Shit." I picked at my leggings that Sam had dressed me in. "And you would rather that than return to heaven?"

"Heaven is not for us nor the ones who fell. We made our choice; there is no do-over because they're bored. There are billions of humans. Those who fell need to forget their ambitions and remind themselves for what they chose to fall."

"Not every demon is a fallen angel," I countered. "I mean, I know little, we all know this, but even I know a demon can be created."

"Conjured more than created. Only one can create."

"God?"

"If that's what you choose to call him."

"What do you call him?"

"Father."

"Is he…good?" I felt blasphemous for even asking it.

"No one thing is all good or all bad. As there is heaven, there is hell. As there is life, there is death. As there is good, there is bad. Always balance. I am not bad, but I am not good. I am a blend of both, as is each living being. The blend of good and bad may alter in any one being; it will never be a fifty-fifty split but a blend of the two which makes mankind and life so incredibly fascinating."

"What's your blend?" I asked him with a smile.

"Sixty-forty," Pen answered immediately as he held his hand up and wagged his finger. "No, I'm not telling you the split."

"No fun!" I laughed as I stood. "I think I may be the same."

"Sweet little Star." Pen gave me an affectionate smile. "You are the closest I have ever seen to all good."

Before I could respond, the door flung open and Zel stood on the threshold. "The room stinks of sex." I met his look of loathing with a wide smile. Grunting in disgust, he turned away. "Come, they are ready."

Pen and I exchanged a look, and as we followed Dark and Murdery from the room, I leaned into Pen. "I say ninety-five percent bad."

Pen chuckled and quickly swallowed his laughter when Zel turned to look at him in anger.

"Ninety-nine," Pen whispered back.

"Ninety-nine point nine," I added.

"Quit it, whatever *it* is," Zel snapped as he tried to ignore our giggles.

We were back in the hall I arrived in. It was empty except for five Watchers. Zel and Pen made seven. "Are there only nine of you?"

"There *were* ten," Zel snarled.

"There are more still." Sam ignored Zel's attitude. "Not all get involved."

"Where are they?"

"None of your fucking business," Zel growled.

"You are a complete arsehole. I've said it before, I will say it forever, go fuck yourself."

Ros looked between the two of us. "I think when you are at full power, Star, you should both fight."

"Agreed." Zel actually looked happy at the idea, which is why I knew it would never happen.

"When do we begin?" I asked, changing the subject immediately. I saw his satisfied smirk, and when he turned to look at Sam, I stuck my tongue out at his back. Zel still flicked me the finger, and I knew he caught me even though I didn't know how.

"Witch."

Rolling my eyes, I made my way over to Sam. "Just once, one time, you could try Star."

"I've tried her, I liked it a lot." Sam was laughing at me and making this all sexual, and I was back to wanting to cause him bodily harm.

"Dick."

"Now don't be greedy," Sam whispered as he pulled me close. Kissing me stopped any more name calling, and I mewled in protest when he grabbed a handful of my butt.

"Who's being greedy now?" I asked softly as we separated.

"Me," Sam said simply before he dropped another kiss on my lips. "You'll be fine."

"I know." I gave him my most confident smile—it was clear I fooled neither him nor myself. He led me into the centre of the circle, which I hadn't even realised had formed, and with a brief kiss to my forehead, Sam stepped back.

Even though I was aware of what was happening this time, and I had been promised no bloodshed, when they all drew their hoods low and their weapons came out, I felt a shiver of fear. Licking my lips, I kept my eyes trained on Sam.

The chanting began. The weird almost Latin that they spoke swelled louder in the empty hall. As I reached for my powers, I could see the air distort as they spoke. As if in a trance, I almost could see the words form in the air. Was that normal?

Something pulled at me, and I pulled back.

Another sharp tug, and I tugged back harder.

You need to let it go.

Hound was beside me, and I wasn't sure if he was here or I was there.

It doesn't feel right, I told him.

It shouldn't, the practice is forbidden.

Trust my Watchers to keep that to themselves. My doubt felt more real. I cried out in pain when I felt a forcible yank, and my hands raised to my chest.

Stop fighting.

How are you here? I asked.

Where else would I be?

The chanting got louder, and my attention snagged on the air around us. I could definitely see words.

I can see it, I told Hound.

Very good, Star. That is most encouraging.

We were in the Void. I noticed some of the Watchers stumbled in surprise, but Sam, Zel and Pen stayed steady.

The Void was not *void* of anything. Where there had been darkness and grey, now there was light, blue, so much blue, and brightness. The Watchers took a step closer to me, tightening the circle as I saw them.

Scavengers.

In my Void?

Fuck that.

Cleanly, I separated myself from my body as I turned to face the shark-teethed demons.

"Take care of me," I told Ros as I felt her fall from me as I shed her like a skin. My powers raced unleashed along my arms. Blue fire danced around me. I locked eyes with the green-eyed demon.

"I'm hungry," I told him.

Wickedness lit his face. "Then let's hunt, witch."

Watchers stood alongside me as we turned and fought Scavengers in my Void. Who sent them, Asmodeous? That would be foolish, he wouldn't play his hand. Or was he desperate? Desperate people made mistakes.

Lightning struck Scavengers, frying them where they stood, as Hound and his fellow hellhounds joined the fray. Ros appeared beside me and handed me the short sword we had practiced with.

It felt right.

Fighting with them made me feel…*right*.

They had slain me. They had lied to me. They had betrayed me.

They had protected me.

Protected me as their brother was tortured and suffered unbearable pain.

As we fought Scavengers in my safe place, they protected me still. When I saw a Scavenger have the audacity to strike Pen and draw blood, my powers had enough.

As I tossed the sword aside, the hellhounds fenced me in as my head threw back and the fire licked along my skin.

I heard someone call "get back," and then my fury was unleashed. In a wide arc, the flames reached out and wiped out the Scavengers. I didn't know if I got them all, but I knew I got a lot.

Weak, I fell to the ground, and I felt gentle hands lift me and hold me close.

"Leave us."

Who was Sam speaking to? I felt rather than saw the hellhounds go. He couldn't command them, could he?

"She did it." *Who spoke?*

"She did, I knew she could." *Sam.*

"We should not have doubted her use."

My use?

"How long will she need before she's ready?"

"A few days." *Was that Pen?*

"We grow impatient."

"Then learn patience." *Definitely Zel.* "Now go before you're caught." *Who needs to go?*

"She really did it." *Ros.*

"She was magnificent." I felt lips caress my forehead.

"Cross will talk her out of it," Zel warned.

"She will not listen."

"How can you be sure?" *Pen?*

"Because I know her."

"This better work," one of them grumbled.

"Trust me, brothers, we did not come so far to stop now." I felt him tighten his hold. "Our brothers will be back with us soon."

"I'll take us there." *Ros again.*

The atmosphere shifted into one I knew, the smell familiar.

"What have you done to her?" Cross demanded. "Put her down immediately."

"She was attacked in the Void."

"She was attacked…" Cross seemed stumped. "Leave us, now. I'll take it from here."

I recognised the feel of the couch underneath me.

"You drained her for your own use." Cross sounded like he was hovering.

"To be all she can be, she needs to be pushed."

"There's pushed and there's *broken*," Cross snapped angrily.

"She has not broken yet," Sam said quietly as his hand stroked over my hair.

"Yet." Cross's tone was sharp. "The operative word there, Watcher, is *yet.*"

Again, I felt them leave.

"They're gone. You can stop pretending."

Sitting up, I looked at Cross and grinned.

"I take it your plan worked?"

"Perfectly."

CHAPTER 23

As Cross produced a glass of wine for me, I leaned back on the couch. "Are they definitely gone?"

"They are. The wards are strengthened; your mother is quite versed in spells when it is her daughter she is protecting."

"My mum, tea leaf reader extraordinaire."

"It is old magic to use the leaves as a protection spell," Cross said in admiration.

"The more that is revealed to me about the world of witchcraft, the more I doubt that my family merely dabble."

"I believe their involvement is minimal but knowledgeable," Cross told me as he settled in his seat. "But enough about that, tell me everything."

As I ran through the last two days with Cross, skipping over the sex with Sam, he listened with rapt attention. "The elements fully responded? You could command them?" he asked me as he leaned forward in interest.

"Everything was as we thought," I told him. "And when we went into the Void, it was blue and white."

Cross's eyes widened fractionally. "The colour of the lightning that you cast?" His fingers tapped off his bottom lip. "And the fire?"

"Blue."

"Completely?"

"Electric blue. I looked like a weird anime character, and my hair went all static with the electricity. I was freaky."

"And the fire destroyed the Scavengers I sent?"

That made me pause. "You sent?" He remained expressionless. "Completely. I'm telling you, between the spell and the fight, I think I'm ready."

He sat back and considered me. "You weren't supposed to have sex," he reprimanded me.

"You could have warned me that when I rejoined my body, I would be a walking, throbbing hormone. The Watchers knew. It wasn't just a case of *ooh I like him*, it was a burning need. I felt like animals must do in heat."

He stared past me as I watched him. "I have never experienced the merging as you have; I apologise my knowledge was lacking." His head dipped in apology. "I should have warned you."

Recalling how insatiable I had been, I shrugged it off. "I wasn't complaining."

"I don't need details," he reminded me primly.

"You kissed me, and you did it well," I started, pausing to take a sip of wine. "Really well, so I know you must have experience."

"Experience? With sex?"

"Yeah." Was it weird to ask Death about his sex life? Probably. Had I already done it? Yup, no taking it back now.

"I am not unversed," he told me as he waited for the follow-on questions we both knew I was too chicken to ask. "Are you done?"

"Yes."

"So, the merge, it hurt?"

"Like you wouldn't imagine, but Zel healed me."

Cross nodded as he thought. "You smell of Samyaza." Pretty sure I would smell of Sam for the rest of my life, but I waited for Cross to finish his train of thought. "It is good that the plan worked."

"Yes, I know where they keep me, I know how to get back into my body, I know the spell to split my soul and body, and I know how much energy I can hold after being there."

"And they suspect nothing?" Cross looked expectant.

"I don't think so, although I wasn't expecting Hound to show up."

"It was necessary. They know he guards you, and it would have been suspicious had he not."

Drinking my wine, I felt somewhat relieved. I truly hadn't expected the hellhounds, and when Hound had obeyed Sam, I had a moment of doubt, but I should have trusted Cross since he had been on board with my plan from the beginning. "Your advice is, what?"

"Your energy is replenishing. You are almost at normal capacity."

I couldn't help but feel like an electronic device that was plugged in to charge. "How long?"

"Hours, maybe less."

"Will they be surprised that I regenerated my energy so fast?"

Cross looked surprised. "You are still going to assist them with their quest?"

"*Quest* sounds like an epic adventure."

"You wish to save the Watchers, even knowing all that you know, after everything I have taught you?"

"I am human, I want to go home."

"They betrayed you once, they will do so again," Cross warned me.

"I am different, I am not who I was." Pulling my hair over my shoulder, I was startled to see it was that white blonde, the same as my real hair. "I fought beside them today, I fought by their side, with them."

"Do not be a fool." Cross sneered as he looked me over. "You are not their equal."

"No, I am not." I recalled my fire, my powers, my fight. "But an ally? I think I am."

"If you do this, you could be captured and tortured. Do you want to die?"

"Of course not, but they have a plan. You know the plan, tell me."

"You are foolish to want this." He was in white today, white linen trousers and a loose white shirt. His feet were as always bare. "Chazaquel, I understand your need to help him, you feel tied to him. Obligated."

"He is my friend, and we know he would sacrifice himself for me." My sadness at the memory of Chaz was not fake.

Cross knew and recognised that, but he still looked grumpy. "The danger with Araqiel has not changed."

"I know. I also know now there are more Watchers than the ones who I have met. I don't know where they are or how many, but the fact that there are more means there are potentially more who wish to get to the tree." Cross was nodding thoughtfully as I spoke, and I knew this wasn't new information for him. "And I think I am sure which Watchers I *do* know want the tree for ascension and those who don't." My hand shook as I reached for my wine. "Pen said he would cut the tree down rather than let anyone ascend."

Cross's eyes lit with…excitement? I studied his reaction as I tried to pretend that I wasn't. "To fell the tree of life upsets not only the balance but the order. It is a bold desire to state."

"I think it's the worst thing that could happen, ever." My anxiety as my companion seemed to weigh the pros and cons of world destruction only increased as he began to smile. "You're freaking me out."

"Am I?"

"Cross, I swear to Christ, if you suddenly go rogue on me, I'm going to be so pissed off!"

His rich laughter made me smile. "Little Star, you are such fun. What would you do to Death if he pissed you off? Enlighten me," he teased.

"I would put you in the body of a human now I know the spell."

Cross sniggered as he watched me. "You think I have a soul?"

Well, that flummoxed me. Didn't he? Didn't we all? Isn't that what made us, *us*? "Yes."

"Why would I have a soul? Who is collecting it? I cannot die."

My brain niggled, and I remembered something Sam said, but I couldn't recall it completely. "Well, I would do something mean to you," I muttered stubbornly and rolled my eyes as he openly laughed at me.

"It may almost be worth upsetting the balance to see you seek retribution." He smiled fondly at me and then grew serious once more. "So, when do you plan on aiding the Watchers?"

"I think they will come for me, whether they think I am ready for them or not."

Cross agreed and we sat in companionable silence for a while, sipping wine and enjoying the quiet.

"I still have so much to teach you," he spoke suddenly.

"I know."

"When this *rescue* mission is over, you should return to me and learn your craft. Only I can teach you this," he reminded me.

"I know. But I need to go home. I need to be me again with my family, my friends." I scowled as I thought of what Sam said about Ruairidh. "I need to make sure my friend is okay."

"Ah, you learned who the alternative was."

"You *knew*?"

"Of course I knew, I am Death."

"It completely freaks me out when you say that so casually. It's like you're saying you want fried eggs for breakfast."

He paused. "What?"

"What do you want for breakfast? Fried eggs." I looked at him as his brow furrowed in concentration. "Who are you? Death. See what I mean?"

"Not at all."

I shrugged. "You know why? Because you are a *being*. A deity if you will."

"Deity?" He rolled it around on his tongue as he considered it. "I like it."

My eyes narrowed as I looked at him. "You think I just called you a god, don't you? And...you already know what you are." Cross's smile was wide and wicked. "That's it, I'm going to bed."

His low laughter followed me out of the room.

THE WATCHERS GAVE me a full day to recover my energy, not knowing that I had recharged within hours. I was willing to work with them, and I believed that this would work, but would I ever trust them again? Not as I once had. Star, the imbecile who had run through Slate like a lost child, had gone. I was Star Elizabeth Archer, and I was so much more than I had been.

More what? I wasn't sure yet, but I was willing to explore it further. The spell they cast as they split my soul from my body rattled around in my head. I didn't understand the language they used, I couldn't write it down if you paid me, but I *knew* it. I knew it, and that knowledge meant I could perform it. The Watchers no longer held my body ransom, and they didn't even know it.

What was it that they said about great power and responsibilities? One was as significant as the other? Was it? Was it really? Because from where I stood on the other side of Cross's glass looking down at the pit, I saw a lot of power and not one being that claimed responsibility for exploiting it.

They were so used to their power, they were so used to *being*, that they forgot why they were here. They came to join with humanity, not exploit it. I was not so foolish to think that I was going to make the world a better place when I took down Asmodeous; there would be another twisted shit to take his place, but I and a few of my friends and family would sleep better, knowing he wasn't down here plotting to escape the clutches of hell.

I wish I knew the witch who cast the spell. She sounded like a good woman. Would her soul be at peace if he was gone, or would she forever linger in the Land of the Souls where the dead waited for their next journey to begin?

I would kill Asmodeous, I would slay Araqiel, and I would ensure that witch's soul found peace. So help me God.

I hesitated. God? My eyes rested on Cross, who was deep in thought in the corner of his couch. Maybe not God, but I had something just as powerful on my side. I had *his* balance.

Never in my life would I have thought that I would be pleased to be on a friendly basis with Death.

How my life had changed since I had been down here.

"You are deep in thought," Cross said as he reached over and picked a book up off of the table.

"Am I?" He may be an ally, but he was still Cross. He was going to lose his shit when he found out my plan.

Which is why I wasn't telling him.

"Witch."

Turning completely from the window, I saw Sam walking towards me. He looked…I had to stop focusing on his looks; the outside wrapping still covered a shady demon.

My demon.

I smiled at my thoughts and at the male in front of me. Soft lips covered mine as he bent and claimed me with a kiss so soft but so possessive. I was clinging to him when he was done.

"I missed you, little witch," he murmured against my lips.

"Me too," I admitted, feeling shy. This softness wasn't us, and I loved it. Too much. I needed to put the brakes on immediately. Stepping back, I put distance between us and saw his surprise at my action. "How is my body?"

"Delightful."

"Ew, you just made that creepy." I headed to the couch to stay out of his reach. Whenever Sam touched me, I lost my mental capacity to think like an adult. Not a good thing to admit about yourself, I knew. Women's lib was screaming at me somewhere for being ruled by a man.

Ruled?

Fuck no.

Influenced…may be more acceptable, but not by much.

"I meant your body is delightful because she, unlike her soul, is quiet."

"Dickhead." I sat down and looked at Cross, who was still studying his book. "Cross?"

"Mm-hmm?"

"The Watcher's here."

"Mm-hmm."

Sam sat alongside me, his leg pressing into mine, and I felt my reaction. Moving slightly, I put a little distance between us. He followed. Swallowing hard, I moved again, again he followed. He wasn't even being subtle. When I was pressed against the side with nowhere else to go, I turned to glare at him, but his satisfied smile and dark eyes dancing with amusement made me ache more.

"You need to stop." I tried to keep my voice low. Cross was engrossed, but he wasn't deaf.

"What did I do?"

Accusations rose ready to spill free, but his smirk made me bite my tongue. He wanted an excuse for me to lose my temper. Why?

"Cross, unless the answer to the meaning of life is in that book, could you put it down?" I asked him more sharply than I intended.

Cross stilled, his head lifting slightly so his gaze met mine. "And if it is the answer to the meaning of life that I seek?"

Huh? Oh shit, what was in the book? His lip twitched. "You're a dick."

He grinned openly as he put the book aside. "Samyaza, too often you come into my home, when will it stop?"

"When you no longer hold her."

"I will always hold her."

"*Her* is still in the room, and I am not, for the millionth time, a possession."

"Shush." Sam's fingers slipped through mine. "We both know who you belong to."

"Is it because of cavemen?" I asked him in bewilderment. "The Neanderthal behaviour? I mean, you've been here since the beginning, but did you mentally stop evolving? Are you stuck in the 'club your woman over the head' phase and haven't matured since then?"

"You like when I'm a brute."

"I like when you don't speak."

"Only you know how to silence me properly." His gaze caught mine in his heated stare, and I needed a distraction.

Was it hot in here?

"Why are you here?" Cross saved me from making a fool of myself. Again.

"I've arranged a meeting with him, and I need the witch."

"Who? What? Where?"

"When and why?" Cross chipped in with amusement.

"What? I just told you. Where? In his domain. Why? Because I asked nicely. When? In about an hour. Who?" He leaned in close, and I held my breath. "Are you ready to meet Satan?"

CHAPTER 24

"Satan?"

"Yeah." His eyes were twinkling with laughter at my goldfish impression.

"The devil?"

"We've had this conversation," Cross interrupted agitatedly. "You are rash to involve him," he directed at Sam.

"*This* prince, I need." Sam levelled Cross with a hard stare. "I would not put her in danger."

"You are the reason she is *in* danger," Cross reminded him.

"Burn," I murmured as I saw Sam glare at Cross, and his eyes flicked to mine in question. "Ignore me."

"Satan gives us leverage. We know how much he and Asmodeous loathe each other, so Satan will be a distraction the Prince of Lust is not expecting. While he is distracted, we move in under the shield of the souls the witch commands, and we free my brothers."

"Then what?" I asked. To me, it was only half a plan.

"Then we aid Satan as he brings Asmodeous down."

"He will kill him?" I asked in surprise.

"The Prince of Wrath has already killed gluttony, so lust will matter not to him."

"And what does he ask of the Watchers in return?" Cross asked shrewdly.

"Protection in case he faces retaliation." Sam shrugged slightly. "It is not an issue, three of us can provide that."

"Which three?" I asked quietly, praying it would be the three who hated me the most.

"It matters not," Sam said to me as he stood. "It's time to go."

I knew the plan, Cross knew the plan, but I was scared. Sam's fingers slipped beneath my chin and tilted my head backwards so he could make eye contact. "Nothing will happen to you."

"I'm going to meet Satan; I don't think you are in the best place to assure me that I am safe."

"It's a simple introduction."

"If you're trying to pass this off as a meet and greet, I'm not listening," I told him as I stood. "Cross?"

"I will not join you. Satan is…a handful."

I laughed out loud. Oh my life, was *that* the understatement of the year? Yes, I was influenced by movies and folklore, but come on, they were taking me to *Satan*. I was going to die. I was sure of it.

"Asmodeous will not be aware that I am in hell?" I asked as Sam reached his hand out, and I hesitated in taking it.

"Satan's taken care of it," Sam assured me.

I wasn't sure that this was something that made me feel better. How had he taken care of it? There were very few details being given my way.

Sam was done waiting, and his hand took mine, and then I was in…*what the fuck was this?*

I had to stop myself from turning completely. I was in a night-club? I was in a low-lit bar with a dance floor, women dancing in cages, nope, not just women—I noticed the ripped abs of a male dancer. Music thumped around us, making my chest reverberate in painful rhythm, which was a trick because I had no rib cage.

Low black leather couches were scattered around with beings and, I noticed, *things*, and as I focused on them, I desperately looked away. Wow. I did not need to see that.

Sam guided me to a staircase, which I hadn't seen as I looked around the club. Was I still in hell, or was I in some glitzy club on earth? Sam held tight to me as he led me up the stairs, and then I was in a box room with an open front that looked out and down to the club floor.

The male was not what I expected. He was blond. I don't know why I thought he would have black hair. Broad shouldered, his shirt pulled taught over his muscular back. He turned when we walked halfway into the box.

I stepped back involuntarily, and Satan smiled.

"Jesus," I breathed as I felt fear grip me in its clutches.

"Nope, definitely not."

Satan was…overwhelming. Was he attractive? I couldn't tell you, because all I could feel was the *wrongness* that exuded from him. It wasn't evil—I wasn't sure anymore what evil was. Was it just too much bad in a split of good and bad, like Pen thought? I didn't know, but what I did know was that Satan was one hundred percent bad. I knew it as brown eyes travelled over my simple jeans and blouse. *Don't judge me,* I had no idea what I was supposed to wear to meet Satan.

"Is she a good fuck?" he asked Sam, and my jaw dropped. Sam's fingers tightened around mine in warning.

"She knows her way around a dick." He shrugged slightly. "But then, they always do."

"Witches, always horny little bitches."

I was in hell. I mean, literally I was, but this was the first time I ever thought I was *in hell.*

"Of course, you look at her like that one more time, Prince of Wrath, and I'll remove your eyes."

Satan laughed.

Is this what a stroke felt like?

"I have never seen you possessive of anything other than your Watchers." Satan looked me over. "She is yours? Her scent reeks of you."

These crotch-sniffing demons would be the death of me. Oh wait…been there.

"She is mine, for now."

For now? Fuck you too, arsehole.

"Do you speak?"

"What do you want me to say?" I asked him coolly, and I was so proud of myself for my attitude.

"I want you to tell me how you, who looks weak and insignificant, will aid me as I strike at the fuckhead, Asmodeous."

"Looks can be deceiving," I answered him.

"I said she can do it, you doubt me?"

"I'm making a move against the fucker who's the bane of my existence. He needs to die."

"Amen."

Was that me? Oops.

But Satan's whole entire demeanour changed towards me. The evil glint in his eyes diminished as he assessed me, really assessed me, and I wasn't at all happy when he smiled at me.

"You are here as he hunts for you?" Satan mused. "You could have given him what he wanted, why didn't you?"

"This isn't why—" Sam started.

Satan shut Sam up with a raised hand. "Shh, I'm talking to the little morsel," he warned quietly. "Answer."

Was this a test? What happened if I failed? Damn it, I was not cut out for this. I met the gaze of Satan and shrugged.

"He said he had burned the witch who cursed him, daily in oil, that he tortured her every day to lift her curse and set him free. And still she did not relent." I wet my lips as I swallowed. "To go through that, to endure that pain, that's more than someone who just doesn't like you. She suffers every day to keep him contained in this realm, and I may be many things, but I'm not stupid. She knows he cannot be set free, and she did what she did to make sure it never happened. To endure that punishment from a demon who is inventing new ways to torture you on a daily basis for *centuries*, I'd be damned if I was lifting it and making everything she has suffered be for nothing. Her sacrifice should not be in vain."

Satan said nothing as he considered me. Had I answered wrongly? I wasn't sure. "And how do you propose we get into his realm undetected?"

He already knew. Sam had already told us, and I knew *this* was a test.

"I believe there may be some animosity between you, and you are the Prince of Wrath, so I'm guessing anger may be your thing. Although wrath is not always anger." I tilted my head when he smiled. "No, he has wronged you in some way. And I think only a fool betrays you." I ploughed on when he said nothing. "I would imagine that you will enter his realm, confront him and cause a distraction. But not for reason of an old slight, I think you will have something more recent to confront him on. He will know, but he won't be expecting you to make a move so soon, because you may be wrath, but you are not rash." I looked at the fallen angel, who scared me to my very bones. "What has he done to you, I wonder? To cause such rage?"

Satan laughed.

Glancing at Sam, I saw his face blank as he watched Satan, his expression giving nothing away, and I felt safe with him by my side. Which I never thought would happen again, and I wondered if my life had become so muddled I now picked the lesser of two evils to feel safe with.

"You'll do, witch, you'll do." Satan turned his back on us. "Three days, Watcher, my army is ready. Make sure you are too." Satan glanced back at me. "Witch, do you want to stay a while?"

"Absolutely not." It was out before I could stop it, and Satan's loud laughter as he turned away from me and back to his perch was enough to have Sam tug my hand and lead me back down the stairs.

We didn't go back to Cross. Instead, we were in the ether, and I looked at Sam in surprise before he had me wrapped in his arms.

"Did I fuck up?" I asked him as he held me tight.

"No, I think I might have."

"How?" I asked fearfully.

"I let him know how much you mean to me. I exposed you to yet another prince of hell, and you're already on too many demons' notice."

Drawing back, I cupped the side of his face with my hand. "Samyaza the Watcher. Are you worried I'm going to leave?" I teased him.

"No." He nipped my bottom lip. "I will never let you leave me, witch." He looked out over the grounds and the surrounding trees. "Satan is a means to an end, the end being Asmodeous. But in order to protect you, I need to keep drawing attention to you. There are worse things out there than the princes of hell," he said grimly.

"Yes, there are Watchers," I replied and held his look when he met mine. It was Sam who looked away first. "Can you guarantee my safety from your own?" He said nothing as he looked at the skyline, and I waited. I was not letting him avoid this conversation. "Sam?"

"No." Stepping back from me, he turned, giving me his back. "I cannot guarantee you safety from them. From me."

My heart felt heavy. "Look at me."

His body stiffened, and then slowly he turned to face me. "They are my brothers."

"I know."

"Yeqon is already lost to us," he started.

"Because of me, I know." I pushed my hair back. "He deserved it, it was not just me that one betrayed."

Sam's eyes flicked my way. "I am sorry I did not listen to you. I am sorry for the hurt that I caused you."

My jaw dropped. "Did you just apologise?"

I saw his small smile and the rueful shake of his head. "I did. I should have done it sooner, but you bring out my worst while you also bring out my best."

"Aww, you say sweet things," I said dryly, and this time his smile was wider. "You want to apologise for the dick comment in the club?"

"No." Sam actually looked surprised. "You do know your way around a dick."

"You *cannot* say that. To me. Or anyone else."

"Why?"

"What do you mean *why*?" I asked in exasperation. "I mean I'm not a slut, I am not someone who sleeps around, and you made me sound slutty to Satan!"

"You care what Satan thinks of you?"

I blinked. Was he serious or was he jealous? "Are you tripping? I feel like you're tripping."

Sam looked at his feet, which had not moved. "Explain."

"I am not interested in Satan, other than I am pretty sure that I now have the face to every nightmare that I have ever had. He scares the crap out of me. You should not have spoken about me to him like I was a bed hopper."

"Bed hopper? Opposed to grasshopper?"

"Shut up."

"Satan likes to annoy me. I try not to rise to his attempts, hence the comment. However, I blew it when I told him I would remove his eyes, because now he knows you mean something to me. For that, I am sorry," Sam said as he pulled me close.

"You went all caveman on me," I teased as I looked up at him. He grunted but said nothing as he played with the end of my hair. "Araqiel will kill me, Sam."

His fingers stilled, and his eyes closed briefly. "I know."

"And what are you going to do to stop it?" I asked him, afraid of the answer.

"I don't know."

Laying my head against his chest, he held me tight. "I don't like that answer," I told him quietly.

"Me neither, little witch. Me neither."

We stayed like that for some time, just wrapped up in each other, saying nothing, and it felt very much like goodbye. Eventually he pulled away from me and took me back to Cross.

Sam kissed me briefly before he left, and I turned to look at Cross and Hound.

"Well?"

Quickly I went through the meeting and afterwards in the ether. Cross listened to it all and said little.

"So now what?" I asked after I couldn't take the prolonged silence anymore.

"The Watcher is right," Cross mused as he sat in his corner of the couch and watched me. "You are on too many demons' notice now. We will need to work harder to keep you safe."

"If Satan takes care of the Asmodeous problem, then maybe the Watchers will ensure that Araqiel stays away from me?"

I avoided looking at Hound. His plan was still the best one as far as I could tell, I just didn't trust anyone enough to share it. Which was not a good feeling to have.

"There are some Watchers who do not want you to succeed."

"Why?"

"You are a witch." Cross ran a hand through his lovely thick hair. "Despite your affinity with the dead, witches are about nature. The natural order of things. For those who fell, it is not the natural order for them to return. The heavens will not allow it, and those above will rain down war if they attempt it."

"Sounds kind of like the end of days." I tried to sound jovial, but I sounded scared shitless.

"It would be similar. They have descended before. The battle was bloody and catastrophic, and it would be so again if they were to return."

"Why are you not stopping the Watchers and those that want to go back then?" I demanded as I paced. I was always going to pace, thank goodness the floor was marble, or there would be a hole in any carpet by now.

"I am Death. I am not Life."

"But you *live* in this world. In all the realms! Don't you care?"

Cross shrugged. "If it is meant to be, then it is meant to be."

"Wow." I shook my head. "I am *so* disappointed in you right now."

He looked confused as to why, and I decided to not bother anymore. "I'm going to the Void. I need to practice."

"You are foolish to aid them," Cross snapped. "You know you are in danger, yet you are willingly putting yourself in danger, and then you reprimand *me* for *my* actions."

"No, I reprimand you for your lack of action," I retorted harshly. "I *am* in danger, and I think I will always be in danger. So if I do not know how to defend myself, then how can I prepare for them when they come?"

"You could sit back and do nothing?"

"I'm not very good at doing nothing."

Cross smiled, and he looked so relaxed I felt edgy. "Then come, let us prepare."

"You'll help me?"

He stood fluidly. "In preparation to be better? Always. In preparation to create war? Never."

I hesitated as I thought about it...his offer was better than nothing. "I'll take what I can get. Let's go."

THE VOID WAS BACK TO BEING NOTHING. I WAS DISAPPOINTED, BUT I saw that Cross was not surprised. Hound sat and watched as I looked around. The Void felt empty to me again, and again I was disheartened. "The colour went away."

"You are not holding your powers," Cross said as he too looked around. "Do you feel anything?"

"No, it's empty." Taking a few steps forward, I looked at him. "Do *you* feel that it is empty?"

"Almost. This can be your first lesson today."

"Okay. What is it?" I bounced on my toes, ready for sparring.

"Clear the Void."

I stopped bouncing. "I just told you it is empty."

"And I just told you that it is not, so…clear the Void."

I was stumped. I had no idea what to do. "Cross?"

"Yes, Star?"

"I don't know how to do that."

"I know. This is why it's your lesson for today."

I chewed the inside of my cheek as I bit back my sarcastic retorts. *Focus. Don't let him mess with you.* "Are you going to give me some pointers?"

"No."

I rolled my head on my shoulders, loosening up. I searched for my powers. Since my angry storming of the Watchers' castle, which made me giggle when I thought about it that way, they had been easier to find, well, they weren't lost. Maybe *feel* was the better terminology. They were easier to feel.

I sensed the familiarity of them as I dipped in and pulled them to me. Cross had tried to tell me that the fact that I associated them as something separate was where I was immediately failing. They were not something alien to me anymore, and in truth, I could wink with the best of them. I had called the elements when I needed them, and I knew that the dead were mine to command.

I'd come a long way from being stabbed on a clifftop in October.

Are you there?

We are here.

I need you to, um, merge.

Merge?

You're my powers, right?

We are yours.

Then you need to be at one with me. Or something.

We are.

Then why can't I feel you all the time?

You block us.

Okay. How do I stop that?

Open your eye.

My eyes *were* open. What the hell were they talking about? I looked around. Cross was sitting on a chair. Honestly, for Death, the man was lazy. Always sitting. Reading. Hound was to the left of him, watching but not participating. I would have welcomed his sarcasm right now, but he was careful when Cross was with us. Another secret to hide.

My eyes are open.

Open your eye.

Now I just had visions of dick jokes and things and wondered if I started laughing hysterically, Cross would kill me himself.

"Cross?"

"Mm-hmm?"

"How do I open my eye?"

His head snapped up, and he beamed at me, and in an instant he was beside me. "They speak to you?"

"They do." He didn't think this was weird. That could be a good thing.

"Tell me."

"They said I block them and I need to open my eyes."

"No the *eye*. Your inner eye." He looked at me in exasperation. "I thought you were a psychic?"

That made so much more sense. "Shut up," I muttered as I closed my eyes. Waited. And then opened them again. "Okay, you need to tell me."

He tried to hide his smile, but I saw it. Cross placed one of his large hands on my forehead and the other on my middle. For being Death, his hands were warm, comfortably so. Well, this could get awkward.

"Close your eyes," he instructed softly. I did as I was told. "Breathe in and out."

"I thought I didn't need to?"

"Star."

"Breathing in and out." I did as I was told. I felt his hand spread across my abdomen, and my breathing picked up.

"Nice and slow," he encouraged.

This was ridiculous. I should not be reacting to him like this, the guy was Death, and I was with Sam…or having sex with Sam…or something.

"Relax, Star," Cross murmured as he stepped closer to me. Him moving to be behind me was not helping me as he pressed me into his chest. I licked my lips, and my head went willingly when he encouraged me to rest it against his chest. "Keep breathing." I did, although I think I sounded more like I was panting than breathing. "Reach inside yourself to where my hand is."

"What?"

"Don't speak. And focus," he said, pulling me in tighter. "Now do you feel my hand?" I nodded. "This is the centre of you, imagine this is where your powers lie. You said it's a pool, yes?" I nodded again. This was weirdly relaxing. "In the palm of my hand are your powers, reach for them."

I did. I felt them stir.

"Is my hand blocking them?" he asked me quietly in my ear.

"Yes," I whispered.

"Move my hand, centre your focus on my hand and move it."

Frowning, I focused. I could feel my powers. I could feel his hand over my shirt. I just couldn't put them together. I gasped when his hand moved, slipping under my shirt, and we were flesh to flesh. Okay, we weren't, but I knew what I meant.

"Where are they?" he asked me.

"In your hand," I replied immediately.

"Take them from me."

Reaching down again, I pulled at my powers and I pushed at Cross's hand. I felt a surge of heat and then a nudge. I stilled as I waited for it to happen again. It didn't. So was that me? Again, I focused on pulling while I pushed. Another flare of heat, another nudge.

"Cross," I whispered excitedly.

"I feel you," he answered as his hand flexed against me. "Keep going."

This time it was easier. The nudge happened almost as the flare happened.

"Good, now, take them and focus on my hand on your forehead."

That was trickier. I liked the feel of his hand on my midriff. I whimpered in protest when he took it away, and he quickly placed it back again. His hand on my head pulled me into his upper body. Almost restrictive but not quite. I liked the feel of his lower hand better.

"Focus, Star," he admonished me as his fingers trailed lazily along my skin.

"I'm trying."

"Harder."

Well, that wasn't productive, wrong word to use. Hot breath warmed my ear. "I said focus," Cross said softly.

"Why am I reacting like this?"

"It's a side effect of your power, you will control it in time," he assured me. And I *was* assured. Because I was pressed so closely to Cross I was almost in his skin. I felt every part of him, and he was completely unaffected by the fact he had me wrapped around him.

"Tell me again," I demanded as his hand moved.

"Take them and push me away."

When his hand slipped upwards, cupping my breast, I almost screamed in frustration. I knew why he was doing it, and it wasn't sexual, but my powers didn't like it. As much as I pulled them higher, their attention was on Cross's thumb, gently rubbing backwards and forward on the underside of my breast.

He's doing it on purpose, I told them.

Open your eye.

I'm trying, but you seem more focused on the fact that Death is feeling me up.

Open your eye.

Agitated with them and Cross, I yanked at them from my middle and thrust them upwards.

Pain blinded me.

Cross held me upright as my knees buckled and I almost fell. Still, I could not see. My powers were stronger as they raced back to where he was now holding a lot of boob.

"No." Clenching my teeth, I tugged again. "Up." A sob broke out of me as they resisted.

I said up.

Open your eye.

I'm trying, you bastards—stop fighting me!

I felt myself slump against Cross. "I can't, they won't let me. They don't like you touching me."

"What are your powers?" Cross asked as he nuzzled my neck.

"Um…"

"Your power is what?"

"Mine."

"Then *own* it." Teeth nipped my neck, and I realised one of my hands had curled into his hair, pulling him down to me. "Finish this."

I pulled my powers. *My* powers. I pulled it from within me, and I forced it, dragged it, up my body, past where long fingers were playing with my nipple, up past my throat where I gasped for breath, over my cheeks that were wet from tears of pain, and finally to my forehead where one hand hadn't moved and was pressing me against his chest.

Pressing.

No.

Not pressing.

Repressing.

Flames awoke within me, and I came alive. With a roar, I pushed him away from me. With a roar, I opened my eyes in the Void. With a roar, my inner eye opened, and I was blinded once again.

Forcing myself to stand strong, I waited.

Dark and grey lifted from the Void. It was once again white and blue, the blue of my flames. Lightning raced everywhere as thunder boomed.

"Why the fuck is my witch half-naked?" Sam demanded as he appeared in front of me.

Looking down, I saw my shirt was wide open, my bra gone, my breasts exposed. "Cross!"

Turning, I saw him beaming at me in pride. "There you are, my beauty. I've been waiting for you."

"Did it work?" I asked him as I hurriedly buttoned up my shirt, ignoring my Watcher.

"Look around, tell me what you see."

The Void was not empty. Holy shit, it was crowded.

"Whoa, Cross?"

"Tell me what you see?"

Where to start? I saw souls. Some looked like actual real live people, but I knew that they were not. I saw wraiths, the reapers from the pit. I saw shadows of Watchers, and I stared at them the longest.

"They are shadows?" I peered closer. "They are in the ether?"

"Very good," Cross praised me. "What else?"

"Souls, some so real it scares me. Wraiths, creepy fuckers, shadows…" I saw them out of the corner of my eye. Shadows of light, which was weird. But the shadows that they cast were white not grey. "Holy fucking shitfuck, is that angels?"

Sam whirled on his feet, weapons drawn.

"Not really. You see the movements of the princes of hell; they are never fully in the Void but skirt its edges."

Sam grunted and put his weapons away.

"They cast light as shadow?" I snorted. "How misleading is that?" Looking at Sam, I assessed his shadow. "And yet your shadow is black."

"Like my heart."

Wanker.

"Why were you having sex with Cross?"

"He was trying to distract my powers so I could gain control."

Sam looked unimpressed. "Uh-huh."

"Look, you don't get a say. It was nothing." I turned to Cross, who had conveniently disappeared. "Dammit."

"So what you're saying is, if I go back to the ether and see a nice buxom blonde, I can just undress her and grope her tits, and you'll be fine?"

Don't do it, Star, do not rise to it.

"Sure."

"Sure." He nodded. "And if I tell her to suck my dick?"

"Make sure she sucks it good."

Sam was watching me, that cocky grin on his face. I was going to stab him, I knew that I was. "Well, I'm glad we had this talk. I don't feel so bad about any indiscretions now."

"Indiscretions?"

He winked at me.

"Who the fuck were you indiscreet with?" I travelled to the ether. I was striding down towards that hall like hell itself was chasing me.

"Witch, you seem vexed," Sam said cordially as he appeared beside me and walked with me.

"Do I?" I gave him a scathing look. "Fuck you and your red-haired whore."

"A threesome? I might not mind, but I didn't have you down for sharing."

I stopped in the middle of my stride, turned and hit him. I didn't just hit him, I *hit* him. And watched with glee as the over-bearing, cheating bastard went flying. Turning, I continued into the hall.

I saw her immediately. Jessica-fucking-wannabe-Rabbit. "You." I marched towards her, and she looked like she would faint. "Did you mess about with my guy?"

"Who?"

"Who? What do you mean who? How many of them do you have sex with?"

"Star, you—"

"Let her continue," Sam cut Der off. "She needs to learn."

"Oh, this is gonna be bad," Ros muttered.

Spinning, I faced him. "Why? Jessica your friend too?"

Ros looked bemused. "No, you really need to think about this."

"I said *enough*," Sam chided him. "Please, witch, carry on."

Narrowing my eyes, I turned back to Mrs Slutty, who was now cowering. "Why are you cowering? Who are you afraid of?" I asked her in surprise. She shook her head frantically and kept her head down. "Are you okay? Look, I'm sorry if I upset you, I just don't want you touching my guy, okay?"

The shivering was out of control.

"I'd back away now," Sam called jovially.

"What?" I looked at him and then the vibrating girl on the floor. "Why? Sam?"

She exploded into motion. One minute, I had red-haired-hourglass-figure-falling-out-of-her-dress harlot, the next I had a three-headed demon with swirly snake heads as hair and about three pairs of arms.

"What the fuck!"

She hissed at me, and all her little snake heads did too.

"Why do you have a three-headed medusa in your hall?" I demanded as I took a step back.

"You want to know if I tasted your Watcher?" she hissed at me as her body undulated like a snake. She was terrifying, but I was sick of guys picking the obvious hussy. If she had touched him, I was ending her and *then* him.

"You better hope the answer is no to that question, because if you've put your scaly body anywhere near him, you're going to die." One of her heads moved like a snake would strike, and I narrowly missed venomous fangs. "Seriously, snake head is what you were coming back to?" I yelled at Sam as I dodged her next attack.

"No. You just don't listen."

"I do listen!"

"And you were the one who was getting her nipples pinched by Death."

"Ew, Star, that's gross." Ros decided to add to the commotion as I ducked again. "I mean, that's necrophilia or something."

"He was helping me unleash my powers!" I cried back as I dropped and kicked my leg out, off-balancing snake head.

"By fucking you?" Sam demanded incredulously.

"Don't be ridiculous. He was provoking my powers." When snake fangs took a chunk of my hair, I'd had enough. "Ros!"

I caught the short sword as he threw it. "Time to end this bitch." Four moves later, and I had three heads at my feet. Glaring at the three Watchers, I nudged one of the heads. "What the hell is she?"

"She *was* one of our best spies." Sam looked at the body as he took out one of his own swords and stabbed each head. "Only way to kill them completely."

"What is it?" I asked again.

"Satan made them centuries ago as weapons in his army. They slither into places unseen."

"She's a weapon?" I asked as I looked down at the body.

"She was." Ros nudged her with his foot. "She wasn't my favourite, but why'd you kill her?"

"He said he was having sex with her."

"With Syra?" Ros looked at me in astonishment and then laughed. "She's sexless."

"What?"

"They are gender-free. You'd have a better chance getting it on with a hellhound."

I turned to Sam. "I killed her, and she was innocent?" I demanded disbelievingly.

"No, she was a spy, and she was spying on *us*. You just took out the garbage."

"You used me?"

"You used yourself. Jealousy? Really? His hands were all over you, but do I go into a fit of hysteria? No. Because I trust you."

"You were angry."

"With Cross. Not with you."

"Oh."

"Yes. *Oh*. Now clean up this mess and go back to practicing." Sam turned away from me. "And tell that bastard to keep his hands to himself."

When he was gone, I looked at Ros and Der. "Oops."

Ros shook his head as he bent down to pick up the whatever-she-was demon. "Nothing is ever dull with you around, witch. Nothing at all."

CHAPTER 26

TIME MAY MOVE DIFFERENTLY IN HELL, BUT EVEN THEN, THREE DAYS passed too quickly. I wasn't sure that I was ready. Cross had been watching me in silence for most of it, and although he had helped me with my training, and my powers were being more malleable, I was still scared.

And who wouldn't be?

I was going to walk into the level of hell ruled by Asmodeous, the prince intent on killing me a trillion times over, and not only free Watchers, but kill *him*. I knew I didn't need to breathe here, but I genuinely needed oxygen. I couldn't catch my breath.

Hound watched me as I paced the bedroom.

"Are they here?"

You will know when they are here.

"Seriously, one of these days, you will just say yes or no. None of this Confucius shit."

You should calm down.

"I probably should." I continued to pace. "I need oxygen."

You have no lungs in this form.

"Hound, we're going to fall out soon."

Meh.

I stopped and looked at the hellhound. "Did you just *meh* me?"

Meh.

"Oh my God, I'm going to kill you."

He laughed. The hellhound laughed at me. With a glare, I turned my back on him. Not the most effective move on my part, but I felt better.

You have your powers. I can feel them.

I nodded but said nothing. My powers were easier to grasp, and the lightning and the thunder were absolutely not in my control, but no one seemed to have noticed that yet, and I wasn't telling them. I mean, if they went spark, spark, boom, boom when I was all witchy, then it was safe to assume that it was me controlling them. Wasn't it?

So what if I didn't have the actual ability to say *lightning, torch this fucker*, or *thunder, deafen this one's bleating*? They came out to play when I was channelling my inner raging bitch, and to date, they had helped me. I knew I should probably bring it to someone's attention; however, since I wasn't actually relying on either element to come to my rescue, what harm was non-admission doing?

I swung my arms in circles to loosen me up. I rolled my head on my shoulders. I bounced from foot to foot. I reminded myself of a heavyweight boxer prepping in his corner of the ring before a big fight.

Only I wasn't a heavyweight boxer.

I was just me.

"I'm going to die."

We all die eventually.

I turned to look at Hound, who was sitting quite calmly watching me. "Really? That's the pep talk?"

Pep talks won't work on you. You're too highly strung. You need Samyaza and five minutes alone.

I had no words. Did I?

When Sam appeared in my room, dressed in his Watcher clothes, I stared dumbstruck between him and Hound. Hound snorted and left the room.

Sam looked at me and the space where Hound had been. "What's wrong?"

I'm pretty sure the hellhound just told me to get laid, was not something I could say out loud. "I'm antsy," I said as I considered him. Maybe Hound was on to something? "I think I need to have my mind, um, taken off…you know, things."

Sam's surprised laughter shook me out of my stupor. Grinning, he walked towards me, his hands circled my waist, and then he was kissing me. *Really* kissing me. Soon I was climbing up his body as he lifted me, and my legs were wrapping around his hips as he pressed me into the wall. Strong fingers were under my shirt as our bodies ground against each other and our kisses got wilder. Hound was right, this was exactly what I needed. My mind was blank, I wasn't thinking of the fact I was probably away to die, for real this time. I was chasing the promise of pleasure only this Watcher could give me.

"I need more," I whispered as I pulled my mouth away.

"I know, I do too, but what I need won't be satisfied with a quick fuck against the wall." Sam peppered my jaw with kisses as he spoke, and my fingers tightened in his hair as I pulled his mouth to mine.

"What if my need will be?" I asked as I took his bottom lip in my teeth and pulled gently.

"You want an orgasm, little witch?" Sam asked me darkly as he cupped between my legs. "Hmm, that what you want?" He began to rub his thumb right where it mattered through my leggings.

My eyes were closed as my head rested on the wall. "Would you judge me terribly if I said yes?"

"No," he whispered against my lips. I heard the rip in the material, and then his fingers were there as I clung to him in desperation. I had a moment of panic when I felt myself slip down the wall, and then his mouth was there, and I no longer cared about anything except how his tongue moved against my core as he held me up. My legs rested over his shoulders, my fingers twisted in his hair, and I basically forgot anything except his name.

It could have been one minute, five minutes or an hour later, but I was in Sam's lap, my arms around him as he sat on the bed and held me as I recovered from the intensity of the orgasm he just gave me.

"Better?" he asked softly as he stroked my too blonde hair.

"Yes," I whispered as I nuzzled into his neck and breathed him in. "I got sex advice from a hellhound."

I heard him rumble with laughter. "You did? I'll have to thank him when we leave."

His comment alerted me to the fact that I just slipped up and told him I could communicate with Hound. *Shit.* Also, Sam mentioning leaving reminded me exactly what I was supposed to be doing. Sam felt me stiffen and tightened his arms around me. "You'll be fine."

"What if I'm not?"

A gentle touch to my chin, and he looked down at me. "Do you think, little witch, that I would let anything happen to you?"

I kissed the palm of his hand before I straightened. "You did stab me."

"You stabbed me, *twice*." He smiled down at me as he pulled me in closer. "Am I upset? You've stabbed me twice, I only stabbed you once, and you think you're the one done wrong by." His eyes danced with mischief, and I started to laugh.

Pushing off his shoulders, I stood and then looked down at my clothes. "Ah shit."

"It's a battle look I haven't seen before," Sam joked as he stood and kissed me briefly. "Come with me."

We went to the ether, and I was in the room where my body lay. Knowing better than to approach, I stayed in the corner and watched my chest rise and fall as it breathed. My eyes were still open, staring at nothing as I lay there immobile.

"You okay?" Sam asked me without looking at me.

"I look so peaceful," I told him quietly. "My hair looks so…odd."

He looked up and over his shoulder. "It's a by-product of being in the different dimensions."

"It doesn't mean that I'm fading though?" I finally voiced the fear that scared me the most. "My hair getting whiter like that, it's not a negative thing?"

"No." I saw his eyes spark with the soft pulsating glow that made my heart race. "It means you're adapting to the surroundings. With Cross, your soul and your powers get stronger. Here, with me, your body gets stronger."

"I breathe here."

He looked at me, and the emotion in his eyes caused me to take a step towards him. A thousand words we had never said passed between us. "Sam…"

"I took these from your home." Sam looked down at a simple pair of black jeans. "They won't do. Wait a moment."

He left the room, and I stood in the corner like a hapless fool. My soul drifted to my body, and although I felt the pull to merge, I was stronger now not to. My fingers traced the side of my face. My skin was smooth, healthy. My hair was thick, clean, brushed. They may have put me in this predicament, but they took care of me, although the vision of Zel brushing my hair made me grin.

Looking up, I saw Sam was back. "Who brushes my hair?"

"I do." Of course he would, no other would be allowed to touch me. Should it thrill me that I knew that to be true?

I reached out for whatever he had gone to fetch. "If this is a long billowing dress, I say no."

Sam held up a pair of leather leggings. "Tough, durable, sexy. You?"

"Leather trousers? Gimme!" Within moments, I was admiring my bum in leather. "Who the hell is this designer? If I knew leather trousers could make my arse look like this, I would have been hitting them up since I got here."

Sam held up boots like his, only better, because these were

obviously designed to be kick-ass while comfortable. "I may weep," I declared as I took them off him and laced them up. Standing, I groaned. "I don't even need my body to know walking in these is going to make me feel weightless."

Green eyes raked over me slowly and with appreciation. "Witch, I think I need some alone time now."

Turning my back to him, I looked at him over my shoulder as I lifted my shirt and wiggled my bum. "You like?" I teased him.

"Witch," Sam groaned. "We need to leave."

It pleased me immensely that he looked like that was the last thing he wanted to do. "Let's go kill things."

"Put you in leather pants, and now you turn all savage on me," he grunted as he took my hand, pulling me into him. "You do not leave me, remember. No matter what, you stay by my side."

"I know, you told me the plan a million times."

"Yes, but when you convince me that you listened at least *one* of those times, then I won't need to repeat it a *million* times." I didn't need to be looking at him to practically *hear* the eye roll.

"Why is the whore dressed like one of us?" Zel snarled when we went back to Cross's domain.

"When does he stop calling me whore?" I asked no one as I hugged Ros and Der in greeting.

"Today," Sam said sharply as he glared at Zel. "Enough. You know the accusation is false. It stops. Today."

They shared a look before Zel grunted and looked away. I think I just witnessed two alphas taking stock of one another, and my alpha winning.

"Are you ready?" Cross asked me as he appeared beside me, and the Watchers gathered in a small group.

"I am." I felt Hound beside me, and I gave Cross a smile. "I have seven Watchers with me, and Satan's army waiting. What can possibly go wrong?"

Cross glanced at the Watchers once before he turned back to me. "You remember what I told you?"

"I do."

"Don't forget."

"I won't."

He pressed a kiss to my forehead, and I felt the brush of power as he pulled back.

"What was that?" Zel demanded as he broke from the group.

"You want souls to veil you?" Cross said, his tone bored. "Then you need my help."

"I thought she was enough?" Zel said as he turned an accusatory glare to Sam.

"Aww, Zel, you say the sweetest things," I joked. "And you tell people you don't like me. Tut tut."

"Enough." Sam had obviously had enough of our bickering. "Are we ready?"

No. Never. Are you kidding? "Yes." *Liar.*

"Witch?"

"Demon?" I answered him as I quickly braided my hair.

"Are *you* ready?" Sam asked me from across the room.

"Take me to Satan," I answered him with a confidence he knew I wasn't feeling, but he gave me a small smile in return. "The actual Satan, not the devil in the corner currently glaring at me," I added as I blew Zel a kiss, and Ros snort laughed so loud that Der jumped in surprise.

As they started to wink out of the room, I turned to Cross once more and hugged him fiercely. "If my soul dies, don't let him get me," I whispered urgently in his ear.

"It is time." Sam stood behind me, but I wasn't moving until Cross acknowledged my plea.

"Follow the plan," Cross told me firmly.

Sam's hand grasped my upper arm lightly. I was still looking at Cross when we travelled to Satan's level of hell.

CHAPTER 27

"You okay?" Sam asked.

"Nope."

"Good, I prefer it when you're honest." Sam dropped his hand from me as we stood apart. "You know what to do?"

"Yes." I saw the blond hair of Satan with an army of horror behind him. There was no other word for it. *Nightmares.* The male was the host of many of my nightmares when I was younger until I convinced myself I found no enjoyment from watching horror movies. Scavengers were scattered amongst his forces, and I shook my head in disgust. I hated them more than anything else I had encountered since my first meeting with the Watchers.

Satan turned to us, and I shivered when he smiled at me in welcome. "You look fucking delicious," he said as he approached us. He sniffed the air once. "Smell it too."

I would never get used to this, this open acknowledgement of sex, and I would therefore always lack a suitable scathing response for him. Sam ignored him, and I opted to do the same. Though it was difficult, because he was *Satan.* When I had been on the clifftop at Dunnottar and met Asmodeous for the first time, I had been scared of him, but it was a healthy fear.

Satan terrified me.

I had no other word for it. I felt the fear of this prince of hell down to my bones. Asmodeous had flames in his eyes when he looked at me, Satan had brown eyes like a normal guy would have. They didn't glow with power. They didn't have pitchforks in them. He looked like someone you would pass in the street and look over your shoulder to check out their arse.

But he *felt* wrong. Malice surrounded him, and I was glad my

237

ability to breathe wasn't a requirement, because the atmosphere of evil that clung to him would choke me.

Satan tilted his head as he looked at me. His eyes danced with mockery, and a small smile played around his mouth. "You look unsettled, witch."

"Do I?" I forced myself to meet his stare. "Little bit of nerves, can you blame me?"

Yup, he knew that was bullshit, but he said nothing, merely dipped his head and turned his attention to Sam.

"Your guard better deliver."

"Your army better remember their role," Sam countered easily. "They fuck up, then *you* fuck up. You don't want to fuck this up, do you, *prince*?" Sam's tone held no respect for someone talking to a prince, and it was obvious what he thought of the royalty in front of him.

"You may have paved the way, Watcher, but remember who you are."

"I never forget." Sam drew up to his full height, and I noticed that Satan was smaller in height. "I know when and why I fell. Do you?"

I was paying more attention. Was Satan one of the demons intent to return to heaven? Surely not. He reeked of ill intent. How he had ever been an angel was too much of a stretch even for my imagination.

"I remember," Satan looked wistful. "It was a fucking glorious day. The blood of Uriel stained my feet." He gave a delighted laugh. "Good times." His demeanour changed in a heartbeat. "Fuck this up for me, and what Asmodeous has planned for her will be nothing." Satan moved closer to Sam, and I gulped. "Do you want her to feel *my* wrath?"

"It's not something I think about," Sam told him, his voice level. "I don't fuck up, and neither will she."

They stayed like that for what felt like eternity, but by the time Satan stepped back, I could have sworn my palms were sweating. I watched him walk back to his army, and I leaned against Sam in relief.

"Fucking hell," I whispered.

"He's just trying to remind me he's got a big dick." Sam grunted in disgust. "This isn't a dick measuring contest."

Did I need images of Satan's dick in my head before a battle? No. Did I now have images of a big-dicked Satan prancing through my head? Yes.

"Need me to remind you whose dick you should be thinking about?" Sam asked me as he checked his weapons, giving me the side eye.

"I thought I could shield my thoughts," I whispered worriedly at him.

"You can, I just know you too well." Sam chuckled as he walked over to the other Watchers.

Arse.

"Do you need anything?" Ros asked me as he fixed his shoulder plates.

"No, I think I'm okay." I gave him a smile, hoping it hid my anxiety, and he gave me a wink as he tightened his straps. "Did you look like this in heaven?" I asked curiously. Ros paused and frowned.

"You mean in appearance?" Pen asked as he came to stand beside me.

"Yeah, I mean, in my head when we first met, Ros was my Viking demon, because he looks like the guy from that show about Vikings. I can't see shaved hair being the 'in thing' up where it's fluffy and light."

Der muttered something under his breath. "Fluffy and light? It's a pity you will never see the reality, young one. You would yearn for your earth."

"I spent time with the Norsemen long before they were

known as Norsemen," Ros told me. "You could say they adopted *my* appearance."

"It freaks me out when you put yourselves in a timeline through history. It reminds me of how…ancient you are."

"Ancient?" Der grinned at Ros. "She's calling us old."

"If you fail to focus on what's ahead, you won't be old for long," Zel snarled behind us.

I looked at their sobering faces in puzzlement. "You're immortal."

"Remove any living thing's head from its shoulders and you're dead." Der spoke casually as he flexed his biceps. "It takes strength and a power very great for it to be done to one of us, but we're about to mess with one of the princes of hell that can do it."

My gaze landed on Satan, who was talking to Sam. "He can kill you?" I asked as I stepped closer to Ros.

"Yup. Him, or another Watcher, another one of the princes of hell, and of course, Death himself."

Cross? Cross could kill them?

"Well, then, let's not encourage Wrath's wrath."

"You'll call for the dead just before we leave this level of hell," Zel spoke to me as he watched Sam and Satan. "We'll ensure we are veiled. Then we will follow him and his army while he attacks Asmodeous." Zel looked at me once. "Are you strong enough?"

"I am ready."

"I didn't ask if you were ready, I asked you if you felt strong enough."

"I am."

"While Satan vents his feelings on his brother, we will get *our* brothers." Zel looked me over. "Then you return to Cross until we come for you."

That was new. "I thought with Asmodeous incapacitated, I would be free."

"You will return to Cross until we come for you." Zel was now giving me his full attention, and I found it hard not to shrink under the coldness in his eyes.

"Fine." I nodded once. "If that's what Sam wants, then fine."

Zel's snort as he walked away told me exactly what he thought of me. *Well, fuck you too.*

As the others spoke and readied themselves, and Sam looked to be patiently trying not to kill Satan himself, I looked around uneasily. Was this what my final moments looked like? On the edge of an army in hell about to invade and battle another army, with the very demons by my side who betrayed me all those months ago.

Is this how my life ended?

Quickly, my hands smoothed over my cheeks before I interlocked my fingers and brought my clasped hands under my chin.

"Star, are you ready?" Pen called as they started to move.

"I am."

The question should have been, were they?

CLOSING MY EYES, I reached for my powers, not so much a reach anymore, they were always there. Waiting. Ready for me to use them. The longer I had been with Cross, the less energy I used to reach for them now. I wondered if Death knew that the elements were not mine to control? *Focus, Star.*

Summoning the souls was painless for me and them. How far I had come from ripping them from their slumber. Now I knew to summon the ones from the Land of the Souls and not the ones from their final resting place.

How much damage had I caused in my ignorance? Opening my eyes, I looked around me and saw them moving between us.

"They are here?" Sam asked as he glanced around.

Cross had explained to me that when the souls were outwith

their dimension, they were not visible to others unless I made it so. On the night that I was stabbed, the Watchers had known they were there but could not see them. Which is why they asked me what I could see.

I had seen them, the souls and Hound.

As the dead walked among them now, I could feel my bond with Hound. We didn't talk about it much. To be fair, Hound wasn't big on idle conversation. Who would have thought that, as I stood at the edge of a level of hell, I was grateful for my bond with a hellhound? The reaper that took me here.

To protect me.

"They are here," I told Sam as he waited. "They are amongst you, two deep as you asked."

Sam's eyes lingered on mine for a moment, and I forced myself to appear calm. He knew me too well, that Watcher, because he moved forward and his lips brushed mine, giving me the reassurance he must have known I needed. "You will be fine," he whispered before he kissed me again. He turned to the others, and I fought down the panic as Satan returned to us.

"It worked," he said as he looked me over. I didn't like the calculating look in his eye, but I kept my face expressionless.

"You doubted me?" With my powers in my hold, my voice was stronger. Gone was the weakness I had shown him earlier. It pissed me off that he noticed, and I didn't miss the knowing smirk he wore as he turned away.

"Time for war."

Had I not felt fear before, I would have most definitely felt it now. Gone were his jeans and shirt, and in their place was clothing very much like the Watchers', only Satan had scales.

My mind couldn't grasp what I was seeing. It wasn't his clothing that had scales, *he* did. His skin was like a reptile, and I was bona fide freaking out. Satan turned to talk to Sam, and I saw that his eyes, which I had noted before where human-like, were now reptilian slits.

This was why he scared me. He was a monster. An actual monster. If I had the ability to sweat, I would have been drenched with fear by now.

"Witch," Sam called for me, and I moved up beside him. "You stay close to me, no matter what you see or what happens. Do not leave my side."

"I know." I was transfixed with Satan, and I couldn't look away.

"Witch?" Sam wasn't budging until I looked at him. I nodded and he looked at Zel. "Azazel, retrieve what is ours."

Zel flung his head back and howled, and then as one, we surged forward. I had been told they would move at speed; they didn't tell me that I would be running. I knew I could move faster in my soul form, but this was like regulated running. Like…exercise.

Thank fuck I was already kind-of-dead or this shit would have killed me.

I didn't know why I expected Asmodeous's level of hell to look like the pit. It didn't. It looked like a massive garden with a huge mansion and smaller houses scattered about. Sculpted land-scaped shrubbery would have never been on my list of "guess what the Prince of Lust has on his level of hell?"

We waited on the edge of Asmodeous's level. I felt like a kid at Disneyland; I just didn't know what to look at first. The angel fountains, the mini maze, the dedicated paths through flowerbeds. Was this real? Was this an illusion?

I heard his roar of anger as he realised that Satan and his army were attacking. The manicured lawns erupted as demons charged upwards from the ground below. From the holes they left in the ground, I saw the red molten rock below. Not an illusion, just a really weird replica of an estate on earth. Why?

As the two armies clashed, very quickly I was grateful the Watchers were not involved in that. All hell had broken loose.

Literally.

How did they know who was who? They all looked the same. They all wore the same. Then Satan's nightmares flooded the battlefield. Sure that victory would be swift for the Prince of Wrath, I almost lost my shit when I saw what Asmodeous countered with.

"Mother of God," I whispered as demons, twisted and misshapen, rushed forward in a wave of attack. They were like a blanket of darkness as they covered the land, and then the two opposing sides clashed in the middle. The noise was unbearable, and I knew that the screams would stay with me for years to come.

"Now," Zel growled as he led the charge of Watchers into the fray, but we were kept to the outer line. I didn't know how they knew where to avoid, but the eight of us and the dead moved fluidly over the ground. None of the things noticed us, the dead did their job, and I ensured I was careful with them as we moved.

Zel led us to one of the smaller houses, and when none of the others hesitated to enter, I thought it was best not to voice my own objections. It was obvious the Watchers had been studying the route for some time, but still it was unnerving to enter into the unknown with apparent disregard. Had they seen the monsters throwing down against each other in the front yard?

We moved upstairs to the upper levels, and I knew Asmodeous was the Prince of Lust, but I saw some things I would never unsee. *They* didn't see me, and thank fuck for that, because I would bet my life on the fact that some of these people were human.

"How?" I asked Pen as he closed a door behind a room where there were a lot of males and only one woman and far too much flesh on display for my mind to process.

"Dimensional split," Pen spoke quietly. "It's on earth but above a ley line, so he can tap straight into this level of hell's energy."

I had questions, but Zel glared at me so fiercely I shut up. *What was a ley line?* There was so much I didn't know.

Bursting through the doors at the top of the house, we were on a rooftop, but we were no longer on top of the house we entered. The landscaped gardens were gone, the war was gone.

Turning in a circle, I looked around.

"Sam?" I heard my hesitation, and I felt someone step closer to me.

"It's an illusion." Ros gave me a tight smile. "Let's go."

The effort to swallow my scream as we ran off the top of the building would have choked me when I cried out in alarm as my feet ran over seemingly empty air.

"Fuck, he knows," Der warned just as another roar of anger erupted all around us.

"Don't lose her!" Sam yelled out as we all ran forward on *air*. "We're still covered."

I staggered when we came to a sudden halt, and I was in the familiar surroundings of the pit.

"Zel?" Sam called.

"I know the way," I told him as I moved to the front. "Follow me."

With confidence, I ran to where I knew Chaz was. Looking up, I saw Cross at his window, looking down. I knew that he saw me, and I faced forward as I covered the ground quickly, the wraiths gathered to me as they moved amongst the souls that kept the Watchers concealed.

In the pit, the one thing I knew that a soul could not conceal.

Was a witch.

CHAPTER 28

I HEARD THE SNARLS AS I LED THE WATCHERS, THE SOULS, AND THE wraiths down to the pit. I kept my focus on the destination ahead and trusted the Watchers behind me to cut down any threat to harm me.

"Star?" Ros asked behind me.

"Trust me," I called over my shoulder as I followed the path I had memorised in my head.

I skidded to a stop when a wall of demons appeared before me. "Shit."

"We've been waiting for you," one of them spoke to me, and its lipless grin was kind of unnerving.

"Well, I hate to disappoint people...*things*," I said as I looked at it.

"Move." I was shoved behind Zel as he unleashed his sword, revealing himself from the shield of souls as he stepped out of it. "When did you become free of the fire?" he asked the demon who had spoken to me.

"We were promised freedom for the death of a witch. *That* witch."

Me? Asmodeous really did hate me.

"You should have stayed in the flames." Zel attacked them. I was jostled as Ros jumped in to help him, but honestly, at first, I wasn't sure if he was helping or hindering Zel.

Then the two of them worked well together. One so pale and one so dark, they were in perfect synchronisation as they fought the demons who had been promised freedom if they delivered my death.

Ros was obviously capable of battle, I mean, he was a Watcher, but Zel? If Satan ever needed replacing, the Prince of Wrath was right in front of me.

I jumped when Pen took my arm, but I shirked him off. "You're still hidden," I whispered as low as I could. "Don't touch me."

"We need to move around them," Pen directed urgently. "Asmodeous is coming."

Nodding, I looked at the mini battle in front of me, but I knew we had to keep moving. "This way." I moved them through a wall that looked solid but was actually an illusion. I had spent weeks staring at these walls, memorising the hidden passageways to get me to my goal.

And my goal was Chaz.

"Witch, how do you know this?" Suriel, who had been quiet on every occasion I had been in the same space as him since the clifftop, spoke to me for the first time.

"Hours of studying."

"Cross knows the way?" Sam asked, moving closer.

I avoided looking up and instead looked at Sam. "Cross *is* the way." I started forward again, and they followed me.

They followed *me.*

When the next wall of demons surged towards me, I stepped aside quickly, and Suriel and Der fought them.

"We must keep moving," I urged them. Sam hesitated and then nodded once. Quickly we advanced. I took another hidden passage, and with no hesitation, I led with confidence much like they had done with the house on the mansion estate. Twisting and turning through a narrow passageway, it was a little bit tight if you were me, never mind a hulking Watcher.

"This witch leads us on a chase," Bara grumbled as he yet again got stuck in the tight space.

"If you start blowing all that hot air around and suck your gut in, you'll move better," I hissed at him.

As Sam hauled Bara out of the end of the passage with a heavy grunt, I fretted at the delay, but I noticed Pen watching me closely. "What?"

"You did not mention this to us," Pen spoke softly.

"What? The pathway to the pit?" I looked between the three of them. "Because I didn't know you wouldn't know the way."

"Let's hurry," Sam moved between us. "The prince is hunting us."

"Not much longer," I told him as I turned my back on the Watchers and once again led them through the twisting paths and corridors that was the pit.

Because the pit of hell was a maze.

A maze that Cross's room looked *down* upon, and from above, I had studied the way to manoeuvre through it, never knowing if I would really need to lead the Watchers through it. I had memorised it to know my escape route should I need it and it was ironic that I now lead them into the pit of hell. A pit where no prince ruled. It was the very bottom of hell, the misery, the harshest punishment.

In the pit, I was weaker. Souls who had been judged and found lacking were led here, and the power of those souls was the only thing juicing my powers right now.

"How much longer?" Pen asked, and all four of us jumped back when the chasm opened suddenly beneath us.

"Jump!" Sam cried as he grabbed me around the waist and powered us over to the other side. But more demons had caught up to us, and Pen and Bara were suddenly fighting them.

My souls were gone and all of us could now be seen. "We're exposed," I told Sam.

"Yeah, I felt the last one go. Can you continue?"

"Of course." I took his hand and led him to the centre of the maze. When we reached the centre, I didn't hesitate and navigated us to the other side.

Asmodeous waited for us. Satan had only distracted him so much, I realised. He knew why we came.

Sam stepped in front of me and drew forth his twin swords of fire. "Stay back," he instructed me.

I didn't need to be told twice.

"You would challenge me, brother, for a witch?"

"I would challenge you for my brothers," Sam said clearly. "*And* a witch."

Did it matter that I came third? No. I was still on the list, and that counted.

"You will lose, Samyaza. She is not worth it. Kill her, and I will free them both."

"They were not yours to take," Sam growled as he moved his feet into his fighting stance. "Chazaquel has suffered too long."

"And Araqiel? Has he not suffered, or do you want him free for your own reasons?" Asmodeous produced a long curved blade. The steel of the blade was half silver, half black, like that of a Samurai sword, but this blade was older than even the ancient Samurai sword masters.

"You lured him to this trap with your web of lies about the Return."

The Return? That's what they were calling it? Seriously, these guys needed to buy an imagination.

"He wants to ascend."

Sam struck and Asmodeous countered. "He will see reason," Sam growled.

"You cannot thwart his plans, Samyaza. How long have you tried?" Asmodeous danced forward, and the two of them stopped speaking as they battled in earnest.

My time was running out.

"Go." Sam's eyes met mine just as Asmodeous struck him and drew blood. "Go!"

Biting my lip, I hesitated, and then as Asmodeous tried to turn to catch me, I saw Sam land a blow that drew blood from the Prince of Lust. Blood that ran black.

"*Go.*"

My feet urged me forward, and I ran, leaving them behind. Chaz was my goal. I ran down to the burning lava at the very lowest level of hell.

The pit was at the very bottom of hell for a reason. It's where the worst things happened. It's where the evillest dwelled. It's where a Watcher screamed in eternal agony. The Watcher who betrayed me more than any of them. The one I had trusted the most. The one I had wanted to love once before I fell for the one that I did love.

As I stood at the edge of the molten lava, I looked at Chaz as his burning flesh melted off of his body, drip by agonising drip.

I had wanted vengeance.

I had wanted their blood.

I had wanted their agony to match the pain of my betrayal.

I never wanted this.

Looking up to the window, Cross gave me a simple nod.

The pit was at the lowest level of hell because it's where a soul burnt to ash.

I was a soul.

With my eyes on Cross, I stepped into the lava. Heat scorched my soul, but I was not burning. Turning my attention from Cross, I made my way to the Watcher who cracked my heart open.

I did not burn in the hellfire. I did not burn. Because Death protected me.

When I reached Chaz, I took a chance and called forth the thunder. The noise covered the sounds of his screams as I cut him from his stakes. The lightning followed, unbidden, as I pulled wooden stakes from his hands and feet.

My powers called the souls to me of the fallen demons that

the Watchers had slain on their way through the maze. Their souls wrapped around the Watcher, and together we moved through the hellfire to the other side.

As the burnt husk was placed on the ground, I heard him whimper in agony. Lifting my head, I looked across the pit and met the forest green gaze of the Watcher I had once sworn vengeance on. They were all there, having defeated the demons in the maze.

Zel stepped into the hellfire and jumped back as he cried out in pain.

"Witch?" Sam called.

"My name is Star," I told him as the wind came. I hadn't called it, but my powers had. As I moved my hand over the body at my feet, the wind soothed and cooled the heat of his burning flesh. Touching my forehead, I pressed my fingers to the mark that Cross had placed upon me. "I have been kissed by Death, and I have been gifted life."

Lifting my hands upwards, the thunder crashed and then the rain fell. It fell on Chaz's body, and my rain replenished his broken body.

"Star, why are you over there?" Pen called as he looked around him, cataloguing, considering, *watching*.

"I heal the one who caused me the most pain." Looking down, I saw the twisted melted flesh smooth out and turn pinker. I didn't have much time. Turning my attention to the seven Watchers across the pit, I smiled. "You stabbed me that night, you say for my protection." I looked them over. Not one of them was marked by their encounter with hell's demons. With fighting a prince of hell. "I didn't need protection. Any one of you could have saved me from Asmodeous's revenge."

Not one of them spoke in their defence.

"You betrayed me." I met each of their stares. "You each

betrayed me, it matters not who struck the blow. You all held that weapon, and you all struck."

"We did what was best for you," Der spoke as he watched me uneasily. "There was more at stake than your feelings," he added.

I nodded as I checked on Chaz. Most of his burns were healing. His eyes were still empty holes, but I knew he would be fine. "You did what you needed to do for *you*."

"Witch."

"Demon?"

"What are you doing?" Sam asked as he took a step forward. "You play games?"

I barked out a laugh at his hypocrisy. "I *really* don't. I play *one* game, Watcher. It's called survival."

"We protect you," Zel snarled.

I met the challenge in his angry stare, and despite our animosity, he did protect me…but not from this. "You do."

I looked at Der. "You do."

My eyes met Ros, who looked pained at my accusations. "You do, as do you," I said to Pen.

"And I?" Sam's voice was heavy with scorn.

"You do," I acknowledged. "You brush my hair as my body lies empty in your keep." As the tear fell free, I looked once more down at Chaz. "You do," I whispered quietly. "From your betrayal, I thought I would never recover, but you risked it all, my friend, you risked it all and even I know that it was too much."

Stepping back, I locked gazes with Suriel. "You do not." He grinned at me with no mirth. I flicked my eyes to Bara. "You do not."

"Witch, what have you done?" Sam asked me in a low warning tone.

When Asmodeous walked out from behind them, all of them turned to look at him, except Sam.

"Would you have told me you hadn't killed him, had I been waiting there on that side for you, demon?"

"Yes."

"Liar."

The battle raged between us in silence. His power was raging around him, his shadows danced wildly as his anger grew, and my lightning crackled in warning.

"How do we cross?" Zel demanded of Pen.

"We can't." Pen was watching the air around us. "She never lost the souls. They barricade us from crossing."

"How?" Der asked in consternation. "She's just one small witch."

Laughter rang around the pit as Satan appeared and walked casually up beside me. "She is not *just* a witch." His snake eyes looked at me, and he grinned. Had he shown me fangs, I wouldn't have been surprised.

"Witch!" Sam's voice had the power of thunder within it. "What have you done?" he asked me again.

"I made a deal."

Turning to Satan, I waited. The bastard drew it out until he flicked his hand, and a Watcher I had never seen before appeared in chains at his feet.

"Araqiel!" Suriel cried as he rushed forward, but the hellfire rose from the pit, forcing him back.

"Tell them," Satan instructed me.

"On the night of a blood moon, nine Watchers struck me down. Three threes. First came the Watchers, then the souls, then the hellhound. I turned three times in a circle of three threes." I could see it even as I spoke. I could feel it. "I was blinded by naivety."

"So tragic," Satan mocked sympathetically.

I ignored him. "I was blinded by love." I looked to the green-eyed demon who broke my heart even as he claimed it as his forever.

"If you love him, free our brothers," Bara demanded.

"It is not that easy," I answered him. "You see, your Father states a law very clearly in his good book that even you Watchers still believe. An eye for an eye."

I looked at Araqiel, who was glaring at me with hate.

"Yeqon." Zel was looking between me and Araqiel. Zel was always smart.

"*You* may have killed Yeqon, but *I* made you strike," I spoke to Sam as I watched Araqiel, "and because of that, *he* will demand his eye."

"I will demand much more, bitch." Araqiel's voice was hard and filled with contempt.

"I know." And I had known. "So I made a deal."

"Witch?" Sam was speaking with a clenched jaw as his shadows tested my barrier.

"Your turn." I turned to Satan.

His laugh was manic as he looked only at Asmodeous. "She was worth the centuries of hunting, well done."

Spikes of darkness pierced Asmodeous's body. He screamed as the spikes twisted under his flesh and dug in like hooks and then *pulled*. Satan snarled something in a language I did not know, and the spikes grew still, even as shadows formed into smoky rope and pulled taught. With a sudden movement, the spikes were tugged and Asmodeous was pulled apart in front of us. As his body was torn to pieces, I dropped my barricade for Satan, who appeared behind Asmodeus, and with a mighty stroke, Satan severed the Prince of Lust's head.

As quickly as it begun, it was over. Satan was beside me again with Asmodeous's head in his left hand, my barricade intact.

"When did she get so much power?" Araqiel demanded gruffly of his brothers.

I watched some of them flounder for an answer; only Zel and Sam were steadfast.

"We made a deal," I reminded Satan.

He moved away from me so he could look at me and Sam, like he was watching a tennis match. "We did." He looked at Sam. "Have you ever heard the saying—it's quirky, but I like it—hell hath no fury like a woman scorned?" Satan pointed at me. "She's one hell of a woman, and she was scorned." Satan bowed to me as he played his game, but I had run out of patience.

The thunder boomed. "Do it," I said forcefully.

"I hope he's worth it and this doesn't kill you." Satan shrugged and almost casually flicked his hand towards Chaz. I heard the cries across the pit before Chaz was beside them. Ros and Pen were on their knees, checking on him and healing him.

Sam didn't move.

Neither did I.

"And Araqiel?" Suriel spoke. "Send him next and keep the witch."

My smile was tight as I heard how easily they would dismiss me.

"He leads a revolt against heaven." I stared at the Watcher who had conspired with Asmodeous to ascend from where they fell. "Which is why Yeqon never fought that hard to free him. Which is why Suriel and Bara did not weep for his return." I turned to see Chaz sit up with aid. He was still healing, but he was safe with his brothers. "You are not strong enough to lose another brother at your hand." I spoke to Sam and saw his eyes narrow at my words. "You took Yeqon's life, and you regret it even though you knew it was right." Moving to Araqiel, I looked to Satan and held my hand out. "An eye for an eye."

"An eye for an eye," he said as he held out a dagger.

"Witch, do not do this," Sam shouted as he stepped forward and ignored the heat of the hellfire as it rose in front of him.

"This is my payment, I made a deal," I spoke to him as I watched Satan.

"What was the deal?" Pen demanded as he watched me hesitate. "Star, let us help you."

"I have to learn to help myself." I couldn't look at them, it was too hard. "With this final act, am I free?" I asked Satan.

"With this, you are free."

"Star! No!" Sam yelled as I cut across Araqiel's throat. Blood gushed over my hands as I dug deeper, and had I been in my body, I would have thrown up everywhere. Instead, I held Satan's stare as I forced the blade deeper, and with a final push, I severed the Watcher's head.

I was not Satan, I didn't need a trophy, I tossed the head to the hellfire and let the body drop at my feet.

"It's done?" I asked him, knowing I had just severed more than the head of a Watcher.

"It's done."

CHAPTER 29

Silence echoed around the pit until Suriel and Bara jumped forward for vengeance, but arms circled their throats and pulled them back. The Watchers turned in surprise as they saw two of their brothers held back by Satan's monsters.

"The debt is paid," Satan declared. "You all know Araqiel would not have rested until she was dead." He addressed Sam, a smile playing around his mouth. "You know you were merely replacing Asmodeous with Araqiel. Does your love not deserve peace?"

"No!" Suriel yelled angrily.

"Do you not deserve peace?" I asked them all. "How long would he have hunted me? How long would you have tried to protect me, my family?" I finally met his heated stare. "How long before you hated the fact you had to protect me?"

"You don't know it would have come to that," Der objected.

"For eternity," Sam spoke quietly as he dipped his head. "He would have sought vengeance for our brother for eternity."

"And will you?" I asked softly. Sam didn't speak, and I looked at the others. "I want to go home. I want to be where I belong."

"You seem to fit in well here," Zel said with scorn.

"Do I, Azazel?" I gave a bitter laugh. "Do I really?"

"You wanted an eye for an eye, witch. I will not rest until you are dead." Suriel spat on the ground.

"I could keep that one," Satan told me conversationally.

"What do you get?" Sam asked Satan as he turned his attention to the prince of hell. "From this. You could have killed Asmodeous years ago. Fuck, you could have killed him in heaven."

"I could, but then…where's the fun?"

"You think you can just leave?" Bara asked me incredulously as he stared at me with undisguised hate. "You're just a witch."

"Actually…" Satan smiled at them all. "She's more. A necromancer *and* a witch."

"So?"

"You should have asked for more." Satan turned to me in pity. "But this is boring me now," he said casually. "You, my delectable morsel, can come visit me whenever you want," he told me as he grabbed my hand. His tongue flicked out and licked the blood off my hand before he pressed his lips to my skin. I felt his smile as Sam growled his warning. "It's been fun."

Satan needed to get out more.

I was alone on one side of the pit, and across from me were seven demons who looked at me in varying degrees of animosity.

"You let him take Suriel," Zel shouted angrily at me.

"Well, he wants to kill me; I'm hardly giving him a gift basket."

"You trust the Prince of Wrath?" Sam asked me.

"No."

"You made a deal with him."

"I did. It's called knowing your enemy."

"Am I your enemy?"

"I don't know. But you taught me to be wary," I said simply.

"That was you being wary?" He looked at my hands, and I saw his jaw clench tightly together.

"Satan scares the shit out of me. Literally terrifies me." Walking forward, I placed my hands in the lava, hissing as I felt the heat, but the only thing that burned was the blood on my hands. "However, he's actually reliable and honest."

"Honest?" Pen scoffed.

"Yes, you see, he's a truly despicable demon, but he knows the honour of a bargain. I told him I would get him into Asmodeous's layer. I told him I would bring with me Watchers, and I told him that I would deliver him Asmodeous to do with what he would, because I knew that the killing blow for Asmodeous may not come from the hand of a Watcher."

"And he told you, what?" Ros asked me as he looked between me and Sam.

"That a Watcher betrays anyone who is not a Watcher," I answered as I placed a hand over my heart and rubbed in memory. "But I learnt that lesson well." I held Sam's closed-off stare. "You sent me to hell, you wanted me to learn, and now you protest when I learn too well."

"What did you get for your bargain?" Pen looked at me all alone on my side of the pit. "Araqiel and Suriel removed?"

"He will not kill Suriel. For me or for anyone else. Satan knows of his part to return to up there." I pointed above me. "That's why he takes him." I looked back to Sam. "But you know that. That's why you still stand here."

"It seems you're not very strong in bargaining power; you gave him another level of hell, revenge on a brother he hates, and a Watcher as a prisoner. All you got was the death of one Watcher, and more enemies," Der said bitterly.

"He gave me one more thing," I told him quietly, and I saw Chaz shakily get to his feet. "Hey," I greeted.

"What else did you get?" Chaz asked as he rubbed his tender flesh at his throat.

I felt tears spill down my cheeks as I watched Chaz stagger and Sam catch him, steadying him. They were broken, they were stunned at my betrayal, and I knew they would never forgive me for making a bargain with Satan behind their back.

"The tree?" Ros said suddenly. "Satan cannot show you the way."

Blinking, I looked at my favourite Viking. "No, he cannot. But do I still need the tree? My enemy is gone."

"Is he?" Sam asked me as anger flashed in his eyes.

"Let it be over," I said quietly. Looking upwards, I watched the souls that I had summoned fade away. "I need to go."

"As soon as you move, you die," Bara warned me.

Wiping my eyes, I gave a small laugh as I nodded. "I knew you would say that." Three hellhounds appeared beside me. "Have you heard nothing?" I asked as I put my hand on Hound's shoulder.

"You command them." Chaz had always been more intuitive than the others.

"Yes." I felt relief when Hound nudged me gently. "They are not just my soldiers, they are my friends."

"And does your master know?" Zel looked us over with disgust. "Does he know you steal his hounds?"

"A hellhound won't stop me killing you, girl," Bara vowed.

Hound stepped forward, and then with a growl, he morphed into his humanoid form. The other two did the same. I had the small pleasure of seeing the Watchers look at them in astonishment.

"Morax." Sam was not surprised.

"No harm will come to her," Hound spoke. "You cannot fight me, Watcher," he spoke to Bara. "Unlike you, I cannot die."

Not even when your head leaves your shoulders? I questioned him in surprise.

Not even then.

Shit. Eternal life? I'm sorry.

As am I.

"You bonded to them?" Pen asked me. "It's why you shield so well so suddenly."

"She is mine." Hound met each of their stares in challenge.

"No." Green eyes lit up the pit. "She is *mine*."

"I am *mine*." I looked between them all. "And I am tired." Hound turned to me and gave me a nod. With a loud sigh, I felt the pull. "Don't come for me," I warned Bara. "You've lost enough. We all have."

"Sam?" Zel asked his leader, his general, as the hellhound switched forms.

"You burnt all your bridges," Sam spoke to me as if we were alone.

"I did."

"You risked everything."

"I had a lot to lose, more to gain."

"Was it worth the gamble?" he asked me.

"No." I felt the pull again. "I lost a lot too." And I had. They would never forget that I took Araqiel's head, which is why Satan insisted it be my hand that killed him. *That* was the price of my freedom from hell and a return to a normal life.

Sam said nothing as he watched me, his eyes flicking over the hellhounds once. "You also gained a lot."

"Sometimes, a girl gets lucky unexpectedly."

I heard the light snort as he broke my stare and looked at his brothers. "Go."

The word shouldn't have caused so much pain. "I'm safe?"

"You? You're never really safe," Sam mocked.

"From you?"

"I will not avenge the death of my brother," Sam said as he held my stare.

"Zel?" He took a long time, but eventually he nodded. I went down the line, all of them agreed, even Bara. "Azazel?" I asked finally. "I need to hear you say it."

"I will not avenge the murder of my fallen brother."

Murder. Wow. "I'm not falling for that," I told him firmly. "Say the words."

"I hate you." He said it simply but there was so much rage. "I hate you and the havoc that you cause. I hate you for the fact that I know you really are so fucking clueless you could destroy us all. I hate you because the actions you took here were actually smart. I hate you for having the sense to be a pissed-off bitch. I hate you for sacrificing everything you had gained so you could save Chazaquel. I hate you for the fact you played a dangerous game and somehow won while you lost what you love most. I hate you for the death of my brothers, my friend, and I hate you because I know why you did it."

"And you hate me more because you would have done the same."

"Go," Zel spat in anger. "Go, rest easy, *Star*, I won't be the demon that brings you nightmares."

Yeah, Satan was a whole other level of crazy I wasn't sure I could deal with.

"Thank you."

"Who got your body?" Sam asked as he stared upward and then huffed. "You still play a game. Keeping us here, distracted with your betrayal while Death retrieves your body."

"Sometimes, not every blow to the heart is physical," I spoke quietly. Hound nudged me and I nodded. "It's a maze." I looked to Pen, who turned and studied the wall behind him. "The window of the room where Cross kept me, it's directly above us. When he showed me Chaz being tortured here, when he knew I would do anything to free him, he showed me the way. I spent days memorising it all. I know there are only two ways out, and I know where the traps are."

"You separated us on purpose," Pen murmured softly as he looked over his shoulder at me with grudging appreciation.

"I was taught how to fight," I answered. "And Watchers taught me to be prepared for treachery."

Cross appeared beside me and smiled at the Watchers across from us. "You have a lot to do," he spoke to them as one. "There are those who still plot to return. You are needed here, you know this, *their* treachery is bigger than this. Than her."

"You think you can take her?" Chaz asked as he looked between Cross and Sam.

"I can," Cross looked at me with a small smile. "She is my disciple." Sam said nothing as he watched Cross reach out and touch my shoulder. "It is time."

"Be safe," I whispered to them before I placed my hand over Cross's. "I'm ready."

I love you, Samyaza.

We were somewhere else, not his usual living room and not the Void. This place, I did not know.

"Am I on earth?"

"Not yet." Cross led the way through the building. I tried to take in details, but my attention was still in the pit. Or on the Watcher who I left in the pit.

"If I'm still in hell, I want a refund," I muttered, and Hound huffed beside me.

Where am I?

Be patient.

"Useless," I mumbled as I looked up at an intricately carved chandelier.

Cross turned to me before we reached wide white double doors. "Try not to speak."

Rude.

We entered a room with a black and white checked marble floor, white walls and billowing gauzy curtains that blew as if there was a wind machine behind them, but there wasn't. When I spotted the grand piano in the corner, I was waiting for the opening chords of an eighties power ballad to start playing.

Instead, I saw the most beautiful woman I had ever seen walk into the room. As she approached, I couldn't take my eyes off of her. I'd never seen hair colour the shade of red she had. I'd never seen anything as flawless as her before. I had a girl crush. Big time.

"Mammon," Cross greeted. He turned to me, his eyes holding a warning. "This is Mammon, she is one of the seven."

Seven? Seven what…oh. "*You're* a prince of hell?" I blurted.

She smiled and I wanted to run. "Prince, princess, queen. Pick."

"Queen?" I asked cautiously.

"Now don't be greedy," Cross chided her, "prince is enough." I understood the not-so-subtle hint. She ruled greed. Why was I here?

"I have the potion you asked for," she told him as amber eyes travelled over me. "I was thinking forty."

"You get five," Cross answered dryly.

"But I always get five."

"Potion."

With a petulant sigh, she handed over a small vial, and I watched Cross slip it into his pocket. When five souls appeared in the room, I realised what he had paid.

"Ooh, these are delicious," she murmured delightedly. "Go now."

We were on the other side of the doors, and when I opened my mouth to ask, Cross shook his head in warning. We were in another room. This one smelled of chlorine and disinfectant. Turning, I saw a machine in the corner, and with a hesitant step, I looked at my body.

"Cross?"

"You're in a coma."

"Why?" I demanded as I approached the bed.

"To sustain a body on earth, requires technology more than Watcher magic," he told me. "Are you ready?" he asked me, and I nodded eagerly.

"Will I still be able to see you?"

"I'm going nowhere. I need to teach you so much." He glanced at Hound. "Your bond with Morax remains too."

"Um..."

"You think I wouldn't notice my reaper bonding to another?"

"Are you angry?" I asked as I waited for the fallout.

"No." Cross looked through the window of the room. "Hurry."

Standing over my body, I felt the pull. With a sigh, I merged and the pain followed.

Opening my eyes, I stared at the acoustic ceiling tiles.

"Star?"

"Mum?"

"Oh baby," my mum whispered and then burst into tears.

"It's okay, Mum." I reached for her hand. "I'm back." Looking around the hospital room, I noticed the colours were less bright than before, but I could feel, I could breathe, I could *live*. "I'm back."

CHAPTER 30

ONCE THEY LET ME OUT OF HOSPITAL FOR MY "MIRACULOUS" recovery from the coma I hadn't been in, I stayed with my mum and dad for a week. It would have been longer if my dad had gotten his way, but eventually he went to work one day, and Mum helped me pack and leave Inverness and return to my cottage.

Dad was the best ever, but it's hard to ground your twenty-five-year-old daughter, and he tried to limit Hound to the garden, even though he couldn't *see* the hellhound, and though Hound had no actual fur, Dad declared he was allergic. It was getting to the stage where I went home or Dad was losing his soul, because Hound was getting closer to taking it.

Within an hour of being back in Slate, I worried about visiting the village. Mum had told me that the village was still recovering from the earthquake. We had all taken a moment as I remembered what had happened and the aftereffects of my actions.

When my phone rang as I bustled about my kitchen and saw the caller ID, I grinned as I answered the phone. "Hi, Dad."

"One hour, it took one hour for my wife to betray me," he joked.

"I needed to come home," I told him carefully.

"I know, I just don't like it."

"I'm completely safe, Dad. The Watchers are gone." The hole they left behind may never be, but that was my choice. He grunted but said nothing. We spoke about nothing controversial at all for five minutes, and then he made me promise that I was to call him when I was going to bed.

Hound was in the back garden acting weird but wasn't

answering any questions. My time in hell had meant I slept through my birthday, Christmas, and Easter. Summer was currently in full bloom all around me. I felt cheated of some of the things I missed. However, it could have been so much worse.

I heard the tentative knock on the door, and Hound was in front of the house within a moment.

It is the useless one.

"It's open," I called to Ruairidh.

I put the kettle on as I readied the mugs for coffee. Hands grabbed me and spun me on the spot. My cry of protest was cut off when my best friend crushed me against him and snogged me.

It *wasn't* a kiss.

It was a sloppy wet snog that I would have fainted for the chance at when I was seventeen. Eight years later, I only wanted one male to kiss me like I was a long cold drink of water on a hot day. It was not this male. There was too much tongue, far too much wetness, and the feeling of wrongness was almost crippling.

"Stop!" I pushed him away from me. "What the actual fuck, Ru?"

He then started crying, and I was back in his smothering embrace. "I love you," he sobbed into my hair.

There was far too much moisture happening in this reunion, and it was making me icky. My chin was wet from his tongue. I mean, seriously, did he know he wasn't a golden retriever and didn't need to lick my face like he was? And he was clammy, which meant he was sweaty, and I had just opened a new body wash this morning, and he was making me feel dirty. And *crying*? Really? He knew I was fine. Mum gave him a weekly update.

She had given me the perfect dead stare when she told me. At first, it had been daily, then every other day, and then he had told her it upset Abby, so could he just get a text on a Sunday?

"Can you stop?" I asked him gently. I couldn't be a bitch because he was my best friend. Even though sometimes he forgot that. When he tried to kiss me again, my powers happily pushed him halfway across the kitchen.

"Star?" Wide fearful eyes met mine. "Why?"

"Stop slobbering over me like a dog. You've never done it before, you're not starting now." Rubbing my hand furiously across my mouth, I glared at him. "Also, I hope you kiss Abby better."

"You used your power on me?"

Okay. Someone wasn't listening. "Because I don't want to be a saliva bucket."

"Why would you try and hurt me?"

What? "What?"

"I love you, you disappear for months and then come back and use your witchcraft to hurt me?"

"Are you drunk?"

"Like you're power drunk?"

"Ru? Are you possessed?" I stepped forward, and he almost fell over his feet to put distance between us.

"Stay away!"

"Are you shitting me?" Was this his way of being funny? As I watched him, I realised he was being serious. "Oh my God, you're *scared* of me."

"Does that make you mad?" he asked me fearfully.

"Get out."

"You're mad!" He looked between me and the door. "I shouldn't have kissed you. It was wrong, I wasn't thinking right."

"Just go." I turned my back and ignored the speed at which he ran out of my house.

When I turned back, Hound was in the kitchen. *You are sad.*

"I am."

He hurt you. Hound's head swivelled to look at the door.

"He can live," I joked as I sat down with my coffee.

Want me to scare him?

I laughed a little at the thought. "I think I just managed that all on my own. Anyway, you're a reaper, not a joker." We sat in silence for a while, and then I noticed the line of souls in my garden. "Hound?"

Yes, Star.

"Why is there a line of souls outside?" I got up and walked to my kitchen window. "Are they here for you?"

No, I brought them to you.

"Why?"

You are a reaper. Reap.

"You want me to process them?" I asked him in astonishment.

You are a necromancer.

I stood and watched them for a long while before I hesitantly walked across to my kitchen door and opened it.

"Hi?"

I spent the day in my back garden, processing souls. Hound was with me the whole time, and throughout the day, the other two hellhounds joined me. Hound had cheated; instead of being at the body at time of "collection" and taking them to the Land of the Souls, he and the others had taken them to me. From the comfort of my back garden, I then processed them up, down, or in limbo.

I was sure Cross would be horrified with the casual chat I was having with the dead before processing them. Plus, he would object to the term "process," but it was the best thing to describe what I was doing. They were like a mini line, and I was the conveyor belt, sorting them into categories.

After the third or fourth soul, I started to feel guilty that I would be the first face you saw in your afterlife, so I quickly brushed my hair and put some lippy on. Hound had been amused but said nothing. He had given me a pointed stare when I started talking to them, but it was all very well and good, Hound telling me my gift would know where to put them, but even I doubted my ability to judge good character.

I mean, my track record was a shit one.

Fell in love with an idiot who didn't value me in any way, stabbed me metaphorically at least three times through my life, and was a truly terrible friend at times.

Fell in love and trusted a demon who betrayed me and literally stabbed me through the heart.

Trusted six Watchers who only ever wanted to use me and who I couldn't trust not to have an agenda.

Made a deal with a prince of hell who terrified me and gave me nightmares…while I was awake.

Stop it.

I looked at Hound, who was sprawled out in the late afternoon sun. "I didn't do anything."

You're wallowing.

"I can't feel sorry for myself for at least a minute?" I asked him as I reached for my coffee cup. I yelped in alarm when Cross moved it out of the way. "How the hell?"

Cross smiled at me in greeting as he looked down at me and then with a raised eyebrow at Hound…Hound, who ignored him or knew he was coming and didn't bother to tell me. His hair was messily styled today, his jaw sharp and clean shaven. He wore black dress trousers and a black shirt, with the sleeves rolled up to his elbow and the top two buttons undone. He did smart casual so well it made me always feel grubby.

"Star," he greeted as he sat at my small patio table. "Some interesting choices you made today."

Which meant he knew I was necromancing in the back garden. "Mad?"

"No, of course not, happy for the help."

"Backlogged?" I joked and lost my smile when he nodded.

"I found your ancestor."

I sat up in my seat quickly. "Gran?" I hadn't seen her since everything had happened, and Hound had told me I wasn't ready for the Void yet in human form, and I wasn't sure I could have coped going to the Land of the Souls and her not being there. Again.

"Ria? Oh, no, she's fine, she's currently at the Waterfall of Solitude." Cross considered me. "Do you want to see her?"

"Of course!" I jumped to my feet and stopped when he remained seated. "What?"

"Where are you going?"

"The Land of the Souls."

Sit down.

Glancing at Hound, I did so, as Cross pressed his perfectly manicured hand to his lips to stop the smile.

"Close your eyes."

I did.

"Think of where you want to be."

I did.

"Star," Cross sighed, and I opened my eyes.

I was in *his* bedroom in the ether. The bed had been stripped bare, and the room was empty—but not unmarked. Angry slashes had been cut into the wall as the bedding I had lain in was shredded around the floor.

"This wasn't what we were talking about," Cross reprimanded me gently.

Closing my eyes against the evidence of his pain, I opened them again at the Waterfall of Solitude on the Land of the Souls. I was surrounded by white again, and I was also very conscious of the fact my bum was sitting on my chair in my garden.

"I'm in both?" I asked Cross quietly.

"Yes, before, you expended too much energy taking your

whole being there. You only need your soul here," he explained as he looked me over. "Do we need to talk about it?"

I knew what he was referring to. "No."

"Fair enough."

We sat in silence as I looked around the familiar waterfall. "I like it here," I told him quietly.

"Yes, it's pleasant." Cross didn't take his eyes off me, waiting, but I didn't mention it. "Curious that you cannot see the colour."

"You don't see it as white?"

He shook his head before he turned away, and I saw the recognition in his face.

"Star, lass?"

Gran!

I raced to her, and my small, sturdy gran caught me as I flung myself at her. "Where have you been?" I sobbed.

"Fixing all kinds of things. Some idiot ran through hell with a guard of Watchers, created havoc, killed higher level demons, made deals with Wrath, and inflamed the anger of the Watchers."

I drew back and looked at Gran; her look was unamused. "Oops?"

"You cannot say *oops*, lass," Gran grumbled as she stepped away from me. "You." She nodded in greeting to Cross, who merely dipped his head. I don't think even I would have had the courage to greet Death as "you."

"Where have you been?" I asked her again.

"Lower levels mostly. Demons are wankers at the best of times, but you mess with their hierarchy, and they think it's an opportunity to advance."

"Ria and some of your ancestors have been helping restore… processing." Cross gave me a look that told me exactly what he thought of my conveyor belt analogy.

"You're a necromancer?" I asked my gran in surprise.

"Good lord, no. I told you, I dealt with the living; the problems of the afterlife were not mine, well, they weren't supposed to be."

Okay, I was getting the memo, I fucked up. "How do you want me to fix it?" I asked them both.

"I think we can take it from here."

I turned to the speaker. Thick black hair hung to her waist, held off of her face with a cloth band that matched the pattern of her full gypsy skirt, which reached to her feet, bare feet. With a white peasant blouse and some silver bracelets on her wrist, she was obviously of Romany descent.

"I am Naomie," she told me with a warm smile. She was stunning, and with that simple smile, I knew who she was.

"It's good to know you are free," I said to her as I watched her settle beside Cross.

"It was a long time, but I knew I could endure."

"Why did you curse him?" I had to know. I couldn't wait any longer. She was the reason I was here. She was the start of it all.

"Vengeance." Naomie shrugged. "Pride?"

"Lust," Cross murmured beside her.

"You loved him?" I asked in shock. I took a step back. "All of this was because, what…Asmodeous rejected you?" Were they serious?

"Asmodeous?" Naomie laughed. "No, I loved another. He took him from me."

I recalled the way Satan had looked at me and the Watchers when he played his part in the pit. "You were scorned?"

"And hell hath no fury like it." Naomie watched me carefully. "You know that."

"You cursed a prince of hell for an eternity in hell because you were rejected in love." Why was I so incredibly disappointed?

"There was more meat on the bones of it, but basically." She wasn't even ashamed.

"Who did he turn against you?" I asked.

"Azazel."

"You trying to catch flies there, girl?" Gran asked me quietly. "Close your mouth."

"You were in love with *Zel*?" It was entirely possible that only dolphins would have been able to understand me, my voice was so high-pitched.

"I am." Naomie's dark eyes watched me shrewdly. "I will *always* be. That is *my* curse."

"Zel?"

"You have trouble imagining the Watcher capable?" Cross asked me as he nodded. "We all do."

"You all misjudge him," Naomie murmured.

"No, I really don't," I blurted. "Jesus fuck, this is all because of *Zel*?"

"He is innocent," Naomie spoke softly.

"Then you don't know him, love," I scoffed. "That hypocritical bastard."

"Azazel is not unaware of who the witch was, but for him, the love died a long time ago," Cross explained. "Before Naomie was a victim of Asmodeous's."

"He never tried to come for you?" I demanded angrily. He could have saved her, any of them could.

"I betrayed him."

Oh. I met her steady gaze and realised what she wasn't saying. "He thought you deserved it," I said bluntly.

"He did."

"Did you?"

"Yes."

Well, there was no coming back from that. "You picked the wrong Watcher for forgiveness," I said bitterly.

"The heart chooses without prejudice."

"The heart is a lump of meat used solely for the purpose of pumping blood around the body," I snapped waspishly. I looked her over again. She was beautiful. She was blunt. She was obviously devious in some way. They would have been perfect together. "Fuck me, I thought it was Asmodeous you scorned."

"I did."

"A love triangle, really?" I walked away from them. "It's so incredibly…mundane!"

Star.

I turned to Hound, who was amongst us. "What is it?"

You must come.

"What is it?" I demanded as I stepped towards him. I could feel the urgency.

They fall.

CHAPTER 31

"WHAT?" I STARED AT HOUND, SURE THAT I HAD MISUNDERSTOOD.

Come.

I was back in my garden, and we were all staring upwards. It was dark now. How long had we been in the Land of the Souls? Small golden lights flashed in the sky, and I felt fear grip my throat as instinct told me these were not stars.

Angels.

Angels were coming. Why?

"Cross?" I asked as I stared up at the sky. "Why are the angels coming?"

"Morax, do not leave her side," Cross instructed and disappeared.

"Gran?" But she was gone too. Naomie remained, her eyes on the golden streaks across the midnight sky. "Any idea?" I asked her softly.

"Trouble. Most definitely trouble." She turned to me and looked me over. "You are strong, much stronger than I ever was. Your magic will come, stop fighting it. You are a witch, and you are a necromancer, you are *both. Embrace* it, Star." She looked back to the sky as the golden lights shone brightly in the night sky. "I'll help you in any way I can, but I cannot stay here. Find me in the Void."

I was in my garden with Hound. What the hell was happening?

"Is it because they know the fallen want to return to heaven?" I asked him quietly.

I do not know.

He watched as I did until the last light of gold had been swallowed in the dark sky. "I'm scared," I admitted as I turned away from the garden and came face to face with Chaz. "Jesus!" I yelped as I jumped. And then I was hugging him closely as I wept in relief.

He held me gently, and then his arms tightened around me, and I was being crushed into his chest as we held each other. "Star," he murmured into my hair.

"I'm sorry, I'm so sorry," I babbled as I pulled back and took in his features, warm blue eyes, perfectly in place, his long brown hair pulled back in his manbun. "I never thought I would be so pleased to see a manbun," I told him as I embraced him again.

I heard his deep laugh, and I felt the kiss on the side of my head. "I have missed you," he told me fondly.

As we separated, Chaz wasn't prepared for the punch I delivered to his shoulder. "Why would you go to Asmodeous? Are you stupid? I thought I was the rash one!"

"I needed to protect you."

"I watched him torture you!" I yelled at him. Chaz gave me a small smile as he knew I was away to launch into a lecture. It stopped me in my tracks. "It's so good to see you smile."

"I'm sorry."

I knew he was saying sorry for the night of the blood moon, and I broke our stare. "Yeah, well, the water's under the bridge." I looked up to the sky. "Did you see?"

"We did."

We. Wrapping my arms around myself, I looked to the house. "You want to come in?"

"Please."

Hound stepped in front of him, and Chaz dipped his head in greeting. "It's been a long time since you made your presence known," he told him. "I mean her no ill will."

Hound didn't immediately move aside, and I held my breath as I waited. With a look that very much portrayed *fuck with her and you fuck with me*, Hound moved to let Chaz past.

My Hound was fierce. I think I loved him more than I realised.

Inside, I made us both a pot of tea. Neither of us spoke, and although I had a gazillion questions, I was content to wait. Which let me know how spooked I was by falling angels. "You're okay?" I asked him as I sat.

"Zel took many days, but between him and Pen, I am myself again." Chaz reached for the pot. "I can pour for you?"

"Thank you," I murmured as I watched him. I may not have been fully aware of my mum's witch powers, but there was no such thing as a teabag in my house. We drank loose leaf tea, out of pots, and God help you if you didn't. "It's lemon, ginger and ginseng."

"A nice, pleasant blend," Chaz told me as he poured.

"Better than what Mum makes us drink," I joked lightly as we sat with our filled cups. "So?"

"Are you angry?" Chaz asked.

"I think I vented it all in the pit," I replied as I looked at my teacup.

"It was warranted."

"Murder?" I scoffed.

"I mourn the loss of my brother Araqiel..." Chaz paused. "But you acted wisely. He would have hunted you."

"I would never have been free," I agreed. "And over Yeqon." I shrugged. "It was an injustice I didn't deserve." I was trying to make light of it, but it hurt. I would always feel bad for what I had done.

"It is done, we understand."

"Does *he*?" I snapped bitterly. "Will Zel? Ever?"

"Yes." Chaz sighed as he sat back. "In time."

"Well, angels are falling, Chaz, and we're sitting drinking tea, going over old ground while you avoid telling me why there are angels falling."

"It is likely that they answer heaven's call," Chaz said carefully. "They have come before."

"They have?" I tried to think of what would make angels leave the comfort of heaven. "When?"

"The flood."

"Oh, genuinely thought you were going to tell me it was for the birth of Jesus."

Chaz laughed. "I have missed you," he told me affectionately.

We shared a sad smile. "So," I started, changing the subject. "You don't seem concerned?"

"Samyaza is not." Chaz ignored my wince at his name. "We could use the aid to be honest. The revolt to return is large and becoming unmanageable. We fear that we are stretched too thin."

"Pen said he would rather cut the tree down," I said softly.

"As would they, I am sure," Chaz told me. "However, we did not fall to destroy."

"No," I agreed. "Will the angels seek out…the Watchers?"

"Unlikely, they are not fond of us. We are deserters."

"You are in danger?" I asked him worriedly.

"Unlikely," he said again. "We always fight back." He winked at me, and I smiled at his confidence.

"You came to tell me not to worry," I said in understanding as I sipped my tea.

"And to say thank you," he acknowledged with a gentle smile. "I know what you sacrificed for me."

I couldn't think of it. I had done it all to save him and save myself. Giving up the Watchers was a small price to pay. Turning away from Sam was worth it, wasn't it? I still didn't know. Would I ever?

"He is my soulmate," I whispered as tears spilled over.

"He is."

It had been the first time I said it aloud, and to hear it

acknowledged broke my heart. A soulmate to a necromancer was so much more than simple love. "It doesn't matter to him."

"He is in denial."

Stubbornest bastard I ever met. "Of course." I let out a bitter laugh. "When is he not?"

Chaz turned in his seat as Cross reappeared. "Watcher," Cross said to him as he looked at me. "You need to come with me, now."

Chaz was on his feet, looking between the two of us. "Why?"

"My business," Cross snapped and reached for me. I didn't hesitate, I took his hand.

The Void was alive with chaos. Turning, I looked around as Cross dropped my hand only to grab my shoulders and spin me, as his eyes ran over me.

"Dammit, Star," he cursed as he stood back. "Why didn't you drink it?"

"What?" I was completely confused. "The tea?"

Hound was beside us, and the Void was quiet and dark. The sudden silence unnerved me.

"Let her go," Cross demanded.

"Who?" I asked in confusion, but I quickly realised he wasn't talking to me.

"I will make you suffer far more than he ever could," Cross warned.

In absolute horror, I watched a dark shadow separate itself from *me*.

"What the hell—"

The shadow morphed into a form. A male form. A malevolent form. "*You?*" I asked in surprise.

Araqiel smiled at me in hatred. "Bitch."

"What the fuck is going on?" I asked Cross.

"His soul alluded me, I could not find it. I've spent days searching for it," Cross looked at Araqiel's soul in disgust. "This is the darkest magic."

"I will have my revenge," Araqiel snarled as he glared at me. "This? This *bitch* will die."

"Reapers!" Cross cried, and Araqiel was swamped by wraiths, and as I watched the struggle, I felt nauseous until finally the Watcher's soul was overcome and he was taken. My nausea didn't pass, and spinning, I threw up.

With my hands on my knees, I turned to look back at Cross. "What is going on?" I ground out through clenched teeth.

"Why didn't you drink the vial?" Cross demanded again.

"What are you talking about? Why don't you tell me what you think I know?" I snapped back.

Hound transformed into his human-like form. "She did, I made sure of it."

"Tell me now!" I screamed in fury as lightning crackled across the Void.

"He must have already been shielding her," Hound spoke. "I did not sense him."

"Neither did I, I've spent *days* searching for him," Cross bit out angrily. "He always was the trickier one."

"I will never speak to either of you again, I mean it."

Cross rubbed his forehead. "Look down," he snapped irritably.

I did. I almost fell backwards. I was no health freak, but I was healthy. Slim. The protruding bump from my stomach was not from a poor diet.

"No."

"Yes," both Cross and Hound spoke at once.

With wide eyes, I looked up at Cross. "*No.*"

"I hear both heartbeats," Cross told me as he paced in frustration. "*Now* I hear you both."

"Araqiel was shielding you, smothering what was happening inside you." Hound was fixated on my stomach.

My *pregnant* stomach.

"He'll kill me."

"Yes." Cross was agitated.

"The ba—" I swallowed. "The *thing* inside me will kill me."

"Possibly." Hound nodded.

"This is why the angels are falling?" I wiped away tears. "They came once before, the flood. Which rid the world of the Nephilim." I remembered Pen's story in the caves below Dunnottar Castle.

"Yes," Cross confirmed.

"What do I do?" I asked. I had never felt so helpless.

"Run." Zel strode towards me, his eyes fierce, his anger evident.

"Zel, I didn't know," I cried as he grabbed me.

"I know, witch. I know." He looked at Hound. "I need you, Morax. They cannot find her. Either of them."

My eyes popped out of my head, or it felt like it. "You're... you're *helping* me?"

"Do you want my help?" Ice blue eyes looked at me and slowly, as my hands touched my tummy, I nodded. Zel gave me a grim look. "The child inside you is innocent."

And I remembered. Azazel, protesting in fury that he didn't kill children. Not even the Nephilim.

"How?" I asked him as I gripped his hand. "They are all going to come for me," I told him. "How do we do this?"

Azazel grinned at me wickedly. "We run."

"And you survive," Cross added grimly. "I will not lose my necromancer," he said firmly.

Zel looked at Cross, and they shared a look of understanding before the Watcher who hated me, the Hound who protected me, and I, the clueless human pregnant witch, ran from the Void and those that would kill me because of whose child I carried inside me.

EPILOGUE

"HOW MUCH LONGER DO YOU THINK BEFORE YOUR STUBBORN ARSE goes and sees her?" Ros joked as he drank his beer. He was three seats down from me at the table, and the others were eating as I sat and drank whisky.

"She made her choice," I told him gruffly as I emptied the crystal glass in one swallow.

"She chose our brother, her friend," Pen spoke quietly. Which was new, he had been very loud and very vocal in his thoughts on her choices. "She knew how we would react to her killing our brother, and she did it anyway for him."

"It's been weeks," Der added.

"It's been a week where she is," Ros added unhelpfully.

I ignored them all.

A week she had been without me. A *week*. I had been without her touch, her smell, her smile, for a lot longer. It was agony to be without her. But then I would recall her slicing my brother's neck before she hacked his head from his shoulders, and I would ignore the craving I had for her as I focused on the anger instead.

Chazaquel approached the table. He was trying to catch Pen's attention, but he was shit at subterfuge.

"Why do you smell like her?" I demanded as I caught her scent.

"I went to thank her for my release," Chaz said simply as he took his seat to the left of me. I ignored Zel's seat sitting empty; he had been gone from the table for too long.

"Did you thank her for killing Yeqon, Araqiel and most likely Suriel too?" Bara grunted as he ate his meal.

"Yes, for that I gave her a handwritten card," Chaz announced sarcastically.

"Wouldn't surprise me. You all seem to be idiots for her cunt."

My power lashed out at him, and I ignored his screams as my swords thrust into his gut and his neck, pinning him to the wall.

"Third time this week," Ros commented dryly as he finished his beer.

"He always was slow in learning," Pen replied.

"And it was them?" I asked Chaz as I watched Bara writhe in pain.

"Yes," Chaz confirmed as he reached for a plate of food. "No contact. Seems to be a platoon at least."

I grunted in acknowledgement as I refilled my glass. We had watched them falling, and I hadn't been concerned.

"About time the fuckers did something," Der said as he looked around. "We're sitting this one out?" he asked me.

"Angels have come before to deal with hell's problems, let them have it." I stood, picking up the bottle. "Cross will keep her off their radar."

The double doors to my hall burst open, and a prick in a golden suit of armour strode across my floor.

Well, that just pissed me off.

My power dropped from Bara and barricaded the angel's progression. "What the fuck do you want?" I asked him.

"Michael demands to speak to you."

"Michael can suck my dick."

"I'd rather remove your head." He walked into the room, and all of my brothers stood. Not in respect but in preparation to fight. Michael the war leader. Michael the favoured one. Michael the giant arsehole who should burn in the pit.

Golden hair swept back from his face and sat on his shoulders, a wide plain, forgettable face, his nose too large, his lips too thin. He looked around us before pale amber eyes met mine. "Your numbers grow smaller." He flicked his eyes around once more. "Where is Azazel? It's been so long."

"What the fuck do you want?" I asked him, thankful that Zel was absent. I wasn't in the mood for their fight.

"Yet again, you have disgraced our Father, your brethren and yourself." Michael sneered at me, and I wished Zel was here after all. "We will take care of the problem you have created, and we will leave. Do not interfere."

"Sure." Bureaucratic bullshit. As always.

His eyes narrowed, but when I didn't say anything further, he simply nodded and left.

"What a giant pain in the arse," Ros muttered after he checked they had left the ether.

"What is it?" I asked Chaz, who was staring at me, eyes wide. "They'll take care of the revolt; it will be nice to sit one out."

"Did you have sex with Star?"

Der's beer sprayed over the table as he choked in surprise. "Fuck me, I was not expecting that."

"I did."

"Here?" Chaz looked frozen on his feet. "When she was human?"

"Yes," I answered as Pen also rose and stared at me in growing horror. "What the fuck is it?"

"She's pregnant?" Pen asked incredulously.

No.

She couldn't be.

I would have known.

"I drank from her," I whispered as my legs lost their strength and I crashed into my seat. "It was the bloodlust."

"She took from you?" Chaz was looking at me with wild panic in his eyes.

"I don't recall, I was in the thrall."

"You fucking idiot!" Ros yelled at me. He was also on his feet. "They've come for *her*. To *kill* her."

"No." I shook my head, numbness washing over me. "No. She can't be."

"We have to stop them," Chaz said as his hands ran through his hair in panic. "They can't—"

"They have to!" I snapped in fury. "You remember what the Nephilim did before, you remember the destruction of *my* children." They had been a blight on earth I was not strong enough to stop...or protect.

"They cannot have Star!" Chaz screamed at me in fury. "I will never allow it."

"She chose me," I snarled back at him. "She didn't fuck you. She fucked me."

"Because you're her soulmate!" he yelled in exasperation. "I don't want to fuck her, you fucking arsehole, I want to protect her."

"A soulmate?" Pen had remained seated through the revelations, thoughtful, pensive. He met my angry stare. "A soulmate could change things?"

"It's not worth the risk," Der spoke quietly. "A Nephilim will destroy it all."

"Where the fuck is Zel?" Ros demanded angrily. "We need to all be here to figure this out."

My eyes landed on the empty seat to my right. He had been missing for days. He refused to talk to me as he seethed in his anger over the death of our brothers.

But now? I knew *exactly* where he was. I wonder if my disloyalty had tasted as bitter to him when I chose the witch over our brothers?

"Weapon up. We need to find them before Michael does." I started to head to my armoury.

"Them?" Bara asked as he looked between us all.

"The witch is under a Watcher's protection." I felt the words burn me as I said them. The taste of betrayal stung my tongue. Looking around the room, I met the stares of them all.

My soldiers.

My army.

"Gather the others," I ordered Der. "We prepare for war."

To be continued...

FROM THE AUTHOR

If you enjoyed this book, it would mean so much if you considered writing a short review and sharing it on your normal retailers site or anywhere else you wanted to share your love of this story and all places books!

Reviews are helpful to other readers, but mean even more to authors, and I would appreciate it so much if you took a moment to share your love of this book!

Eve x

ACKNOWLEDGMENTS

As always it's not a one woman venture to get a book out into the world, so I would like to thank the people who help me get this piece of my imagination into your hands.

Anna, the cover is beautiful. I love it. Thank you.

Helayna, your editing expertise is gratefully received each and every time and I love our conversations during the editing process (and of course in general).

To Shauna, Ashley and Wildfire Marketing for the promo tours, the sign up and the management, thank you so much.

To the bloggers, reviewers, and bookstagrammers out there who have supported this launch, thank you so much. I appreciate each and every one of you.

To my beta girls, Renée, Julie, Katy & Amber, thank you for being my support team.

Mr M, for putting up with the endless nights, the continuing stress, the worry and the ongoing caffeine addiction. Thank you always, for the unwavering support, for the reminder to let the negativity go and for constantly being by my side to support me when I'm in danger of letting the demons win.

And finally, to my readers. Thank you from the bottom of my heart for continuing to pick up my books and lose yourself in the pages of a world I have created, it's an amazing gift that you give me each and every time you read my words.

Love Eve x

About the Author

Eve L. Mitchell is a USA Today Bestselling author who writes contemporary romance and urban fantasy.

Being an avid reader from a young age, Eve still considers herself to be a reader first. She believes there is nothing better than getting that new book either on your e-reader or in your hands, and the fact she may bring that excitement to a fellow reader, fills her with wonder. She writes under a pen name because otherwise her Secret Agent status will be revoked.

Eve lives in the North East of Scotland, with her three coffee machines and her significant other, Mr. M. She enjoys NFL Football, music and having long conversations with the voices in her head, which sometimes turn into the stories she writes.

If you want to keep up to date with all things Eve, to be the first to hear about updates from Eve sign up for her newsletter.

All the books; both fantasy and contemporary:
https://bit.ly/Evesnewsletter
Just contemporary romance book news:
https://bit.ly/Evesromancenewsletter
Just Fantasy books news:
https://bit.ly/Evesfantasynewsletter

Connect with all things Eve here: https://bit.ly/Eveslinks

Creatures of evil roam the shadows - the Drakhyn. They may look like humans, but their taloned hands and razor-sharp teeth serve one purpose only; killing.

A Sentinel's purpose is to patrol and protect. They are highly trained soldiers with superior skills and abilities. Whether they be Vampyres, Lycan, Castors or gifted Akrhyn, their purpose is the same; hunt the Drakhyn and rid the world of their evil presence.

GET THE SERIES
WWW.EVELMITCHELL.COM

FROM BOOK 1:

They hunted me down.
Six demons who believe I can cast a spell to lift a blood curse.
But I'm merely a clairvoyant who can summon the dead.

Being thrust into the world of demons is terrifying, intimidating, alluring…
Their leader refuses to believe I cannot understand the spell.
He's infuriating—but there is something about him that calls to me.
An attraction that scares me.

GET THE SERIES
WWW.EVELMITCHELL.COM

FROM BOOK 1: You'd think the universe would toss me a break after the year I'd had.

I made a plan, one that would give me a fresh start in a new town where no one knew me.
It should have been simple, but nothing is ever as easy as it should be when starting over.
New town, new school, and a new life. It sounded easy enough, or I'd thought it had.

It wasn't.

GET THE SERIES
WWW.EVELMITCHELL.COM

FROM BOOK 1: I knew the moment I saw Aiden that he was the kind of man who would break a woman's heart. With his looks he could grace the cover of any book or magazine.

Even as I got to know him, his hard no nonsense attitude was alluring. He was as captivating as he was intense. My pulse raced and my stomach fluttered when I was near him. Having his attention was as intoxicating as it was overwhelming.

Yes, Aiden would break a woman's heart. If she let him.

Maybe, even if she didn't.